HIDDEN
HARM

HIDDEN HARM

The Gartside Series

Ben Byrne

for my family

ACKNOWLEDGEMENTS

Writing a novel is a big project and is only made possible by the contribution of many people who lend insight and encouragement along the way. Emma, Jack and Finn thank you for letting me have time to write, despite the fact it is as liable to make me miserable as it is to bring light into our lives.

I am hugely grateful to my own 'Pro Team' of Sian, Siobhan, Conor, Claudene and Chris for the ongoing feedback and improvements you helped me to make throughout the editing process. Chris, thank you in particular for your careful eye and for your fantastic cover design.

There were a host of people who I must also thank for feedback on earlier drafts of the novel: Sarah G, Julie, Chris S, Gavin S, Mike B, Mike O, Damian, Mark, Susie, Kate, Polly, Sarah W, Layla, Fi, Rosie, Dan N, Dan P (a most critical friend), and my siblings Jim, Fran, Mary and Cathy. Nick, thank you for the invaluable advice of an established author.

I hope you can take some pride from finally seeing the finished product.

Ben

THURSDAY 10TH MAY

2pm

"I spend too much time with sex offenders."

Tom Collins repeated to himself the conclusion he had long since reached about his chosen profession. He was reminded of it as he surveyed his next destination: a charmless block of maisonettes on the out of town estate known as The Gartside. 'The Darkside' was what many called it.

He looked back to the case notes on his lap, as he struggled to focus on the facts, the essential details that he could hold on to, amid a sea of lies, allegations and alibis. Instead he saw only a jumble of words, from which jumped the occasional descriptor, to spark a torrent of intrusive memories: "unlawful sexual intercourse", "indecent assault", "domestic violence". With each, Collins was reminded of another time, another case, from more than a decade spent as a social worker with the most damaged and damaging residents of the Gartside.

Tom Collins' working day consisted of unpicking the facts from the fantasies of a range of disturbing and sometimes dangerous people. This meant listening to the justifications of the mother who had sold her child for sex so that she could get her next fix, or the complaint of the rapist who thinks it's "not fair" that he can't return to his home, next door to the babysitter who, five years earlier, he had left broken, defiled and gasping for what was so nearly her final breath.

"What a way to earn a living?" Collins mused to himself. "It's not a vocation, it's a life sentence."

He looked out of his car window to number eighty-four with its small patch of lawn, railed by a low fence. Weeds fought their way over and under the decaying wooden barrier. A crisp packet here, a coke can there, a free paper and a discarded baby's bottle; all nestled amongst the unruly grass. Condensation stuck the grey net curtains to the front windows.

Those windows looked as if they had never been opened, never served their purpose of letting light and air into that house; a house he already knew would be dark and dank inside. It appeared so completely sealed to the outside world. He found it hard to imagine the front door opening and being able to enter. Harder still to think of returning again to the light without being sullied, without taking away the patina of that house's silent secrets, stories with no end, clinging like a second skin.

This was the world Tom Collins had chosen to inhabit. He didn't just do the sex cases, he mixed it up with violence, neglect and various sorts and shades of abuse. What he referred to as the "hard end of the mad, sad and bad". This was forensic social work, his specialism, which earned him his place alongside police officers and other social workers on the new-look Joint Child Protection Unit. He had the skills to work with the troublesome parents and build relationships with their needy kids; when necessary being ready to whisk them out of home.

The handle his colleagues had self-applied for the unit was the 'Pro Team', and, in lighter moments, at the end of a good shift, Collins would describe himself as a "crime-fighting, super-social worker". Most of the time, however, he felt more like society's rag-and-bone man: "bring out your junk", social junk. People we would rather didn't exist, but they do exist, and many of them have kids, or have access to other people's. It was Collins' responsibility to keep those children safe, and he was fearless in fulfilling his task.

Before leaving the car he looked again at his case notes, forcing himself to engage his brain with the circumstances of this family, disaggregating them from all those who had come before. Tom Collins knew too well that for all the patterns, for the all too predictable excuses he had heard in so many different homes, every case is unique. Forget that

3

and you will miss the clues that will lead you to the truth for the family in front of you. Reviewing the evidence in the file on his lap, Collins focused on the unique features of the Chilcott family.

Father: Alexander Chilcott: Age 44
Mother: Carol Chilcott: Age 32

Children:
Daniel Alexander Chilcott: Age 14
Crystal Carol Chilcott: Age 11
Kevin Chilcott: Age 8
Kylie Marie Chilcott: Age 8

The police and social services had numerous reports of the troubled and troublesome Chilcott family. Their principal interest was the activities of the father, Alex. He had a penchant for exposing himself in Gartside Park. On top of this there was his history of domestic abuse towards Carol. There were multiple police call outs from their early days, although these had become less frequent in recent years. Collins' guess was either people had given up reporting the violence, or Alex Chilcott had such control over his wife and family, he didn't need to use his fists any more.

What had brought Tom Collins to the Chilcotts' door was a new allegation that Alex Chilcott had been up to his tricks again. He was seen waving his wand in Gartside Park, terrifying a couple of school girls who were hurrying to be home before dark. He had done it before, it was his 'MO', as the police officers on the Pro Team called it, and all just a short walk from his home. Not that Mr Chilcott had admitted to it. He was at home; his wife vouched for that.

"He's an agoraphobic with doctors' certificates to prove it," she had told the investigating officer. "He's had psychologists try to get him out of the house for years but there's no budging him."

The only people to ID Alex Chilcott outside of his house in the last five years were these two school girls, who had seen him pulling at his penis in Gartside Park. "It was that weirdo who lives in Gartside Gardens." They were sure of it, having been warned about him by their parents, as had all the children on the estate.

Even though they picked him out in an ID parade it didn't get to court, as CPS wouldn't run with it. It was the girls' word against Alex and Carol Chilcotts': not sure they would get a conviction, especially with his agoraphobia. In the end it wasn't 'in the public interest' to go to trial for a flashing offence; when there was a fair chance the Crown might not win. That didn't mean it didn't happen. It didn't make Alex Chilcott any less worrying for those, like Tom Collins, who were concerned for the Chilcotts' children and other people's. He closed the file and headed out of his car to start his latest assignment.

Collins cut an incongruous figure on the Chilcotts' doorstep. Looking younger than his thirty eight years, he had a certain style, in his charcoal suit and crisp white cotton shirt. His need to be ready to make one of his frequent court appearances meant this was often his attire. It also suited Collins to have deliberately cultivated an image in recent years that marked him out in his profession, and demonstrated he had cleaned up his act. The new Audi A4 he was driving was part of the package. He turned back and looked at it now, hoping it would remain untouched while he was in the house.

The streets of the estate were empty on this bright early summer's afternoon. Collins had been on far worse estates. The sprawling, grey concrete warrens of south east London, where he had trained, were much more intimidating. There was, for him, nonetheless, a harshness to this semi-rural impoverishment, that outstripped the inner city. It was the contrast, the juxtaposition of a redundant white working class in the midst of moneyed middle England, a blot on the genteel landscape.

Collins knew better than anyone that it wasn't just the city streets that could be dangerous. There was plenty creeping and crawling around the lanes of leafy suburbs and provincial towns that you wouldn't want your daughter to stumble across on her way home. Worse, though, happened off those streets, behind closed doors, away from prying eyes; the hidden harm in the shrouded silence of family homes. It was Tom Collins' job to make those secrets public, to expose the abusers and protect the children. He knew some of his colleagues thought of him as too unorthodox, but he was good at getting to the heart of a family's untold stories. On occasions, though, even he found the silence impenetrable. Sometimes those secrets were too deep and too dark to ever find the light of day.

Collins took a deep breath and knocked firmly on the door of number eighty-four. There was no sound inside, no movement visible through the frosted panel. He waited, listening, but nothing. He caught himself in a thought.

They're out. I can put off the day when I'll have to face into this house.

He knew that he was only stalling, delaying the inevitable. He knocked again more loudly. This time there was a response. Muffled voices, a woman and a man, a door slammed inside, then a shout from the woman.

"All right, all right, you don't need to take the bloody door off, I'm coming."

Another minute passed before the figure of Carol Chilcott, a woman who would soon come to be so familiar to him, approached the other side of the door.

Collins listened as Carol fiddled with locks and chains, before levering the stiff door open, just wide enough for her shrew-like face to emerge from the shadows of the dark hallway. Still in her early thirties, there was little evidence left of the striking looks which had made her a favourite of the local boys in the Gartside Gang. Carol's brown hair hung below her shoulders and fell limply across one side of her face. Her strong cheekbones now protruded too far, when, as a younger woman, they would have been part of her charm. Black sunken eyes darted about anxiously, like those of a small rodent emerging from its burrow.

Collins had found out a great deal about Carol Chilcott in the preceding days, but the face that confronted him now spoke more eloquently of the life she had led than any case file possibly could. It said "I am tired, I am scared, I don't want to let you in – into this house or into my life – because you will make the pain worse, not better."

And so, Tom Collins crossed the threshold and entered the Chilcotts' world, becoming the latest agent in the strange, sad, saga, played out behind the door of number eighty-four.

2.45pm

Carol Chilcott stood trembling behind her front door. Thoughts tumbled over feelings, fear barely checked by relief that the social worker had gone. She had done her job, for now.

He's gone. Pull the chain and fix it closed. Do the mortise lock and put the catch down on the Yale. Hands are shaking. Still shaking, bloody shaking. I could see him looking at them, as I was reading the papers he gave me. Looking and thinking it means something. Means he was right about me and my family.

She told herself to breathe.

Have a blow girl, you did all right.

8

The arsehole's got nothing. Thinks he knows it all, thinks he knows it all, but he doesn't know half of it. He thinks he can come in here and sort this family out. Thinks he can protect my kids better than I can?

Carol steadied herself knowing, having kept the social worker at bay, it was now her husband she would have to try to pacify.

Take your time. Get yourself straight before you go in and face Al. He'll be sat back in his armchair already. Staring, just staring. He'll tell me I got something wrong, that my big mouth will get us all in trouble; get him banged up and the kids taken off us. Bet he didn't miss a word from behind the door. I did just what we said though. He can't say I didn't.

Silly cow, course he can. Course he will. "You fucked up. You deserve a drowning." That's what he'll say. "You don't deserve to breathe the same air as me. You're stealing my air, you fucking thick, thieving, cow. You're going to be breathing water, you bitch." That's what you've got coming.

Carol countered her own fears.

No not today. You've done all right. That social worker got nothing, you were good. No water today. Don't, don't even think about it.

But she was thinking about it. Her nose pressed against the bottom of a half full bath, lungs screaming for air. Being left to lie on the bathroom floor, wanting to be dead, bath water cloudy with blood and puke. But then the touch of a towel on her face, wiping away the blood and the tears. A hand holding her hand. Her boy's hand. Her Daniel. No words. Just her baby boy.

I can do it for him. I can do it for them. Keep going, keep breathing. It's my air too. It's Dan's air.

Just go in there, tell him it went well. "We've got nothing to worry about Al. Let them do their child protection investigation. They've done enough of them in the past and nothing's changed."

Carol admitted to herself that this social worker seemed different. He seemed like he had actually done his homework. He had the list of all the times the police have been called by the neighbours, knew of all of Alex's previous, and about all the other times the kids had been on social services' books.

What do they know that they haven't always known, or thought they've known? So he wants to spend some time with Dan. It's not like Dan's going to say anything is it? He barely speaks. It's not like he's going to start talking to some snooping social worker.

"It will be all right Al. Nothing to get annoyed about. Honest, it'll be all right."

Go on. Go back in there. Tell him there's nothing to worry about. Just open the door girl. Deep breath. It'll be all right.

Carol steadied herself. Having mastered her emotions to open the door to Tom Collins, she now had to find some strength to do it again. To manage herself, to be able to hold in check her husband's rage.

3pm

On the drive back to the office, Tom Collins reflected on his time in the Chilcott house. It was worse than he had imagined. Worse than his colleagues said it would be. It was like stepping into a sarcophagus. When he insisted that the interview could not take place on the doorstep, Carol reluctantly ushered him into the front room. She pointed for him to sit on the small marmalade coloured sofa, which no doubt had been purchased by someone at least thirty years earlier, before being sent to a charity shop, from where it had come to the Chilcotts.

The room was a claustrophobic assault on his senses, a dizzying array of ordered chaos. An imposing widescreen television dominated one wall and directly opposite it, against the other wall, was a bulky black leather armchair, its regular occupant's impression permanently imprinted on its cushion. An occasional table stood to its right, with an ashtray containing a dozen cigarette ends, and next to it green papers and an Old Holborn tobacco tin. There was nowhere else to sit in the room other than the two-seater sofa, occupied by Tom Collins. Carol chose to get a kitchen chair, rather than sit in the armchair, or next to Collins on the sofa.

The only other furniture in the room was a sideboard, on top of which was a picture of the Chillcotts' youngest children, the twins, in school uniform, when they were five or six years old. Their smiling faces looked out of place against the bleak backdrop. Collins guessed the picture had been placed there while he stood on the doorstep. There were no other pictures, no ornaments, no evidence that this was a family home.

What took the place of familiar household items were newspapers. Next to the picture of the twins was a pile of newspapers, on top of which was the local Gazette from 2010. In the corner to the side of the television was another stack. Down to Collins' right, on the floor by the sofa, thirty or forty more newspapers, greying with age, topped by a copy of the Sun from July 2012. As Collins looked around he noticed more neat piles of yesteryear's newspapers, patiently awaiting their reader's return.

While Collins waited for Carol to come back in from the kitchen a noise upstairs made him avert his gaze from the piles of newspapers, and caused him to look up at the ceiling. A large yellowing patch above his head suggested water had come through from above. It stretched out from the centre of the room to the wall, and had caused the woodchip to peel, all the way along to the window. The Chilcotts could have had this damage seen to by the council, but Collins suspected they were unwilling to open their doors to workmen.

Collins looked at the window with its condensation and yellowing net curtains, wishing he was on the other side in the sunlight, gulping in air filled with the scent of blossom and grass-cuttings from Gartside Park. Nothing on the inside of the window betrayed the fact that nature was in riot, bursting with new life, only yards away. The window may as well have been a wall for all the light it allowed to penetrate this oppressive cave; it was a dead eye to the world outside.

Carol put the metal chair she had fetched from the kitchen five feet away from Collins and perched herself on the edge of it. She reminded him of the whippet he had got from the rescue kennels, back when he was still with Janet and Jamie. It had that look that Carol had: always watchful, always ready to run for cover.

Collins quickly realised that her husband had Carol exactly where he wanted her. Despite the haunted look behind her eyes, she remained ever vigilant, impervious to his various lines of enquiry.

Carol wearily explained that, yes, they'd had problems earlier in their marriage and had some bust ups, "but who doesn't?"

"Poor Al is terrible with his nerves and these days the doctors have got him on so much medication he couldn't hurt a flea."

As for those schoolgirls, they were "just like all the others around here" who had it in for her family.

"Anyway, Al's agoraphobic, how's he going to flash at anyone in a park?"

And so it went on. The kids went to school like any other kids.

"Daniel hasn't been well the last few weeks, but he's feeling better. That's why he's out playing now."

"So what if they say he won't talk at school? He's not quiet at home, you can never shut him up. He's always been a shy sort in public though."

"Yes, you can come and see him, but don't expect much out of him, he's no good with strangers."

All the while she fought to keep her hands still. All the while her eyes darted around the room.

"The noise upstairs? That's only Al going to the bathroom…No you can't see him, he's not a well man."

"Anyway, I can't sit here talking, I need to get ready to get the kids from school," she said, as soon as she felt she had answered enough questions to be able to terminate the interview. Collins was appalled at the thought of children coming back to this dark, dispiriting shell of a home. There was no sign that children inhabited this place at all.

"Where are their toys, Carol?" Collins challenged.

Carol countered, "I keep a tidy house. I can't be tripping over toys all the time. They've got things in their bedrooms if they want to play. You think there should be toys and mess everywhere because we're poor. Well we may be poor, but we're decent people, and we don't need you telling us how to live our lives."

"I'm not here to tell you how to live your life Carol, I'm here to make sure your children are safe, and that they are able to thrive. What I know about Daniel, in particular, makes me believe he's not thriving. His school is worried, he's stopped communicating with anyone, and now he's stopped turning up. So, until I'm satisfied that he and the rest of your children are getting what they need to grow up like any other kids, you are going to have to put up with me. I'll be back at four o'clock tomorrow to meet Daniel. Make sure he's here please."

As he said it, Collins was aware he was another man coming into Carol's life, making threats, throwing his weight around to make her do what he wanted. It didn't sit well with him, but he knew he couldn't let her fob him off, as so many before had been.

With that Collins left her and headed back to the office. He wound down the driver's window, determined to exchange the deep, nicotine-heavy fug, which had filled his lungs in the Chilcotts', for something resembling fresh air. The cool draught through the window reminded him that summer was still to fully take hold. He left the window down as he drove the five miles to his office. His journey took him through the increasingly suburban landscape, passing the detached mock Tudor piles, and more modest rows of semis, on the edge of Queenstown, or 'Town', as it was known to locals. All of which sat in contrast to what he had left behind on the Gartside. The breeze in his face brought tears to his eyes. Tears which in any case had been close to the surface since he had left that house.

Already he hated Alex Chilcott. For Tom Collins he was taking shape as an irredeemable bogey man, who was destroying his children's chances of having anything resembling a happy or healthy childhood. What took Collins by surprise was his realisation that he hated Carol Chilcott too: hated her for protecting her husband, hated her for allowing herself and her children to suffer in that house, hated her for refusing to be rescued. If she wouldn't do anything to protect her kids, then he would.

3.30pm

Tom Collins was still seething when he got back to the office. His boss, Dave Andrews, was on the phone in his room. Collins wasn't standing on ceremony and barged in, banging the door closed behind him. Andrews quickly terminated his call.

"Tom, you've been to the Chilcotts' then?" he said, before Collins had the chance to launch his initial assault. "How's Mr. C's newspaper collection coming on?"

Dave Andrews had been Collins' boss for more than a decade, but he was here long before Collins, long before any of them. At fifty-eight he had done well to survive the punishing world of child abuse and child abusers. His trick was to keep some distance, retain some perspective. As he had said to all of the team, at one time or another, "we're not the ones who are hurting these kids, we're not the ones to blame when bad things happen." And they weren't, but were they doing enough?

Collins always wanted to do better. He knew that he didn't always get it right and somewhere, sometime, he would inevitably have left a vulnerable child behind, with that, oh so plausible, daddy and mummy, to face some unspeakable pain. But he didn't get Andrews' detachment; unlike Andrews, Collins took it personally. That's why he knew he wouldn't be doing this job in twenty years' time when he was Andrews' age. He would have burnt himself out, or busted someone up, and been kicked out long before then.

Collins wasn't in the mood for que sera sera today.

"Don't joke about it Dave. Yes I've been to the Chilcotts'. How the hell have they been allowed to bring up children? The place is like a fucking morgue." Collins was unable to prevent himself from raising his voice.

Andrews was ready though. He knew Collins well enough to be sure he would come back from the visit raging. He wasn't the only firebrand social worker he had dealt with in his time and he knew how this conversation would go. He leaned back in his chair, opening up his portly frame, hand massaging the back of his balding grey pate.

"Tom, we've done everything we could over the years. We've conferenced them, we've had them on child protection plans, we've had those kids as open cases most of their lives. We had them in proceedings once, back when I was a practitioner, but we've never had enough to persuade a judge to take them into care. I've been through this case with legal enough times."

As ever, Andrews was being his reasonable self. For Collins though being reasonable wasn't good enough, sometimes you had to go with your gut and your passion, sometimes you had to fight. After experiencing the Chilcotts' house he was up for a fight.

"You can't leave kids with parents like that, in a place like that. They must be stunted in every way. You can't be a child in a place like that, and everyone is entitled to a childhood."

He was tumbling over his words, wanting to get them out urgently, wanting them to force his boss behind his cause.

Still Andrews remained unmoved. "Tom, lots of children have shitty childhoods. We can't take them all into care, you know that, and let's be honest we don't always do too well with the ones we do take away, do we?"

Collins wanted to shake him, he wanted to physically propel him into action, but of course he couldn't do that. That was what was so infuriating about his job. He couldn't shake his boss by the lapels, just like he couldn't punch paedophiles in the balls, couldn't threaten wife-beaters with a good hiding. As Andrews would say "that's what makes us different from them". Instead of fists and knives and broken bottles, Collins' weapons were words, and if he was lucky a court order. So it was words he would have to rely on to persuade Andrews that they could not let the Chilcotts' situation continue.

"Dave, don't talk to me like I'm an idiot. I know child protection and I know significant harm. I know just from reading that file and stepping through that front door, that's significant harm. And what's more this department knows it, and it's let it happen to those kids since Daniel was born, fourteen years ago."

But still Andrews batted him away, just as Carol Chilcott had done an hour earlier.

"We know Alex Chilcott is an odd man but there's never been any evidence he's done anything to his own children. You can't go to a family court and say we want to take the kids away because the house is dark and dingy."

"He's a sex offender, Dave, and a domestic abuser, that's a good enough starting point isn't it?"

"Half the men on our books have got a history of domestic violence and, yes, he's a flasher, who could have an unhealthy interest in teenage girls, but that's still not enough for the courts to make a Care Order. We've been here before with this family."

"Well, he's got two girls at home. Doesn't that bother you?"

Collins couldn't believe that his boss could have allowed this to go on, on his patch and under his nose. He might have been one of social work's survivors but Collins never thought he was callous or indifferent.

Finally, he saw some movement, finally Andrews was coming around to the cause.

"Of course it bothers me and it bothers the Director." Andrews' tone was no longer the soothing tenor to which Collins had become accustomed. Now Andrews' fury matched his own, his voice rumbling with a pent up anger.

"That's why we created the Pro Team to get to the bottom of cases like this. That's why we've sent you into the Chilcotts', Tom, to nail that bastard once and for all."

"To do what you and our esteemed Director, Frazer Campbell, should have done years ago."

The younger man continued to glare at his boss. Andrews had failed those kids and now, too late, he wanted Collins to try and make up for the mess he'd left behind.

"Get me the evidence Tom and I'll back you."

"I will and you better," Collins said, his dark eyes still fixed angrily on his boss's.

As Collins turned to leave the room, Andrews shouted him a parting instruction.

"But Tom, do it by the book."

Collins left Andrews' office determined to puncture the silence of the Chilcott house, open the windows and throw light upon the secrets that those parents had worked so hard to keep under wraps. He knew the task was a tough one and would have to start with breaking the silence of a selective mute.

5.15pm

Collins spent the afternoon re-visiting the numerous case files on the Chilcotts that had been brought up from storage.

Carol had been quizzed by twenty or more social workers over the years, starting from her first encounters, when still herself a teenager, who stayed out at night with the boys in Gartside Park. They had asked her why she kept running away, why the police would find her off her face on drink or drugs, in the park, or in Town, in the middle of the night. "Is there something wrong at home Carol?" Maybe no one had asked in a way that made her feel able to tell them. Maybe the fact they kept taking her back there, to a home from where she kept running away, made her think she couldn't trust these people, who said they just wanted to protect her.

Either way, she voted with her feet, and as soon as she was sixteen moved in with her boyfriend, Alex. He was twenty-eight and had his own flat. What the file didn't say, but Collins guessed, was that Chilcott had been having sex with Carol long before she was sixteen. He would have told her he would always look after her, always keep her safe, she could trust him. Within six months they were married. Her parents may have been quick to give their consent but Collins didn't imagine they had gone to the wedding.

By the time Carol was seventeen, Daniel was born, and soon enough social services were back, this time wanting to protect him. Neighbours had heard arguments from the Chilcotts' flat and police had been called to a number of these 'domestics'. No statements, no charges, but social services had to be informed. More questions, but this time they would have been accompanied by threats.

"You need to tell us what has gone on between you and your husband Carol, we need to be know your baby is safe, or we'll have to take action to make sure he is safe."

Carol would have guessed what this "action" was. She knew that given the chance they would take Daniel into care.

Collins tried to put himself in the shoes of that frightened and suffering seventeen year old girl. She would have known that if she gave the social workers any idea what Alex was like, they would whisk Daniel away. She would lose the one thing in the world she loved and be left alone with her abusive husband.

Did she ever have another choice? Could she have broken away back then and made a life for herself and Daniel? Collins asked himself those questions, as he stared out his third floor office window, towards the hills that rose beyond the Gartside. He knew how those conversations would have landed with a young mother. From when he first looked into her face, Collins had been confirmed in his belief that, even back then, she would already have been too terrified to tell the truth. Terrified of her husband, terrified of the social workers, terrified of losing her baby.

So Carol said nothing and learned to live with the abuse. What went on in the house stayed in the house. Collins wondered what she knew of her husband's activities when he slipped out at night and guessed that she didn't want to know, didn't want it to be her business. Her business was bringing up Daniel, keeping him safe, and then Crystal came along, and finally the twins. Her life's course was set; a buffer between a violent husband and four children who had to be sheltered from his wrath, protected from his cruelty, and at the same time kept out of care. Collins knew she would do what she needed to do to maintain her precarious status quo.

The records showed that the Chilcott children had been on and off social services books since Daniel had been born. There had been one attempt to get a Care Order ten years earlier, but the proceedings had fizzled out. Concerns from health visitors, teachers and school nurses persisted, nonetheless. Police referrals to social services were made each time the old man was suspected of having crept out at dusk and made a nuisance of himself in the park, or when the neighbours had rung to say he and Carol were having another fight. Nothing proven, nothing to substantiate the suspicion that the kids were being harmed, just more concerns.

The children seemed to get more troubled as they got older, with the most worrying being Daniel, the fourteen year old. His school was at a loss as to what to do with him. Not that he was naughty in class, just vacant, withdrawn, a non-participant, who seemed to communicate with no one. His homework usually got done, but the suspicion was someone else was doing it for him. Now he had withdrawn from school to the extent that he had not yet been back for the first two weeks since the Easter break. The younger siblings had similar but less obviously concerning behaviour in school. It might be that their problems would become more pronounced as they got older, but for now it was Daniel who was causing the most concern. He was the one with whom Collins was going to start.

Collins turned his attention back to the police file to read the account of Chilcott's last conviction, five year's earlier. Collins was drawn to a familiar name in the case summary: PC Tara Sharma. Now Sergeant Sharma, and a colleague on the Pro Team, Tara was sat just across the aisle of their open plan office.

The police had received reports that a flasher had been spotted in Gartside Park, emerging from the shadows and the shrubbery. He would always disappear by the time officers arrived, so they set up a sting. Tara Sharma was sent into the park, in plain clothes, just as it was getting dark. Sure enough, Chilcott appeared at the edge of the wooded area the kids call 'Hangman's Hollow'. As he exposed himself he was apprehended by Sharma's colleagues, who had been ready to pounce, when she hit her radio.

Collins called to her across the office. "Tara, we've re-opened a CP enquiry into the Chilcott family: eighty-four Gartside Gardens. You've had dealings with the old man haven't you? Alex Chilcott."

Sharma stopped typing the report she had been working on. She took some time before answering, "yeah, I think I remember him."

"And? You can normally do better than that Tara. You're like a walking encyclopaedia of every sex pest between London and Birmingham."

"A paedo-pedia" shouted their colleague, Stan, from behind Collins; ever eager to bring some humour to what could otherwise be a tough work place.

"Thanks Stan, very tasteful as ever," said Collins scornfully.

Before Collins got to quiz Sharma any further, she had hastily got up and was heading for the door, clutching an armful of files.

"Tara?" Collins called after her, as she disappeared through the office door.

"CPS" she shouted back, waving one of the files as she went.

Collins watched her go before returning to the papers in front of him. Chilcott had got probation for the last offence. "Just another flasher", "no real menace", would have been the prevailing view in the magistrates' court. Of course the social workers were concerned by Alex Chilcott's worrying behaviour. The Chilcott kids were assessed again. Regular home visits followed and protection plans were formulated. But Carol said he was a great dad, "he may be quiet, and not want to make a show for bloody social services, but he loves those kids." Not enough reason to take them away, not enough reason to split up the family. In time Alex Chilcott got his probation done, with the help of home visits, because of his agoraphobia. Without any other incidents the social workers backed off; moved on to the next hard case: the baby boy down the road with the hard to explain bruising, and the girl whose mummy tells her she wishes they were both dead.

Collins' instinct was that the Chilcotts' children's situation was far worse than anyone had appreciated. His home visit had told him all he needed to know, and now this was underlined from his reading of all the old case files. He also knew that without some tangible evidence he, like all those who had come before him, would be unable to stop the harm that was being done to those children.

10.15pm

Daniel's room was in darkness. He did his best to see through the net curtains in his bedroom, just as he had earlier, as Tom Collins had driven away from Gartside Gardens. He remembered being surprised at his expensive car. He had him down as a copper, only the police had decent cars, but his mum had said he was a social worker.

He knew exactly how the interview with his mum would have gone. Her making excuses for his dad, "no he can't be disturbed" not after all the stress he's been caused by "those silly girls making up stories". Daniel had heard it enough times. All the while his father would have had his ear right against the back of the front room door, listening for a slip up by his mum. It was the same any time that the school, or social workers, or police came around to the house. The only time they ever got to speak to his dad was when they had an arrest warrant.

That bloke probably won't be back. Just a routine enquiry. He's done his job, checked everything was OK. Mum will have told him we're all doing very well thank you. "He's a very caring father, only wishes he could do more with the kids but it's his agoraphobia you see". Something like that. I wonder if they know she's talking shit? They're probably not bothered. All part of the job, having people lie to you. He's checked it out now. Everyone's still alive. They've got nothing they can pin on him. Carry on like before.

His mum had managed to keep his dad in check that afternoon. She had persuaded him that no damage had been done, but Daniel knew from her pleading and his threats, she had just forestalled the inevitable. This was his father's preferred time, once the lights were out, and he didn't have the inconvenience of the little ones, screaming and crying, while he beat their mother up. This way they just cried into their pillows.

It was still all quiet for now, but Daniel knew that at any minute the noise was likely to start to build from downstairs.

If I hear him running that bath, I swear I'll kill him.

27

As he thought it, Daniel pulled an 8 inch bowie knife from under his mattress. He held it flat against the inside of his forearm. He liked the feel of it: cold, hard, powerful. He pointed the blade, and traced a line from his wrist down to his elbow; just a line, no blood.

You wouldn't cut? You're a pussy.

I would.

Yeah would you? Why you and not him?

I want to know what it feels like. I want to know what it will feel like for him, when I do cut him open.

Daniel could now hear the first noises from the front room. It was just a low rumble: threats, swearing, a bang on the table. He wished it would stop at that, but he knew there was more to come.

Just leave her alone, you bastard. Have a growl, like the big ugly bear that you are, then crawl back to your cave.

Daniel knew his mum would be pleading now. She'd be telling him she did well, telling him there's no need. Daniel knew his father would be a millimetre from snapping.

If he touches her I'll kill him.

He could hear more clearly now from downstairs, "No Al. No Al. Please Al."

The bastard. The fucking bastard.

The noise was closer. Daniel could see it in his mind's eye.

On the stairs now. He'd have her by the hair, dragging her up, step by step.

Don't scream mum. I can't listen to you scream.

Fucking knife. What you fucking for? For cutting cunts like him. Then do it. Fucking do it. He's outside the door. Do it.

"Not the bath Al. Not the bath."

Not the bath. You bastard.

"Please Al. There's no need. Please Al."

There's no point in pleading with that bastard.

Daniel held the knife flat, an inch from his face. He could see the outline of his own reflection.

That's him, looking out from that knife at you. That's him in you, in that reflection. You're his son all right. You're a fucking coward, fucking yellow. You're too shit scared to do anything to him. Just stay in here and piss the bed again then.

I can't bear the screaming. Stop screaming mum.

Fucking bath taps now. Puke and blood and tears. It should be his blood.

Daniel couldn't look at himself in the knife's reflection any more. He lowered the point to the inside of his forearm and for the first time made an incision that drew blood; opening up a thick, ruby-red stream, that drove its way down his inner arm, and pooled beneath his elbow, dripping on to his bed sheet.

Cut then knife. Cut. Show me what you can do. Open up my arm then.

It should be his blood, not mine, not mum's, his.

FRIDAY 11TH MAY

6.30am

Carol Chilcott looked at herself in the bedroom mirror.

"Mirror, mirror on the wall who's the fairest of them all?" she mumbled, as she stared deep into her tired eyes; stared beyond the bags, and the red rims, deep into her own soul.

Where did looks ever get you anyway? Fingered in the Parky's hut on Gartside while you were still at primary school, fucked by every one of the Gartside Boys by the time you were fourteen.

"What good were your looks? You're better off without them," she said to her reflection.

Carol examined the fingerprints on each side of her face and around her neck. She guessed that they would bruise by tomorrow. It wasn't like Alex to leave marks that could be seen.

He's getting careless, or madder, or angrier.

Carol confronted her greatest fear, facing into the thought that was never far from her mind.

What if he kills you? I swear another ten seconds under that water and you weren't coming back. What good will all this have been if you're dead? What about the kids then? No mum and a dad in prison for murdering her; that's if the bastard doesn't get off with it? What will it all have been for then? Suffering at the hands of that pig all these years, to leave the kids as orphans.

No, he won't kill me and he won't break me. He can carry on with his water torture. I'll survive and one day, when I've got the strength and the money, we'll be gone.

"Stop kidding yourself," Carol whispered disparagingly to her reflected self.

You know the only way you're leaving him is in a box. The only life you've got is with Alex Chilcott. That was your choice and there's no way out of it now.

Carol pressed on with cleaning her face up.

Come on girl, find some make-up from somewhere to cover up those marks. Bloody social worker is coming back later.

Carol had been surprised by Tom Collins. He seemed a bit sharper than the rest, not the usual snotty nosed student, who had barely read the file, they normally sent around. This one had actually done his homework.

He will probably notice the make-up and that will start him thinking. Better that than he spots the fingerprints down the side of your face though.

Carol was relieved that at least there had been no police last night. Alex was getting more violent again, ramping up her punishment, but the neighbours didn't seem to bother with the police any more.

"What's the point?" they must think. "She still stays with him, won't ever press charges, it's her look out in the end," is probably what they said.

It was getting light. She knew she had to get the bathroom cleaned up before the kids got up. She thought about the pools of water on the bathroom floor. Bath water mixed with her blood and with her sick.

Get it clean. Get it behind you. Hopefully he won't blow like that again for a while.

It was time to face out of the bedroom. Carol knew that Alex would be asleep in the armchair. The TV would still be on. It was always on. Those papers and the TV. That was Alex's world. She had seen Tom Collins eyeing up the papers, "there's no crime in keeping newspapers. It's just a collection, like other people have collections," she had said to him.

Collins didn't look convinced. He seemed more bothered than the other social workers. He looked angry.

Don't know what he's got to be angry about, with his smart car and smart suit. He's not the one walking on egg shells, trying

33

to make sure he doesn't get strangled or drowned, trying to keep this family together with social services breathing down his neck, and a lunatic who's listening on the other side of the front room door.

Collins was pushy too.

How had he said it?

"To be blunt Mrs Chilcott you're going to have to work with me, whether you like it, or not. I will get to the bottom of what's going on for your children, so you're better off being honest with me now."

Be honest with him. Don't make me laugh. Why would I ever be honest with a social worker? If they can't work out what's going on in this family, after all this time, it doesn't make you want to tell them anything does it? I would have told them twenty years ago. I wanted to tell them, but they just kept putting me back home. Sending me back for more.

And what would you do anyway, Mr. Collins, if I told you? Told you when your interrogation finishes the next one will begin. When you're done threatening me, he'll start. If I'm lucky I'll still be alive tomorrow Mr. Collins. Is that what you want to hear?

What would you do if I told you about the bath, lungs full of cold water, choking it in, puking it out? Crawling to my bedroom. Pushing a chair against the door handle and praying to be left alone. Lying shaking, barely able to breathe, because every time I breathe I want to be sick, and I hear him pushing at the door. Hoping to god the chair does its job. Hoping he'll just grunt and curse, and I'll hear his feet on the stairs, retreating to his armchair. Hoping that it will just be the threats through the door, "don't sleep, I'm coming back for you". I couldn't sleep anyway, you bastard. How could I sleep with every bit of my body crying out like it is?

Worst though, Mr. Collins, are the nights he is determined to have me; to ram in that final nail to complete my humiliation. The chair gives way under his force and there he is in the doorway. I don't look, can't look, but I know the picture exactly, his silhouette enormous, as he enters the blacked out room.

I know what's coming next. I want my shaking body to be still, but the harder I try, the more it shakes. It's like convulsions, my body is protesting against what it has been through and what it is about to endure. I hear the buckle of his belt open, the zip of his fly, the muffled bunching of denim down his legs to his ankles, and then the slap of elastic from his underpants on the back of his thighs. Shoes, socks, t-shirt and jumper still in place; he stands at the back of the bed. Throwing off the duvet, he pulls my calves towards him. I keep the pillow hugged tight to my face, as I'm dragged to where he wants me, face down in front of him.

And then it begins. Hard, pummelling strokes, thrust at the place of his choosing; more often above rather than below. As he says when he's working up to one of his explosions, "Anywhere else is a waste of time. I can't feel anything anymore."

How long it lasts I don't know. The agony feels endless. The pain stretches on into the distance, with every thrust and with every handful of hair he grabs at its roots. But it does stop: when he tenses, and releases my hair, and the elastic of his pants slaps the bottom of his back, and his trousers are pulled back up, and the fly is sealed, and the buckle is fastened, and the door closes; and I am left to shake and retch into my pillow.

Those are the worst nights, Mr. Collins; drowned nearly dead, then raped in my own bed. What will you do with that story Mr. Collins? Me in a refuge and the kids in care? Al wouldn't let that happen anyway. "I'd kill you all before I'd let them take you, and you try leaving, and you know I'd find you." He's said it enough times, "over your dead body" and then that cruel smile as he thinks about the best way to do it.

And that's just the violence, but I could tell you so much more Mr. Collins. About the nights when he slips out to prowl around Gartside Park, or about his other collection he has hidden away. I could tell you so much more about the scared little lives my children have to lead, but if I did I'd probably never get to be with them again. So no, I won't "be honest" with you Mr. Collins, it's too late for that.

Carol moved the chair from behind the bedroom door and faced out on to the landing. She got the mop for the bathroom and confronted the scene of her assault.

"Little jobs," she told herself. "One step at a time. You can do it girl."

7.00am

Daniel heard the familiar sound of the mop and bucket being pulled from the landing cupboard and filled in the bathroom.

She's still alive then. I'm still alive then. The morning's here and we can start again with family life. Creep around, hoping he won't kick off again for a while.

So you did it then big man? Spilt blood like you promised? Shame it was yours, eh? Blood all over your sheets. Makes a change from piss, though, I suppose.

Daniel lay in his blood stained sheets, repeating the arguments he had had with himself so many times before, and berating himself for his failure to be a man.

It can't go on like this. Someone is going to die in this house soon. Either you're going to do it, or he is. Have some balls. Take control of your life for once. Control. That's always been his. Total control. You could have control. You and that favourite knife of yours under the pillow. Except you're just too shit scared.

"Dan, wake up. You've got to go in today."

Daniel knew that his mother would be in, to hunt him out of bed any minute, to try to get him off to school. That's when she would see the blood on the bedsheet draped around his forearm. Daniel looked at the wound. It wasn't a big cut and he thought it could probably be covered with a plaster.

"Dan I mean it, you're going to school today."

It's that social worker who came around yesterday. It will have spooked her and now she'll make me go in, to make it look better. Go in for what? To give the kids someone to pick on. "Pikey Dan, with the sicko dad." It will make their day.

The teachers are as bad. Most of them are cunts. Think the same as the kids, just say it in a different way. "Nice of you to join us today Mr. Chilcott. Shame your mother still hasn't managed to get you any school shoes." Worst are the ones who say they care. Always want me to talk to them, tell them what's bothering me. "Is there a problem at home Daniel? If you'd just talk to us, we might be able to help."

They can't help. Nobody can help. So just keep quiet. Say nothing. Nothing at all.

"Right Daniel, you better be up."

Here she comes.

As Carol pushed through the bedroom door she saw the makeshift tourniquet around her son's forearm.

"Oh god Dan, what have you done? Where's this blood from? Oh Dan."

Daniel immediately realised that his cut was felt by his mother as yet another assault.

"Don't cry mum. It's not that bad. See, it's just the skin."

"Why have you cut yourself Dan? Why?"

Carol had so recently stopped herself from crying and now the dam began to break again, as she held her son and began to sob.

Daniel fumbled for words, struggling to say why cutting himself felt like the right thing to do. The only thing he could do.

"I can't stand the noise mum. I can't stand it. What he does to you."

"It won't last forever Dan. It won't. One day we'll be away from here."

"One day he'll kill you mum."

There it was, the truth that Carol so often fought to deny. There it was spoken now by her beloved baby boy.

"He won't son." Carol fought to get the words out, between tears and snot and her shallow breaths.

"I wouldn't let him. Not for me, but for you and the others. I won't let him."

Carol fought to gain some composure. "Come on Dan, let's get this cleaned up."

Daniel didn't want to let go of her. He just wanted her to keep holding him. This was the one time it felt all right. The one time.

Just hold me mum.

Carol let go of her son, turning her attention to his cut.

"We'll get this cleaned up. Under your school jumper no one will know it's there. If you've got games, I'll give you a note. You've got to go in today, though, Dan. That social worker is a bit different from the rest, so we'll have to watch out. I want you back in school today, and then back here for four o'clock, because he's coming to see you."

"What's he interested in me for? Thought he'd be more bothered about the girls, seeing as it's young girls that the Bastard's interested in."

"Don't ever say that Dan. He might be a bastard but he's never touched your sisters and he's never going to."

Daniel lifted his eyes to his mother's as he confronted her with another truth she had spent years fighting away.

"Not yet maybe, mum, not yet."

"Never, hear me, never. Over my dead body."

"Yeah, that's what he says too."

Carol had faced too many truths already this morning and knew that her one way to cope was to keep on going.

"Come on let's find you a plaster and get you to school. When that social worker comes, you won't say anything about last night, or show him your cut, will you Dan? It won't do any of us any good. They'd just take you and the others away from me and god knows what your dad would do then?"

"Don't call him my dad. Bastard's his name." Daniel snapped at his mother. "What am I going to say to him anyway? Course I won't say nothing to the social worker. I never say nothing to anyone."

Carol looked lovingly at her poor wounded little boy, and her heart broke one more time, but somehow, from somewhere, she managed to find a smile.

"Good lad. We'll get there in the end. We'll get there."

4.50pm

Collins was late for the four o'clock appointment he had arranged with Carol Chilcott. His plans for the day had been blown out of the water when he received notice from CPS that the proceedings against one of his sex cases, Carl Johnson, were about to be withdrawn, and he would be released from custody. This meant, without a conviction, Collins would need an interim order from the family court to stop Johnson going back to the family home on the Gartside. Collins also had to go to St Christopher's to let Mickey Johnson know the news; his disclosure about his father wasn't going to make it to a criminal trial, and he was about to be released.

Hurriedly he phoned around colleagues to get a message to Carol Chilcott to let her know he would be late. He wanted to limit the opportunity for excuses for Daniel to duck out of their meeting. Tara Sharma was on the estate and helped him out. He made a mental note to insist to Carol Chilcott that she give him her mobile number, which she had thus far withheld, so that he wouldn't have to scrabble around like this each time a crisis messed up his diary.

Back outside eighty-four Gartside Gardens, Collins tried to focus on the task in hand; flipping from the detailed exercise of providing evidence to the court, to the job of finding a way to engage, what he knew, would be a reluctant teenager. Now, knowing what it was like inside, the Chilcotts' place looked sadder and more spirit-sapping than ever. Collins was determined that this time he wasn't going in. He knew, if he was to have any chance of getting the kid to talk, his meeting with Daniel needed to happen away from the house. He took a deep breath and knocked hard.

Carol took her time to respond. As she poked her head around the front door, Collins noticed she was wearing make-up, which did something to take the edge off the tiredness and fear that had been so evident in her face the previous day. He hazarded an informed guess that the make-up had been applied to hide bruising, which meant that Alex had been at it again.

"Turn up when it suits, eh? Don't worry about us or our plans," Carol said by way of welcome.

"Tara got a message to you I hope?" Collins replied.

"Yeah, she stuck a note through the door. Looked like she was too la-di-da to risk having to actually speak to any of us." Collins got the impression Carol was enjoying the chance to put one over on him and the system he represented. He moved the conversation on to the reason for his visit.

"Is he here?"

"He's here, but he doesn't want to talk," Carol answered firmly.

"Who? Your husband or your son?"

Collins knew who she meant, but wanted to remind Carol he needed to speak with her husband in the course of his work. He also wanted to redress the balance in their verbal jousting. As expected, this shot across the bows sent Carol's defences up.

"No, Al's in his bed, you can't see him, but Daniel is here. Like I say, he won't have anything to tell you. He doesn't talk to people he doesn't know."

"Send him out Carol. We'll see if he's got anything to say. Don't worry, I won't keep him out too long."

After several minutes, and evidence of cajoling from inside, Daniel reluctantly emerged into the light: a slight, pale figure. He had on a pair of jeans, ripped through wear rather than design, a black hoody that dwarfed his meagre frame and a pair of threadbare trainers. Collins would have taken him for eleven or twelve years old, not fourteen. His thick black hair was unruly and fell so far over his eyes that Collins wondered how he could see at all. In any event, there was no attempt at eye contact, as Daniel stood hunched, head down, with his hands in the pockets of his hoody. Collins could make out the tale-tell pimples around Daniel's nose that suggested he had been abusing aerosols.

Daniel looked much as Collins had expected, from what he had read about the boy, and what he had experienced so many times when presented with children who had been neglected and traumatised. Yet still his heart ached for the pathetic little figure in front of him. That he never lost that pain, when encountering children who had been abused, surprised him. It was supposed to wear off, you were supposed to become hardened to it. Otherwise how do you survive in this job? That was how Dave Andrews was still doing it, but Collins knew that would never be his way. While he was in this job he knew it was always going to hurt. That was what made him good at it, but it was also what made him vulnerable.

"Hello Daniel, I'm Tom. I've heard a lot about you. Good to meet you at last." Collins said it with feeling, like he had really waited all his life to meet this scrawny, injured teenager, like he was the most important person in the world.

In reply Daniel gave a barely visible nod of his head.

"We need to have a talk Daniel. Do you prefer Daniel or Dan?"

No response.

"Well your mum calls you Dan. So if that's OK, I'll go with Dan?"

Daniel was staring at an empty milk cartoon beside the doorstep.

"Let's have a little walk and see how we get on Dan."

Collins turned and started down the path to the gate. He looked back to see Daniel, still on the doorstep, still staring at the milk carton.

"Come on Dan. I've been looking forward to meeting you. Come on, we'll take a walk down the precinct and get a bar of chocolate and a can of coke, if you fancy that?"

Daniel took a few tentative steps towards Collins, who opened the gate with a wide smile, and ushered him through.

"Good lad. I'm going old school – Mars Bar. What about you? Drifter, Twix or are you going to join me in the stars? Galaxy, Milky Way? Why do they name so many chocolates after things in the solar system? What's that about?"

Collins looked across at Daniel, not expecting an answer, but leaving space for the boy to communicate in some form. On the short walk to the newsagents their conversation followed this same pattern: Collins sharing memories of previous times on Gartside, his visits to St Christopher's, Daniel's secondary school, and asking how Daniel was feeling having gone back in after his time off. Daniel's contribution to this conversation was no more than the occasional shrug of his shoulders, until Collins probed some more about school.

"Because you did go in today, didn't you Dan?"

Daniel gave a small nod.

"But you didn't stay too long? I spoke with Mr Everard, your Year Head. He said they didn't see you after about ten o'clock."

Daniel shot Collins a glance, before hastily returning his eyes to the pavement. They were almost at the shop door, and Collins was happy to leave the question hanging for now. He had let Daniel know he was well-briefed on his movements, and would continue to build from here, when the time was right.

The newsagent's had the same left behind feel as the rest of the estate. Many of the shelves were half empty, and the Sikh proprietor had the resigned air of a man who knew it wouldn't matter how many hours he sat behind his counter: he was always destined to struggle on the slim pickings of the estate's customers. Daniel wasted no time in picking a bar of chocolate and taking a can of coke from the fridge. At the counter he fiddled with a bag of crisps, and Collins recognised adding to the haul might enhance his chances of communicating with the boy.

"Crisps as well eh? This really will be a feast. How about, if you have the crisps, you tell me where you were when you should have been in school today?"

Daniel continued to finger the various packets in front of him. Collins wasn't sure if he was deciding on whether to accept the deal or just struggling to choose a flavour. Eventually Daniel picked one and put it beside the rest of Collins' purchases on the counter.

Collins enthusiastically greeted Daniel's selection, "Bacon Wheat Crunchies, the crisp of kings. Good choice my man."

They sat next to each other on a metal bench in the deserted precinct, overlooked by the three high rise blocks of Gartside Towers, which stood at the heart of the estate. Daniel went for his chocolate bar first.

"Mint Aero. I prefer the plain myself but each to his own," Collins mused, as the boy hungrily bit into his chocolate. "Aero, not quite in the stars but if you've got the money, you'll soon be able to take an Aero-plane into outer space". He winced at his poor attempt at humour. Daniel remained unmoved.

Collins looked at the run down surroundings of the precinct. "It would be no bad thing to get a plane out of this place, eh? You ever been on a plane Dan?"

Daniel shock his head. It wasn't a big movement, and it wasn't a verbal contribution to the conversation, but it was the most that Collins had got thus far.

"One day, eh Dan. I was older than you when I went on a plane for the first time. It's something to look forward to. It's beautiful when you get up there."

Collins right arm swept across the surrounding view.

"All this, these tower blocks, the estate, Town, it's tiny when you get up there. It gives you a different perspective on things. You realise we're just like little ants charging about, bumping into each other down here, but we're part of this great big green island, that's all hills and rivers and fields, which is part of this beautiful planet of oceans and mountains and deserts."

Like the needle settling on the well-worn grove of a record, Collins was warming to a familiar theme. One he had shared with countless teenagers over the years.

"When you're up there, you think anything is possible: and it is Dan. Life can be what you want it to be. You've got to believe and you've got to be brave."

Collins had said what he had wanted to say to frame the work he planned to embark on with Daniel. He stopped on his monologue, and started on his chocolate bar, while Daniel opened his crisps. He knew Daniel could talk, if he wanted to, and he knew he would talk, if he felt safe enough to do so. He also knew it could take time. As they sat and munched, Collins moved the conversation on to more challenging terrain.

"Mr Everard is worried about you and so is your form tutor. They like you Dan, they say you're a good lad, but that you've stopped interacting with the other kids, you don't look well and now you've stopped turning up for school."

Daniel had his head turned away from Collins, staring blankly towards the hills that started to gently rise beyond the last houses on the far end of the estate.

"I'm not expecting you to spill your guts about everything that's going on for you Dan, and everything that goes on at home. You've just met me. Why should you trust me?" Collins sensed that this was exactly the question that Daniel was asking himself.

"In time I want you to be able to talk to me, but let's just take it slow. You don't have to say anything for now, if you don't want to, or maybe if it's easiest, just nod or shake your head."

Daniel didn't respond.

"So Dan here's what I think's happening. It's my best guess from all I know about you. You tell me if I'm right or wrong." Collins started to outline his assessment of Daniel's situation to see if he could provoke a response.

"Your dad hits your mum, bullies her, frightens her. Am I right?"

Daniel kept staring into the distance without acknowledging the question.

"You love your mum, and she loves you and your brother and sisters, so you don't want social workers to know how bad it is at home, in case we take you away."

Still nothing from Daniel.

"It's not just that your dad's violent though, is it? He does strange things, frightening things, and that makes you and your mum worry about what else he'll do?

Daniel's stare remained fixed but Collins noticed he was having to work hard to keep himself still. He could see his breathing had quickened, and his hands and feet had started to twitch. He knew he was following a fertile seam.

"He's a frightening man to live with, and you don't know who he'll hurt next, and you don't know how far he's capable of going. Are you worried something really bad is going to happen, Dan?"

At this Daniel put his head in his hands, as a sign he could take no more. Collins knew he had hit the spot, but knew he needed to stop now.

"Okay Dan, I wanted you to know that I know." Collins paused to emphasise his point. He knew. They both knew, and that knowing, could be the start of something.

"It's not your responsibility to hold on to this stuff on your own. You're fourteen years old, you should be having a life, enjoying being a teenager. You didn't tell me, you haven't dropped anyone in it. You just need to know that I know."

"Come on let's get you home. Don't worry, I'll tell your mum you said nothing. Well you didn't did you? We're going to do this together Dan, in your time and we are going to make sure you, your mum and the little ones are looked after. You're not going to be punished for what your dad does."

As he said it, Collins put a hand on Daniel's shoulder, and the boy raised his head from his hands.

As they got up from the bench Collins reminded Daniel of their deal in the newsagents.

"One thing Dan. We said if I got you the crisps you'd tell me where you went when you left school this morning."

Collins wasn't actually sure whether Daniel had really entered into this pact, but he thought it was worth a try. Daniel said nothing but looked over his shoulder, at the nearest of the tower blocks, and nodded towards one of the higher floors.

"Oh Parkside Point," Collins smiled. "Were you up there for the view across the hills?" He winked at Daniel, grateful that the silent child was starting to give up his secrets.

They walked back without Collins feeling the need to fill the silence now. They had shared something. They had made a start.

As they approached Collins' car he noticed Daniel's interest. "My pride and joy, the A4. I only got her a couple of months ago." Daniel peered inside through the blacked out window into the driver's side. "I'll take you for a spin next time. Same time Monday."

And then they were outside Daniel's front door. They stood hesitantly on the doorstep. It was clear that their shared knowledge of what went on in that house was weighing heavily on each of them.

Collins could have taken Daniel there and then and tried to get an Emergency Protection Order. But what additional evidence did he actually have, other than the sense that the boy's body language confirmed his hypothesis? How much more vulnerable would he be making Carol and the kids if he acted in haste now? And so he stood with his hands in his pockets, looking at Daniel, asking himself what he could do for the best.

"If he kicks off, you or your mum have got to call the police. It's the only way to keep you safe for now. Keep working with me and we'll get a better plan for the long-term."

Collins felt sick as he said it, felt like he was pushing the boy over the top to face his fate in no man's land.

Daniel pushed the key into the lock before turning to look at Collins. Briefly, for the first time since they had met, he held eye contact with his new social worker. Then he was gone, sucked back in to the black-hole that was his home.

5.15pm

As Collins started the drive from Gartside into Queenstown, he asked himself what he had learned from his hour with Daniel Chilcott. Beyond feeling he had confirmed for himself his belief that Alex Chilcott continued to be a highly volatile domestic abuser, he didn't have much. Certainly not enough to convince Dave Andrews to get off his backside and take some meaningful action.

He did feel like he had connected with Daniel. He guessed more so than any other adult had managed to connect with Daniel for a long time. Daniel may not have uttered a word, but Collins felt he had made those first hard yards, which would enable him to get close to Daniel and through him unlock the world of the Chilcott family.

Collins thought about his own son Jamie. A year younger than Daniel, but bigger, stronger and with so much more energy and life about him. Collins visualised Jamie on a football pitch: throwing himself into tackles, charging up and down demanding the ball, the centre of the action. Poor Daniel, you couldn't imagine him in any team game. He would be blown away, or would melt into the margins, until disappearing all together. No doubt that had been his experience at school, in games and in the classroom, or left to sit alone when the others paired up for school trips. No wonder the kid didn't want to go in.

Not that all was tranquil in Jamie's life either. It was six months since Tom Collins had been invited to watch his son play football. For much of that time he had been incommunicado, unwilling to talk to his dad, because of one of the many fall outs between Collins and his estranged wife Janet. This was the pattern that had been established since they separated two years ago; Collins desperate to see his son and treading on egg-shells with Janet, so that he could retain his relationship with Jamie. When things broke down with Janet it was Collins' punishment from wife and son to shut down all communication with Jamie.

Collins spent the rest of the drive to Town flipping between the stories of the two boys. One whose father was a monster who had destroyed his life, and the other…Collins knew that there were times Jamie thought that of him and Janet certainly did.

6.15pm

Back in the office Collins added some urgent notes to the system so that the weekend duty team were warned of the dangers at the Chilcott home. He also called through to police intelligence to update the risk flag on the house, and spoke to the inspector on weekend duty, to ask for patrols to keep an extra eye on the location. It wasn't that Carol or the kids were necessarily in any more danger than they had been before, but now Collins knew about it, or at least thought he knew about it, he needed to make sure all that could be done was being done, while they were all still in that house.

Collins thought about Carol. Should he have gone back in to talk to her about her abuse? About outreach support or the chance to go to a refuge? He knew from everything Carol had been through, and everything she had said to him, how should would have responded to that. She was beyond prising herself away from Alex Chilcott, the chance of that had surely gone many years before. Her best hope was that they could get Chilcott locked up. Collins knew it was more likely that he would be able to get a Care Order on the kids, but that would mean leaving her on her own with her husband. That wasn't the result Collins wanted, but his first responsibility was to those children.

There was one tangible lead that Collins got from Daniel. Something was attracting a fourteen year old boy to the top of Parkside Point, when he was supposed to be at school. The chances were he wasn't the only school kid going up there either. That was worth checking out with his police colleagues to see who they knew up in those flats. Collins wandered over to the only police officer left in the office at 6pm on a Friday, PC Joe Bowles, known to his colleagues as 'Stan'.

"Stan have you got anyone you're interested in up near the top of Parkside Point?"

Bowles twiddled an imaginary moustache in the manner of a down at heel Poirot. His crumpled white shirt, bearing the ketchup stain from his lunch time burger, barely covered his expanding girth, making him look the antithesis of the sophisticated Belgian detective.

"Let me have a think," he mused in his South Wales lilt. "Just from my computer-like memory of all things criminal on the Darkside: I can give you cannabis and pills at number forty-two, small time fence knocking out hooky gear at forty-four, for Class A's you'd want number forty-seven, and I can offer you a most charming registered sex offender at number forty-nine. What do you fancy? Take your pick?"

"I've got a fourteen year old boy who's going up there when he should be at school. I hope it's not the nonce," Collins replied, turning down the corners of his mouth into a grimace as he did so.

"Tut-tut, you're jumping to conclusions Thomas. I said he was a sex offender, I never said he was a paedophile. This gentleman's interests are in adult females. Unfortunately for him, and them, these are not females who are interested in what he has to offer; and therefore, he has had to use coercive means to procure their sexual services."

"Drop the flowery bollocks, Stan. I take it you're saying he's got no interest in teenage boys. What about the others?"

"My best guess would be number forty-two. There's often teenagers coming and going. It's petty dealing, on the bottom rung of the food chain. We wouldn't be interested if there weren't kids involved."

"As it seems one of my boys is a regular visitor, I might pop up to number forty-two to acquaint myself with the tenant. What's the name?"

"Damon Hartley, you might know him from your old youth offending days when you started here. Probably one of your graduates?"

At this Collins' heart sank. Damon Hartley had been one of his very first cases when he came to the patch, as a newly qualified social worker. 'Damo', as his mates knew him, was Tom Collins' first mission. He had poured hundreds of hours into him and his mum: getting them moved out of Gartside to make a new start, getting him off the gear, helping him to get an apprenticeship. Thirteen years since he had said a fond farewell he was back, and pushing drugs to school kids.

Like Daniel an hour earlier, Collins sunk his head into his hands, pushing back his thick black hair and rubbing his palms on his eyelids.

"Damon Hartley, one of my great successes. What's the point of this bloody work Stan? What is the point? We're wasting our time."

Bowles put an avuncular arm around his younger colleague's shoulder.

"The point is that we give kids a chance that they would never have had otherwise. We give them a chance to get away from the mess, and abuse, and hurt. It doesn't mean it will all turn out peachy, but at least they've had a chance that they would never have had." Bowles smiled down at Collins, radiating his usual hope and good sense.

"Come on Tommo, it's been a long week. Call it a day. I'd offer to buy you a pint, but I know you wouldn't thank me."

"Yeah, yeah. I've got ten minutes of notes to write up and I'll switch off. I'll get down the gym. Healthy body, healthy mind and all that," Collins replied, in as positive a manner as he could manage.

"I'll have one for you Tom." With that Bowles manoeuvred his ample frame out of the office door and Collins was alone.

He sat motionless as he stared towards the green of the distant hills, which sucked in the soft evening glow of the sinking sun to their west. In front of the hills he could pick out the slate grey of the Gartside towers. He thought of the lives being led, the deals being done, and the hearts being broken in those towers, which from where he sat were no more than tiny lego bricks. Daniel might already be back up there, getting high or getting low, with Damon. All the hope that Collins had for Damon and for himself when he first arrived here, all for what?

Collins' reflections were interrupted by a ping from his mobile phone. It was a text from Tara Sharma.

"TIME TO STOP WORKING!"

He smiled. It wasn't like Tara to get in touch with him outside of office hours. Why was she contacting him now? What he knew of her was that she worked amazingly hard, she was a valued colleague and a damn good copper. Beyond that he knew little else about her, other than she was very clear: work was work and home was home.

He texted her back. "How do you know I'm still working?"

Her immediate response, "Because I'm outside and your car's here. I need to talk to you. See you out here in five?"

He looked out of the third floor office widow to the car park, and there was Tara propped against the bonnet of her Polo. She waved and beckoned for him to hurry.

Collins was intrigued. This was out of character for Tara.

It must be something important if she wanted to talk at seven o'clock on a Friday evening.

He shut down his computer and started to make his way out of the office. He decided to take a brief detour on route, to check the toilet mirror, to make sure he was looking presentable. He wasn't entirely happy with what he saw staring back at him; he looked tired from a long week's work and could see evidence of the onset of middle age. His thick black hair had the first strands of grey appearing, and the creases around his eyes were an ever more permanent feature.

For all that, his strong physique filled his well-cut suit, and Tara's arrival had brought a glint to his eye, which had been missing of late. Collins grandmother had told him he was one of the 'black Irish', a throwback to a descendant cast ashore on the west coast of Ireland by the retreating Spanish armada. His legacy was brown, almost black, eyes, set in dark features.

Collins' felt his looks were somewhat tarnished by a deep scar above his right eye. The mark left by the stitches was a reminder of a past he was trying hard to leave behind. He wondered what Tara Sharma would make of that past.

7pm

As he made his way out to the car park, Tom Collins admitted to himself that he wasn't just intrigued, he was excited. Tara Sharma was a world unto herself, Collins' most exotic and enigmatic colleague. Fiercely dedicated to her work and her career, Sharma was a formidable operator, who was marked out for further promotion in the police.

Her physical appearance complemented her professional persona. Always impeccably turned out, her long black hair meticulously tied in a bunch behind her head, trouser suit crisp and elegant. That she was beautiful, strikingly so, no one would question, but nor would anyone dare to notice. Collins had a strong sense of the force field around Tara, which told him and any other would-be suitors, not to go there. She was here to work; what she looked like, what she did outside of work, including who and how she loved, were strictly off limits. Tara Sharma's whole demeanour told you she was not to be messed with.

As Collins let himself out into the car park he could see Tara standing next to her car. She had obviously been home to change after work. The trouser suit had been exchanged for black jeans and top, and for the first time in the year he had known her, she had let loose her hair to fall in waves below her shoulders. Collins had spent the last year pretending to be oblivious to Sharma's dark eyes and warm, blemishless brown skin, but now in front of him, in her out of work attire, he couldn't help but be brought up short.

"Tara, I'm not used to seeing you on a Friday night. What can I do for you?" Collins did his best to retain his normal, neutral attitude to Sharma: always friendly but never too friendly, a generous colleague but not too eager, always keen to be helpful but not the slightest bit desperate. It was a tight-rope he sensed was going to get even more difficult to walk.

"I wanted to talk to you Tom." Sharma lacked her normal certainty. She sounded unsure how she wanted to take this conversation forward. "It's stuff I wanted to say out of the office".

Collins' mind was now working overtime; he could feel small electric tremors rippling through his upper torso. These were dimly remembered sensations that took Collins back to his much younger self.

"Can we get a drink somewhere quiet?" Sharma suggested. She immediately followed with, "It doesn't have to be a pub, we could get a coffee." As she said it, she averted her eyes from his.

He knew what she meant. Despite Tara Sharma's own hermetically sealed private life, she clearly had knowledge of his, and knew that he didn't drink and why he didn't drink.

"It's okay, I'm not frightened of pubs, it's just my pints are lime and soda these days," he said with a smile to acknowledge he knew that she knew, and it wasn't a taboo subject.

Collins' history meant he was able to tell which pubs in Town would still be quiet at this time on a Friday, and where Tara would be able to unburden herself of what she needed to tell him, without being disturbed; either by after work revellers, or worse, by any of the clientele of the Pro Team.

"The snug in the back bar of the Foresters should be perfect," he suggested.

And so it was, that Tom Collins found himself sitting facing what, in the short walk from the office car park, he had acknowledged to himself might well be the woman of his dreams; in the deserted snug of the Foresters, waiting to hear what was on Tara Sharma's mind.

Collins was taken by surprise by her opening. "Tom, you want to get to the bottom of the Chilcott case don't you?"

While Collins was disappointed that Sharma had clearly not come to tell him of her secret attraction to him, his interest was immediately provoked by his own immersion in the Chilcott case.

"Of course I do Tara. You know I don't do anything by halves. It's a bloody mess, and I'm going to put a line under the last fourteen years that we've failed to protect those kids."

"Good Tom. I know you won't let anything get in your way. That's why I wanted to talk to you. I knew I could trust you to do the right thing."

Collins was heartened by the opinion Tara clearly had of his work and his principles. Maybe there was a personal dimension to this conversation after all.

"What you asked me earlier in the office, what did I remember of the Chilcott case? I remember every detail. Not that anyone else has been interested in what I thought about Alex Chilcott, or whether I thought his kids were safe."

Collins was now fully in forensic social work mode. "I'm interested Tara. Tell me everything I need to know, and I promise you I'll use it in the right way."

Sharma's initial hesitancy was gone now and she spoke with certainty, as if recalling for a court her encounter with Alex Chilcott.

"We had several reports of this flasher in Gartside Park, who'd appear at dusk. We had a strong feeling it was Chilcott, despite all the psychs saying he was housebound. The only way to prove it was to catch him in the act, and so we set up an operation with me going in, pretending to be a member of the public on my way home from work.

I had criss-crossed the park a couple of times between six and seven o'clock and I was on the narrow path by the bushes, next to what they call Hangman's Hollow. Out steps this bloke in front of me. He was late thirties, big build, leather jacket. It was getting dark, but I could see him clear enough. He's just stood there on the path in front of me and in his right hand he's got his erect penis."

Tara stopped, as if to draw breath, recoiling from the image now back in front of her eyes, but determined to continue nonetheless.

"Then he's started walking towards me, pulling at it in his fist, slowly, ever so slowly. Tom, I've caught flashers in the past, pathetic old men, fiddling with their sad, wrinkled little dicks. Old gits who needed a slap around the face and a cold shower. He wasn't like that. He stared straight at me, straight through me, and all the while he held it, like a knife."

She paused again.

"I swear he was going to rape me. He was within ten feet when I hit the radio to get the boys in. Even then, with lights and shouts, and the sound of half a dozen coppers running across the ground to take him down, he just stared at me, his cock still pointing at me."

Tara sounded angry now, angry that she was still plagued by the image of Chilcott defiant in front of her.

"I had my CS gas out and I just wish I'd blistered his face with the spray, made those cold, dead eyes weep. I didn't, I just held his stare and you know what? Five years later I can see those eyes, like I can see yours now. All I could see in his eyes was hatred. He hates women and he hates the world. He's not a flasher Tom, he's a rapist and a psychopath." Sharma said it with absolute conviction.

Collins looked into Tara's dark eyes and saw she was clearly still affected by her encounter with Chilcott, still filled with a combination of dread and loathing.

"Did anyone understand that this was an attempted rape? Did you ever get any help afterwards?"

"I told my boss what I've told you, that Chilcott was a dangerous man. I told him we needed to push for attempted rape, but he said CPS would never run with it. I told Dave Andrews as well. Said that those children would never be safe in that house and he just gave me that, 'processes need to be followed', 'we'll put them on a CP plan' crap. Those kids should have been out of that house that night, but they all sat on their hands, and five years later they're still there."

Tara continued, as Collins struggled to make sense of the reasons why Chilcott had been left to prey upon his family and community.

"He pleaded guilty to indecent exposure, flashing, and no one ever got to hear my account of how I was seconds away from Chilcott attempting to rape me. He got a bit of probation, and here we are, he's still hanging around that park, and those poor kids are still at home. I didn't just leave it, though, I've made sure the top brass know my view, but nothing's been done."

The anger Collins had felt when he left the Chilcotts' after his first visit, the anger he had vented in his boss's office, was back now. This was worse than he had thought. Andrews had first hand evidence from a good cop of how dangerous Chilcott was, yet still he'd done nothing of use for those kids.

"I don't get it Tara. It's plain for anyone to see that the man's dangerous. Why is it that we can't get him banged up, or those kids away from him? Is it incompetence or something worse?"

"I don't know Tom, I don't know. It's your turn to have a go now though. We've got to keep trying right?" Sharma's energy seemed spent from her effort in re-visiting the

Chilcott arrest, and now her head bowed as her response to Collins tailed off.

"We'll get those kids out and we'll get him put away. I just wish we weren't leaving them there for another weekend, knowing what we know."

Collins was himself in reflective mode now, considering again the imminent danger that Carol and her children were facing. He also realised the significance of Tara going to the house and dropping her note in.

"Sorry Tara, had I known I would never have asked you to go to that house today. I can see why you didn't knock on the door."

Sharma's reply was definite.

"I'm not going to behave any differently because it's him. That would be letting him win. I didn't need to knock. If I had needed to knock, and go in, I would have."

Collins saw a flicker of anger in Tara's eyes, but told himself it was directed at Alex Chilcott and not him.

Tara had finished her drink and Collins wondered if, now he was appraised of the facts of the Chilcott case, she was going to pull up the drawbridge again and retire to her private world.

"Another lime and soda?" he asked. "Or you can have something stronger, you don't need to abstain on my behalf," he said, flashing what he hoped was his most inviting smile.

She returned his smile but politely declined another drink. "I need to get to the gym. Anyway I'm not one for the booze. You're not the only one with a story."

Collins was surprised Tara Sharma chose to share a further intimacy, but not that she was now retreating back to her own world, which he knew he would never share. With that she was rising to go.

"Thanks for listening Tom. I needed you to know that stuff about Chilcott."

"Thanks for trusting me with it Tara," Collins said, by way of goodbye.

Sharma half turned to him as she opened the snug door to leave, and with a slightly mischievous smile playing on her lips said, "Maybe another lime and soda some time?"

Again Collins found himself taken aback by Sharma; wondering if perhaps there had been a sub-text to their case discussion. Maybe she was showing him a crack in her beautifully sculpted exterior, because she felt it was time she let some light in.

He sat for a moment looking at the last dregs in his glass. The optics behind the empty bar reminded him that he needed to be moving on, lest he get too comfortable, and let his hard won sobriety complacently slip away. Collins headed for the door.

7.50pm

Friday nights were always the hardest for Collins. His muscle memory still expected to see the working week off with a booze binge; out with mates having the craic, washing the hard stories and the tough cases away. While on weekdays, in the evenings, there was football to be played, a bike ride, the gym or a run; none of these hit the mark on a Friday night when the rest of Town was partying. Tonight he had briefly hoped to be spending more of the evening with Tara, but now, at barely 8pm, the night stretched ahead of him.

While his job was definitely not nine-to-five, it was supposed to be just Monday to Friday. There was always more to be done, of course, and weekends could easily be filled with report writing, case notes, and assessments, but this really didn't offer an appealing alternative to a night on the sauce, after a hard week at work. Without a family to go home to, and few friends who wouldn't by now be half-cut, Collins was a man on his own with time on his hands.

As he made his way back to his car he tried not to think about having a drink, a proper drink, and, the more he tried to suppress it, the more the longing grew. After nearly two years, he was slowly getting used to being around alcohol and the people drinking it, but perhaps, in the inviting snug with Tara, he had flown too close to the flame. It had reminded him of all he missed. He was starting to feel that yearning for the soft fire at the back of his throat, that he knew was his, from just one shot of whiskey. He walked with head down amongst the bustling evening streets. Every time he looked up he found himself staring in the window of a pub, or a wine bar, where the customers were drinking deeply and enjoying life.

As he passed his old haunt, the Orange Tree, he imagined himself at the bar, tumbler of Irish whiskey in hand. Down in one, the bitter joy as the soothing elixir hit his system, the relief and the release. And then? He knew what then: another and another and another. Because it couldn't stop at one, or three, or even five, he knew that he couldn't let it start.

He thought back to a particular night in the Orange Tree, four years ago. The last words he remembered were from Liam, the young Irish barman.

"I think you've done that bottle of Paddy, Tom. Probably time you called it a night."

Thereafter it was a blur. He was told he had got in an argument as he stumbled towards the door. He dimly recalled having taken offence to the aggressive way a man had been addressing his female partner. That had always been the way if Collins was going to get into an altercation; righting the world's wrongs, once he had consumed a belly full of beer and whiskey. Collins woke in St Mary's hospital, having been felled by a bottle smashed across the side of his face. The doctor's said he was lucky not to have lost his eye.

He touched the scar, as a reminder of why he couldn't be drawn back to prop up that bar. It was another two years after the incident before he finally stopped drinking, a move which coincided with leaving his wife and son.

He turned away from the Orange Tree and picked up pace to escape the tentacles that seemed to snap at him from every doorway, dragging him back to the place from which he had fought so hard to escape, and yet so wanted to return.

At last he was at his car, a cool sweat on his brow and breathless from his flight from his imagined pursuers. Collins started to drive. He didn't know where. There was nothing to take him back to the meagre flat he currently called home. He found himself heading for the ring road, towards Corton, on the north side of Town. Without thinking, or at least without a conscious decision, he turned into Duke Street. These were the roads he had taken hundreds of times after work, the roads back to his old home with Janet and Jamie on Carlisle Place.

As he turned off Duke Street he slowed, wondering what he would find when he arrived, wondering why he was back here in a place where he had long since lost any visiting rights. It was several months since he had had any personal contact with Janet, as she insisted that everything now went through their respective solicitors. It was eight weeks since his last scarring conversation with Jamie.

The latest confrontation with Janet had been over money: specifically the fact that Collins was now driving what Janet described as his "crisis car". Her suggestion being, his purchase had been an act of vanity by a man desperate to forestall the onset of middle age. A purchase Janet said represented taking food out their son's mouth. For his part, Collins felt he had already bent over backwards to keep Janet in the style she felt was hers by right, and that the car was a reasonable reward for having stayed off the drink for two years.

As he pulled up outside the house, Collins again felt both the comfort of familiarity and the sting of loss, which accompanied every visit to Carlisle Place. The street was deserted, but almost all the houses were well lit, with occupants going about their family business. Number twenty-one was no different, with lights on around the semi-detached house, and the warm glow of the television emanating from the front room. He could see movement in Jamie's bedroom, and imagined that Janet was ensconced in front of one of her favourite police dramas in the lounge.

Now he was here, Collins didn't know what he had come for. His safest bet would be to drive straight off again, but he knew he had been drawn here for a reason. He could sit in the hope of seeing a glimpse of his son, or more ambitiously, he could knock on the door and try to speak to him. Before he could dwell on the pros and cons, he was propelling himself out of his car and up the path to the front door, desperate to see Jamie.

He knocked, too fast and for too long. He hadn't meant to cause alarm, but he was now in a state of agitation, conveyed in his urgent banging on the door.

Within seconds Collins found himself face-to-face with his estranged wife for the first time in over a year. Janet looked the same and yet so different; her face was drawn, with eyes which had wearied but hair and makeup sculpted to tell another story, one of youthful vitality and grasping the chance of a fresh start. For all the changes this was still unmistakably Janet, the woman he had lived with for nearly half his life.

"What are you doing here? You've got no reason. Jamie doesn't want to see you and I don't suppose you've come to see me." Janet spoke as if she had been expecting this conversation, as if she had long prepared for him to turn up in the night on the doorstep.

"Poor Tom, have you had to have a little drink to make you feel better about what you've done to us and now I bet you feel all sad?" Her scathing tone was familiar to Collins, from the nights when he returned home dead drunk, or the mornings when he had to face back to explain why he hadn't got home the night before.

"I'm not drunk Janet. I haven't had a drink, not tonight, not in two years. I just want to see my boy."

Janet visibly hardened at the realisation that this wasn't the drunk, remorseful Tom, who was begging forgiveness, and would plead to be let back into the family home. This was the treacherous husband who she had battled to keep sober. The man who had damaged them and then deserted them. He was here still wanting the best of both worlds;

to have his own life, away from her, away from them, but still wanting the easy relationship with his son. No way: he might be sober now, but how long would that last? He would let him down, just like he had let them down so many times before. No way: not his way, this was going to be done Janet's way.

"Just go before I call the police. Trust me, you are the last person on earth he wants to see."

"That's not true. He loves me and I love him. He's my son. He needs his dad. Just let me speak to him please Janet."

Collins was desperate now, but knew that Janet was going to hold the line. He shouted beyond her to the top of the stairs, to where he imagined Jamie was sitting listening.

"Just let me speak to him." Frustration had caused Collins to raise his voice. "Just let me speak to him, or –". He stopped mid-sentence. He didn't know what he would do, or what he could do. Janet seized on his hesitation.

"Or what? Or you'll hit me again?" She glared at him, challenging him to do something, or say something, in reply.

Collins refused to respond to the allegation, to the memory she demanded he summon forth from thin air, a memory she wanted to create. He looked away from her to the stairs beyond, to where he continued to call.

"Jamie, talk to me son, Jamie, it's your dad. I'm missing you so badly, please talk to me."

"I'm serious Tom, go or I'll call the police. That won't look good at work will it? When you're the saint who's supposed to protect women from their scary husbands?"

He barely heard her words, appealing instead to the space behind her, in the hope that his son would respond.

"Jamie, please son, talk to me."

Behind Janet, Collins saw a shrouded figure approaching slowly down the darkened staircase.

"Jamie, Jamie, come here son. Jamie, I've missed you so much."

Jamie held his father's eyes, while he reached an arm around his mother's shoulder. "Close the door mum, I've got nothing to say to him."

With that, Janet pushed the door closed, with Jamie and herself on one side and with Collins standing staring, in silence now, on the other.

9.30pm

Collins dragged himself off the doorstep and back into his car. He had done what he had told himself so many times not to do. He had long feared that he would turn up on Janet's doorstep drunk, his resolve to be away dissolved by alcohol, drawn back by the lure of familiarity, to the family he had walked out on two years earlier. Ironic then that it was not a drunken relapse that propelled him back, but the absence of alcohol, as if he could only deal with so much loss at one time. If he couldn't have a drink, then he wanted to have his son, but, as Janet had said when he first left, he could not have his cake and eat it. It was either the whole family, wife and child, or a meagre alternative, with a non-existent relationship with his ex-wife and a horribly fractured one with his thirteen year old son.

He sat staring at nothing. His heart was thumping, adrenalin coursing through his veins; anger, mixed with an excruciating grief for all he had lost, all that was gone, all that could not be put together again. So she had said it. She had come out with the fabrication she had hinted was in the pipeline: the claim that he had hit her. This was the trump card he suspected she would choose to play when she most needed it. In the course of the to-ing and fro-ing between solicitors there had been accusations of marital disharmony, distress caused by his drinking and his erratic and sometimes threatening behaviour. Collins had suspected when the ante needed to be upped, it might turn to allegations of more specific abuse.

He examined his conscience. He hadn't been a good husband, he accepted that, but he had tried his best and, when it became irreparable, he had done the right thing by getting out. He pored over memories of those hardest times towards the end, when he would come home in the wee hours, or sometimes after dawn, to be confronted by Janet furious that he had let himself go again, furious that a promise to be home, a promise to be sober, had so easily been washed away.

He saw her now, shouting into his face, "You've fucking done it again, haven't you, Tom? Just roll up when you fancy it, roll-out of some party, or some tarts bed, and come home to your wife and son still pissed? You piece of shit, you don't deserve us."

Apology would be followed by denial, followed by another apology, and slowly things would settle before the next big blow out and the next big blow up. It was never violent though.

He thought hard on it. What was the worst that had happened? Was there ever anything physical? Collins remembered shouting at Janet to leave him in peace, and pushing her away, during one of their more heated confrontations. Nothing that could equate to domestic violence and, in any event, he felt she gave as good as she got during those arguments. That was why he had to get away from her. He didn't want a life with her and he couldn't imagine getting clean while they were together. Now he could see those arguments were going to be brought up as evidence of his abuse, to ensure she got exactly the divorce she wanted, and to make sure Collins saw little, or nothing, of his son.

Collins couldn't say how long he sat staring into the darkness before rousing himself to turn on his engine. He knew lingering outside the house would give Janet a reason to call the police and have him pulled in for harassment. Collins drove the car on auto-pilot, not knowing where he was going next, or following any considered course.

As he made his way along Duke Street he saw blue lights pass him in the opposite direction. It was that time on a Friday night: when merriment was turning to malevolence, where old scores were being settled, and new wounds being opened.

Collins felt crushed that his son, his little Jamie, the person in the world he loved more than anyone, more than anything, could so coldly cast him aside. He realised that if Janet was now painting him as an abuser, this rift with Jamie might become permanent. He felt that without Jamie he was nothing, and it had all been for nothing. He had destroyed the thing most precious to him.

And so he drove, not knowing and not caring where he was going.

Collins first realised where he was when he saw the looming towers of the Gartside estate. As the last light of the day slipped away, the three twelve story blocks looked like ancient monoliths against the hills on the southern horizon. He knew he was being propelled by impotent rage; away from the wreckage of his own family, and towards those other wrecked lives that he was responsible for on the Gartside. Another set of people he was failing to protect from the cruelty of a harsh world.

He stopped outside Parkside Point and thought about Damon, his first hard case after he qualified, whom he had clearly failed to divert from a life wasted in crime and drugs. He wondered what had happened to him in the intervening years to derail his progress. Collins decided, having caused one scene on a doorstep already tonight, now was not the time to reacquaint himself with Damon. That would have to wait until the working week re-commenced on Monday.

So what was there for him on Gartside at this time of night? What had brought him here? Without finding a satisfactory answer he drove on, until he came to a stop in Gartside Gardens. He turned his lights and engine off, parking obliquely across from the Chilcotts', and sat in the darkness. He could make out the glow of the TV from the front room, but beyond this there were no other lights on in the house. The old man was in front of the box again. Collins guessed he would be on his own, with Carol making herself scarce in the kitchen, or having taken herself to bed. Collins wondered about Daniel. Was he in there in his darkened room, or would he be out, maybe up the top of Parkside Point with Damon, getting wasted?

Collins decided to sit and watch for a few minutes. He wound down his window, not knowing what he was expecting to see or hear, but feeling this was where he needed to be. This was the one place where he felt he could be of use to someone. Despite his emotional state, Collins knew his time here was limited, he couldn't stay too long for fear of being spotted. Staking out your clients' homes at the wrong end of a Friday night was not the domain of a social worker, even one on the Pro Team, so he needed to be careful.

10.15pm

The 10pm lights out having now past, Daniel sat on the side of his bed, with just his torch lighting his room. The curfew was another one of Alex Chilcott's petty tyrannies: a further means of control over the details of his wife and children's lives.

With nothing else to do when the lights went out, Daniel had taken to sniffing aerosols under his bed covers. He liked the heady rush; the intoxicating dizziness made him feel light, like he could fly up above the house, over the estate and over the hills. He thought about the social worker earlier, all his talk of getting a plane, and being able to look down on the world. He smiled as he flashed his torch to the deodorants on his windowsill.

There's only one way I'm getting high enough to look down on this shithole. Fucking planes. I haven't got the bus fare into Town. I'm never going to be getting on a plane.

Daniel had been thinking about Collins for most of the time since he had left him. He wished he hadn't let on about going to Parkside. He guessed that Collins would be using that 'intelligence' already. Social workers and police, they were as bad as each other. He'd had the grilling from his mum when he got in, as his dad sat brooding in his armchair. "I said nothing, so there's nothing to talk about," he insisted to her. "See Al. He's a good lad, nothing to worry about."

There was something about Collins. He was friendly enough, most of them were, but he didn't mess around. He said it how it was, and he had already worked out more about his dad than any of the others had over the years. He was the first one who Daniel could imagine talking to, and him actually getting it, and doing something.

And then what? Once you've shouted your mouth off and blabbed about what the Bastard does? What then? Hell that's what, one way or another, it will be hell.

It's already hell.

It'll be worse. If the Bastard doesn't kill us, then they'll split us up, and then where will mum be? With him and no kids. Or dead. Is that what you want?

The only way for Daniel to put a stop to this interminable argument with himself, for a short time at least, was an aerosol high. He walked across the room to the permanently locked window to get a can to spray. Pushing his net curtains aside, he wiped away condensation, to get a view of the car, which had just pulled up across the road. He was surprised to see it was a black Audi A4, the same as the one Collins drove. He continued to wipe the window to get a better look. The street lights picked out the new year's registration plates, and it had the blacked out windows too. Daniel was sure it was Collins. He didn't seem to be coming to knock on the door, he was just sitting with his window wound down, watching and listening.

Daniel's mind raced, looking for an explanation for why his social worker was in his car outside his house at ten-thirty on a Friday night. Had he come to see if he could catch his father in the act? Collins knew what sort of man his dad was, and Daniel had as much as confirmed it when they had met earlier. Daniel was thrilled at the thought that he really wasn't just another soft social worker, he was walking the talk.

Daniel switched off his torch and stood watching Collins from his darkened room; watching Collins watching over them. Maybe the end of this hell wasn't another layer of worse pain. Maybe there was another way. Daniel dared to hope.

As he did so, he heard the familiar rumble from downstairs. The inquisition was starting. His dad had sat stewing all day. He was always worse when there were people asking questions, "in my face", "getting in my business", so Daniel was expecting something as a result of his outing with Collins, and now was the appointed time for him to kick off. Daniel braced himself. He couldn't bear to hear his mum pleading again, but maybe it had to happen for Collins to come to the rescue, and catch him red-handed.

"Liar!" he heard his dad roar, and then a brief silence, punctured by a yelp from his mum, and a pleading, "No Al, no".

He watched Collins, hoping he could hear the escalating commotion from outside, and then a thud and a loud cry. Daniel's stomach was churning and his racing heart was causing his body to shake.

He stared beseechingly at Collins' car.

Come on. Come on. This is what you're here for isn't it? This is your chance. Do something.

To Daniel's astonishment he saw Collins' headlights come on, as the engine started, and the Audi swung around and headed out of Gartside Gardens. Daniel's guardian angel had split at the first sign of trouble, and he was alone again; left to listen to the sound of his mother being tortured by his father.

Bastards, bastards, bastards. Fucking social worker, you're no better than him. Another fucking coward. Another bastard.

Daniel looked at the deodorant but left it on the window-sill. He didn't want the relief of getting high any more, he needed the release that he could only get from cutting.

The noise downstairs had subsided for the moment. Daniel imagined the scene; his mother curled up in the corner of the front room, sobbing gently. She would be trying not to make too much noise, so as not to further perturb her husband. Conscious, even while nursing her bruised body, not to disturb the piles of newspapers that she lay between, for fear of provoking another assault.

Daniel examined his blade with reverence; his guardian angel may have deserted him, but his avenging angel was still at his side.

One day Bastard, you'll feel this blade.

Tonight it was Daniel's turn to feel the blade again. He uncovered the wound on his left arm. It was still raw with blood, dried in clumps along the two inch incision. He took the knife in his left hand, and found the spot half way down the inside of his right forearm, which matched the left arm. He winced as he felt the prick against his skin. The first spot of blood appeared at the point of his blade. His heart was thumping, but already he sensed the on rushing freedom from letting loose his blood. He held the knife more tightly and started to slice through his white skin. The light in the room turned blue then red, and blue and then red again. His head was swirling with noise and colours. He no longer knew where his body ended and the world started.

A repeated banging on the front door brought Daniel back into the room. Behind the knocking were mechanical voices on a short-wave radio. Slowly he realised the lights in his room were from a police car. There was no noise in the house in response to the knocking. He knew as soon as his father had seen the lights he would have been making his way out. Daniel thought he heard the slamming of the door into the back garden, signalling his father's departure.

Daniel pictured his mother gathering herself to open the door to the police officers. The huge effort just to get herself off the floor, to straighten her clothes, pushing her hair down over her face to cover the reddening marks. Then to open the door to two burly police officers, who would want an arrest or, if not that, at least a plausible explanation for having been called out. Having been kicked and punched, she would have to explain away the noise in the house as "the kids", or "the old man having a bit of a paddy". "No he's not here now, getting a walk, best thing to clear his head." "Absolutely nothing to worry about here, we're all just fine."

That was the pattern with police on the doorstep, and at least their coming out would end the violence, for this evening.

Tonight, they were being extra thorough, checking that the kids were all safe. Daniel heard heavy footsteps on the stairs.

A woman's voice, "Can I come in Daniel? I just want to make sure you're okay."

Daniel quickly jumped under his bed cover as the police officer put her head around the door and turned the light on.

"Sorry to disturb you Daniel. We do need to see you; to make sure you're safe and well." She looked inquisitively around the room and at Daniel with the duvet pulled up to his chin. Her eyes rested upon the blood that had freshly fallen on the duvet cover.

"Daniel, where's this blood from? Is there anything you want to tell me?"

"He's fine. He just gets nose bleeds, poor kid." Carol was behind the officer in the doorway.

"Have you had another one, Dan? You should have told me."

"Mrs Chilcott, I was speaking to Daniel. Daniel is everything okay?"

As Daniel nodded, the police officer's radio screeched instructions for units to get to another incident back in Town.

"We'll get someone around to have a chat with you on Monday, Daniel."

With that the police were gone, and the Chilcott household returned to its hushed and darkened state. In Daniel's room Carol Chilcott cradled her son's head in her lap; stroking his thick black locks with the tender intensity of a mother's love for her first born. Daniel lay still, wishing the moment would never end.

11pm

Tom Collins closed the door of his flat. He instinctively made for the fridge to get a beer. Even after two years the habits of his previous life were proving hard to shake. He let go of the handle on the fridge door and turned instead to fill the kettle. As he listened to the hissing of the boiling water, he lent against the sink in the small kitchen, rubbing the back of his head in an agitated manner. As he turned he saw his tortured reflection in the kitchen window.

"Get a fucking grip man," he muttered to himself.

It had, admittedly, been an emotional day, ending with one of the hardest decisions of his professional career. When he heard Carol Chilcott crying out, every fibre of his being was pushing him into that house to confront Alex Chilcott. He was furious, raring to get in there, to get in his face and confront him with the truth of his abuse.

But then he was dragged back to the reality of the situation. He was a social worker not a police officer, he had no business being there at gone ten o'clock on a Friday night. How would he account for his presence in the midst of the Chilcotts' domestic incident? He had primed his police colleagues that it could kick off there over the weekend. The best he could do was call 999, as a concerned member of the public, worried by the noises emanating from the Chilcott household, and then make himself scarce. Collins was not long out of Gartside Gardens when he saw the blue flashing lights coming in the opposite direction. He hoped he had at least put a stop to Alex Chilcott's violence for the night, and he would now have further evidence to build his case that the Chilcott kids were not safe.

Collins lay back on his single bed and stared at the ceiling, and tried to make sense of all that had happened to him in the course of the day. He thought about his lost boys at work; poor suffering Daniel, and his predecessor, the returning ghost of Damon Hartley. Collins considered his thankless task in trying to again liberate a child from a hopeless situation; trying to buck the odds to set his life on a better course. It didn't seem to have worked for Damon, and he didn't rate Daniel's chances highly either.

Then there was his own lost boy, the one he had left behind, in the ruins of what used to be the Collins' family home. Was Jamie going to join the ranks of Daniel and Damon, quitting school and taking drugs as an act of defiance against his absent father?

Collins suddenly felt desperately alone. For much of his married life he had imagined the freedom of cutting loose, of being unshackled, and now here he was on his own, in a pokey flat, with only his solitary sober thoughts for company. He struggled to find hope or consolation in his professional or his personal life.

"It's enough to drive a man to drink," he said to himself, as he reached for the tea he had placed on his bedside cabinet.

Collins found some comfort from turning his thoughts to his first out of work encounter with Tara Sharma. She at least seemed to find something admirable in him, as someone she could trust, and had held out the hope that there might be a further rendezvous outside of work. Tara also appeared to be his one firm ally in his quest to nail Alex Chilcott. Collins knew he was pinning a great deal on his hook up with Tara, thinking she might hold the key to change his fortunes at work and just possibly in his personal life too. Perhaps he was being fanciful, but if he couldn't fantasise alone in his bachelor pad on a Friday night, then what was the point of being alone, in a bachelor pad, on a Friday night? It was at least a positive thought to end the week on, and one which started to soothe him towards sleep.

11.30pm

Tara Sharma was struggling to sleep. Her conversation with Tom Collins had shifted something deep inside her. She had become expert at blocking out the memory of her confrontation with Alex Chilcott, and to have re-live it for Collins had re-surfaced images and emotions she had successfully suppressed. She knew, however, it wasn't just the memories of Chilcott that were now preventing her from sleeping. Collins had awakened other emotions Tara had long fought off.

She tried to get in touch with what she was feeling. Tara had not had a serious relationship in nearly ten years. She had for so long closed off the possibility of being drawn to share her life with someone else. Instead she concentrated first on recovery, and then, on making a success of her career. Attachment meant loss, love meant pain, and with that pain came the need to self-medicate. Without the danger of emotional engagement, Tara could focus on work and live on the adrenalin that provided. This, supplemented by a demanding exercise regime, had kept her safe and moving forward.

Now she felt the pull of emotional involvement and it frightened, and yet, excited her. Half-forgotten sensations moved through her, as she toyed with possibilities. Tara recognised Tom Collins was a good looking man, but there were plenty of them. She had never had difficulty in getting the attention of attractive would-be partners. If it wasn't his looks, then what was it that had rekindled these feelings in her?

Tara had felt it as she turned back to him from the door of the snug in the Foresters. She looked at him and saw a soul in pain, working hard to do the right thing, to be better than his past. Tara knew that feeling, and sensed that she and Collins were on the same journey, fellow travellers, and possibly kindred spirits. Tara knew that Collins might be trouble, and she had been burned before by her attraction to trouble. She tossed and turned between her bed sheets as she wrestled with her confounding cocktail of emotions.

SATURDAY 12TH MAY

5.15am

Collins awoke fully dressed on top of his bed covers with the first light of a bright May morning streaming through the open curtains. He looked around, struggling at first to remember where he was; to fit the place and his life together in his mind. It came back to him soon enough. This place, this life, was the outcome of a choice he had made two years earlier.

His mind went back, as it so often did, to another Saturday morning, fourteen years before, and another momentous choice he had made. A choice which had ultimately led him here, to this lonely, solitary existence. He thought about the fork in the road his life had taken that day and about the life that his ghost, who took the other path, might be leading.

Collins was back there again now, on that sultry Friday night in July which had been so full of promise. Newly qualified, he and Janet had moved to Queenstown when he got his job a year earlier. They had met at university and were wed before they had finished their courses. Two years into marriage, the dizzying whirlwind of their heady romance already seemed a distant memory, and Collins was getting distracted. He had also by this point acquired a taste for drink and hadn't taken long to fall in with a crew who liked to party hard.

It was closing time when they rolled out of the Star and down the road to one of Squeaky's infamous parties. Squeaky had inherited the house just off Duke's Street from his mother, and he made ample use of the opportunity this offered him. His stood out from the other houses in the suburban terrace, not only because of the scrap that collected in his front garden, but because of the constant comings and goings of friends and business associates. Squeaky's business was keeping the immediate neighbourhood supplied with illicit substances. He was a small time, disorganised supplier who, with the imminent arrival on the scene of cheap and plentiful cocaine, was just waiting to be gobbled up by a bigger fish. For now though, Squeaky was 'the man'.

Before turning the corner into his road, Collins heard the music that signalled Squeaky's party was in full flow. The front door was open; this was clearly not a ticket only affair. It wasn't yet midnight but the scene was already one of carnage. Empty cans covered every space in the kitchen. Half-drunk bottles of lager littered the front room, where people milled around, tripping over the bodies of comrades who had already fallen. The height of the Ecstasy era had passed but there were still plenty of people taking a variety of pills, looking for their euphoric high. Typically what they actually found, having mixed uppers and downers and a bellyful of booze, was a corner to curl up in.

The music boomed: Ballearic beats well-suited to the sticky night and sweaty guests. Collins was soon assailed by Squeaky who was in an advanced state of intoxication. His black curly fringe flopped across his bearded face. His broken front tooth gave him a piratical air, which was enhanced by the sense that, like a man who has been too long at sea, he needed a damn good wash. As his ironic sobriquet suggested, Squeaky was anything but squeaky clean. When his host managed to fix both eyes on Collins, he dragged him close and hollered.

"I'm so fucking glad you're here. Tommo, you're the fucking man!"

His accent betrayed the fact that his parents had wasted good money on his education. He held Collins in a beery, sweaty clench, contemplating what he had just said, as if unpicking one of life's great riddles, before ploughing on.

"No, no, what am I saying? I'm the fucking 'man' and I'm fucking glad that I'm here. In fact I'm glad we're both fucking here."

Another conundrum solved. In awe of his own powers of reasoning Squeaky rolled away from Collins to tell another guest about their joint good fortune in being here and him being the "fucking man" and all.

Collins had a bottle of cold white wine poking out of his inside jacket pocket which, with a little help from his mate behind the bar, he had liberated from the Star. He poured himself a glass and took a wander upstairs to see if things were a little calmer up there.

What he found was a scene more bizarre than downstairs. In one room four people were huddled in front of a TV monitor playing Donkey Kong on computer. Shaun, who had the controls, whooped wildly with each barrel he jumped, his eyes white and wide, unfathomed pools for pupils. He screeched as Mario missed a jump and was consumed by fire. The three people playing with him echoed his cries. Lit by the monitor their faces looked ghoulish in the otherwise darkened room. Behind them, in shrouded corners and on the two mattresses laid on the floor, bodies wriggled, intertwined like maggots falling over each other in a bait tray.

In the second bedroom a similar scene was played out, while a Vietnam War film filled the room with shouted dialogue above helicopter drone. Two men who Collins didn't know sat transfixed by the action, while behind them a couple writhed on Squeaky's parents' marital bed. Collins sensed there were others too, in the murky recesses of the room, but he couldn't bring himself to investigate any further.

This was heavy going. He was just pleasantly tipsy and looking for a couple more drinks, but it seemed he had walked into a hedonistic whirlpool of excess and everyone was off their faces. Collins knew that the guys he had come with from the pub would by now have scored, and would be trying their damndest to get as wrecked as the other revellers. He made his way out into the garden, having decided to drink his wine before slipping back to his own marital bed, where Janet would be waiting for him. To be at home by 1am, after a Friday night out, would represent a bit of an early night; not quite deserving of Brownie points, but not far off.

The warm night had encouraged a number of guests out to the garden. A guy called Lionel had got hold of a guitar, and had half-remembered Dylan's 'Like a Rolling Stone'. In his version the words petered out after the first verse, and only returned when it came to an oft-repeated chorus. Joining in, when the mood took them, the few people listening clearly didn't care about the right words or the order that Dylan had chosen to put them in. Lionel's friend, the charmingly nicknamed "Gusset", put it eloquently.

"You don't have to be a hard on about it, just sing, coz singing's cool."

Collins certainly didn't think you could argue with that, or at least knew there was no point in bothering to try.

As he replayed the night's events, all those years on, Collins slowed the action down to recall his first sight of the woman who still haunted him. As he surveyed the garden he was struck by the sight of a petite girl, with dark ringlets, neatly bunched on top of her head. She appeared entirely at ease with her surroundings, her composed contentment at odds with the chaotic environment. She looked a couple of years younger than him, maybe early twenties, with a posture that suggested ballet dancing or at least regular yoga. She was sitting on an upturned milk crate and looked like a different species to the slouched, unruly, good-timers around her. She was smiling and swaying gently to the music; self-assured and self-possessed, quietly taking in the scene, rather than being lost in it, as everyone else he had seen since coming through the door had so clearly been lost. It may have been relative to the dull dough that surrounded her, but she just shone.

Collins caught her eye and held her gaze for a moment. She smiled and her eyes twinkled invitingly. He wasn't sure if that look was just a shared appreciation by a fellow party-goer of the craziness all around them, or was it something more? Did that look say,

"this is mad isn't it, and you and me are about the only ones here who can see it?"

Or did it say,

"this is mad isn't it, and you and me are about the only ones here who can see it, maybe we should fuck?"

Collins decided there was only one way to find out. For the first time since taking his marriage vows two years earlier, he surreptitiously removed his wedding ring, slipping it in his front pocket. He didn't know where his encounter with this beautiful, enigmatic stranger might lead, but he thought the prospects were far better without his wedding ring on. Waving his bottle of wine in her direction he mouthed, "do you want some?" She nodded and Collins made his way over to her. The girl pulled another makeshift piece of garden furniture close up beside her milk crate. Collins could hear the sound of opportunity knocking.

He still remembered his opening gambit as being woefully poor. "You look a bit out of place here" he blurted out, over-excitedly. She took pity on him and came close, speaking in a hushed, almost secretive tone.

"It wasn't quite what I was expecting. My mate, Lily, lives a few doors up and we thought it would be a bit of fun."

Those first few words can tell you so much about a person. That "bit of fun" spoke volumes. What Collins heard was this slight, straight-backed girl, looked forward with optimism, she was willing to try new experiences, she thought the world was going to be good to her. With a few words she had thrilled him with a glimpse of what might be.

Within seconds of meeting her his mind was already racing, full of possibilities. Minutes earlier he had been in the house, where it seemed the more depraved scenes from Sodom and Gomorrah were being re-created. Now his head was full of images of a simple, wholesome, contented future with this enchanting girl, with her enticing almond eyes, and dark hair so beautifully bunched on top of her head. Even the act of having just wedged his wedding ring into his front pocket didn't manage to detract from the purity of the fast evolving fantasy Collins was creating for himself.

She continued in the same intimate tone. "Lily's certainly got in the mood, the last I saw of her she was hogging a massive joint someone had made the mistake of giving her. What about you; is this what you were expecting?"

"No, not at all" Collins lied. He'd been to Squeaky's parties before, and while this was pretty extreme, you kind of knew what you were going to get.

"No, I didn't expect to be spending the night with the living dead," he continued. "It's like a zombie film, and we're the only ones who haven't been zombified."

Her laugh encouraged him to carry on.

"I just thought I'd come out tonight and have a bit of a drink and a laugh."

"Well that's exactly what we'll do," she said. Now that she was smiling broadly he could see her perfectly formed teeth flashing from behind her full lips. Collins held her gaze again and beamed back. This was good.

"I'm up for that," he replied. By now he was up for anything.

She said her name was Holly.

"I'm Tom and it's a pleasure to meet you. I was just starting to think about going home."

Collins cursed himself. What had he said that for? This had started him thinking about home, which was less than ten minutes' walk away. Janet was there, and he didn't want to think about her right now. He just wanted to think about Holly. Now she was probably thinking about his home, and if there was a wife, girlfriend, kids?

"Hey but nothing there to rush back to," he spluttered. He felt a mild tremor of regret at his weasel words. Married life may not have been as he hoped, but did that mean he could just do as he pleased? He told himself to get off the subject of home.

Collins was saved by the crash of Lionel, who had by now started to drift off, falling backwards from his wooden crate. "Another zombie bites the dust", he threw in quickly. This started them on a conversation about the various states of deterioration that surrounded them. They laughed at people trying to negotiate their way in and out of the backdoor of the house, most stumbling on the step as they did so. One still remained crumpled in a heap where he had gone over.

The zombie spotting and avoiding the un-dead kept them going through their first bottle of wine, and one that Collins freed from Squeaky's, not-so-secret, secret stash. The 'avoiding the un-dead game' took the form of deflecting the attention of wasted guests who would periodically approach and try to strike up random conversations. One such reveller, who hailed from Glasgow, made a stab at interaction with the obscure, "have you got any of the erm, you know, the erm, dupty-doo?"

"Sorry Snagler," Collins shook his head as if empathising with his plight, "right out of dupty-doo mate."

"Ah, nay matter, let's get skooshed!" he shouted, before wandering off to have another incoherent conversation, this time with the sleeping Lionel.

"I think he's already at least double-skooshed, and god help us if he finds any dupty-doo," Collins said, sniggering conspiratorially with Holly.

Often when approached by the un-dead it was enough to just pretend not to hear and they would forget that they had spoken. With the more persistent it required standing up and turning them around, before giving a gentle push in the direction of the bottom of the garden, and off they would trundle to mumble into the shrubbery.

Collins hadn't realised they had finished the game, but Holly clearly thought they had, as she put her hand on top of his and declared, "I'm going back to Lilly's. I want to go to bed."

Before Collins had the chance to consider whether he was included in that arrangement she continued, looking deep into his eyes from beneath her long lashes, "maybe you'd like to come too?"

And there it was, the offer he was hoping she would make, was now his to accept or decline. Looking back, he would like to say, now his imagined coupling with this pretty stranger was to become a reality, he felt torn by a moral dilemma, or that his wedding vows echoed loudly in his ears. But no, he only thought of Holly, the rest of the world had ceased to exist.

They left the zombies behind and walked the short distance to Lilly's hand-in-hand. Alone now, under the light of the street lamps, what they were about to do suddenly felt more real. For Collins there was still no pang of conscience, instead just excitement, tinged with that male anxiety that trusts everything will be in working order. They let themselves into Lilly's with the key from beneath the flowerpot. Holly led Collins up the stairs to a small, plainly decorated room, with a single bed occupying the whole of one wall.

"It's not the four-poster in the master bedroom for us I'm afraid. More of a monk's cell."

He grinned: she was funny, and clever and pretty. This was not a combination Collins was familiar with in girls who were susceptible to his charms, but he liked it. He liked it a lot. If he were at the bingo he would have shouted "house" by now. Collins realised he really wanted to kiss Holly. Holding her hand had sent sparks through his veins that had made him tingle, and now he so wanted to touch those soft, full lips with his.

He did it and from then was completely lost in her: no thoughts, no fears, no conscience.

He knew, fourteen years on, it could be a trick that fickle memory plays; changing events to suit its purpose, but he remembered no hard edges, no fumbling, no awkward transitions. Instead as he played back his internal tape he saw only rhythm, grace and symmetry, until, sated, they fell asleep in each other's arms.

He woke early on that Saturday morning too, with sunlight peeping around the curtain on to their un-nuptial bed. It was 6am. He recalled once again those initial feelings, as he came around, on his first morning as an adulterer. Still not shame or guilt, instead, a thrill at the sight of Holly lying curled naked next to him. Collins knew he had to get home, but couldn't bear to leave the soft, warm body beside him.

Holly lay with her back to him. He cuddled in behind her, moulding himself to the curves of her back and her legs. She squeezed his hand but made no other movement. There they lay, as he fought off the urge to melt into sleep, all the while having to listen to the voice in his head telling him, "the longer you stay here the worse it will be when you go home."

He knew to stay any longer would be dangerous. It was now the morning after; this was new territory for him, and he had no idea how Janet would react. He kissed the top of Holly's back and uncoiled himself. As he stood up from the bed, Holly spoke softly into her pillow, her back still turned to him. "Someone waiting at home for you?"

That was the question they had both ignored last night, and one that he hoped he could get away without dealing with this morning. His tired brain suddenly needed to be at its most agile. It whirred into action, computing the various potential outcomes to the answers he could give to that question. He wanted to see her again, and he didn't want to have to lie about being married but, if in order to see her again he had to lie (only for a short time of course) then that might have to be the way. The unknown variable was her attitude to his being married. She didn't ask last night, so maybe she wasn't that bothered? Equally, he wasn't wearing a wedding ring, so why should she have thought he was married?

"Yes, there is someone," he offered, "but I would really like to see you again, and we can talk about where we go from here."

She sat up and turned to him, drawing the bedsheet around her. "I'd like to see you again too, Tom." Hearing her say his name gave him that same thrill he had felt when she first took his hand.

"I really like you," she continued. "Last night was wonderful, all of it. But you've got to know, I don't do the whole two-timing shit. Either it's us alone, or not at all."

"Yes, I understand. I wouldn't want it any other way. We'll talk. How about the Roebuck, it's quiet, tomorrow at eight?"

She agreed, and they kissed; just lips and the briefest touch of tongues, just for a few seconds, but now, so many years later, he could still taste it; still feel her supple lips pressing into his. Collins turned as he exited the bedroom door, and caught that picture of her, which was in his mind's eye now. Propped up on two pillows, the bed sheet tucked under her elbows, covering her nipples but showing just enough of the porcelain flesh of her neck and shoulders, and the inviting tops of her breasts. Her brown ringlets fell across her face, and onto the pillow behind. She looked for all the world like a beautiful English rose: plucked in full bloom.

He could see now, as he saw then, that half-smile that played on her mouth and eyes, but he could also see a sadness in those soft features. She knew that the cocoon they had inhabited last night; in which they had ridden pleasure's smooth curves, where there were no questions, no future or past, just the moment, leading on to their heady, intoxicating climax; she knew that it had gone. Gone with the morning light; sullied by the real world, which demands commitments, decisions, linear progress from one action to the next; taking us further and further away from the blank page on which we can experience anew, afresh, without regret.

Collins left the house without washing. He had said goodbye, and it felt too late to find the bathroom and start to scrub up. Now though, on the street, he wished he was at least going home clean. He felt conflicting emotions as he walked away from Squeaky's terraced row, and started the short journey home. He was unclean; the sex of last night still clung to his skin, he had to face home having spent a first night without explanation away from his wife. He was in trouble. Yet, when he thought of Holly, he thrilled at what they had shared, and the possibilities for what could lay ahead for them. He clenched his fist in his pocket as a mark of his triumph.

By the time Collins reached the bottom of Squeaky's road, and turned into Duke Street, anxiety was increasingly tempering his sense of elation.

So much sooner than he wished he was outside his own front door in Carlisle Place. He pushed the key in as quietly as he could, undoing the lock, before carefully shutting the door behind him. It was 7am on a Saturday morning, there was no reason for Janet to be awake, but he knew that she would not have slept well while he was still out, and may even be up waiting for him. He headed straight for the bathroom. As he closed the door, Collins heard his wife shout his name from the bedroom.

"Tom?"

He locked the bathroom door pretending not to hear her call. He leant his palms on top of the sink, and stared in the mirror. His eyelids were heavy from too little sleep and too much wine. His sharp brown eyes seemed to have dimmed overnight, and sat sullenly looking back at him.

All he could find to say to himself was, "You look like shit". What had he been thinking? This was his life, and there was no point getting lost in fanciful thoughts about a future with the girl with almond eyes and perfect teeth. Surrounded now by the familiar possessions that filled his home: the dirty laundry, the toothbrushes, the football boots; the reality of his situation struck him hard. Still not guilt, more a case of realising the massive contrast between this, the life he had chosen, here, with his wife, and that promise of something else held out by his encounter with Holly. The gap between the two felt immense, and he would have to decide which side he wanted to be on.

For the first but not the last time in his married life, he gave himself something akin to a standing bed-bath in front of the sink: a good scrub below, a light sponge over the upper body, while remembering to give the face a proper wash to remove the whiff of unfamiliar perfume. That first morning it felt clinical; a washing away of the joy of the previous night.

As he turned to open the bathroom door he saw his bare wedding ring finger. He shoved a hand in his front pocket, and searched hurriedly for the gold band he had removed at Squeaky's. Desperately he fumbled in his jeans. Had he dropped it at Squeaky's, or was it on the bedroom floor next to Holly's bed, having fallen from his pocket while he hastily removed his trousers? Suddenly he was faced with the prospect of not only having to explain his night's absence, but having to also explain why he was no longer wearing a wedding ring.

"Tom?" Janet called again from the bedroom.

In increasing panic, scenarios flashed through Collins' mind. There would be no hiding his naked ring finger, so he would need an alibi. One of Squeaky's dishonest mates had stolen the ring while he slept. No, too far-fetched. He would just have to play dumb and be shocked at the discovery the ring was no longer on his finger. It all looked so shabby. Maybe he should come clean: this was his way out, and would resolve his dilemma about staying or going. All this had shot through his mind in a matter of seconds, as he rifled urgently, again and again, through his pockets.

"Tom? What are you doing?" Janet called more insistently now.

Finally as he turned the front pockets of his jeans out, from the deepest recess, the ring appeared, and fell on the floor in front of him. Collins, hands shaking, rapidly slipped it back on and took a deep breath, before leaving the bathroom, to make his way down the hall to face in to the marital bedroom.

As he pushed the bedroom door, he wished that on the other side it was Holly, waiting expectantly, not Janet, waiting for an explanation. She was sat up in bed, pyjamas on, knees in front of her and cover pulled half way over her body.

"What happened to you?" her voice betrayed a ruined night's sleep.

"Sorry, Jan, I've just woken up on Squeaky's front room floor. I feel like shit." Collins rubbed the back of his head, as evidence that he did, indeed, feel like shit. He continued massaging the nape of his neck to offer what he thought by now must be conclusive proof that he felt rough, because he'd slept on Squeaky's floor.

Janet didn't say anything, but he felt her eyes boring into him, as he performed his charade.

He carried on with his explanation. He hadn't wanted to blurt it all out at once, as that was clearly the way a guilty man would behave, so he held some back, but now he would have to offer further elucidation.

"I just had a little toke on one of his joints and the rest was history, I just curled up in a ball. Christ knows what was in it?"

She smiled, a smile full of understanding. It wasn't his fault after all. Now she could see her husband had wanted to come home, but been foiled by his grossly irresponsible host, who had again lived up to his reputation.

"Come on get into bed, we'll have a lazy morning," she said, pulling back the duvet. "You have a lie down and I'll get us some tea." She left the room, and he got undressed, making himself comfortable.

The bed was warm; just like the one he had left a few minutes earlier. He put his head on the pillow and thought about Holly, still lying in that bed down the road. He imagined he was still coiled around her, pressed against her warm back, her ringlets brushing against his face. When he closed his eyes it was easy. It was Holly and him, always just Holly and him; in bed, at a pub, in a restaurant: talking, laughing, at ease with each other. But when Collins opened his eyes he was surrounded by discarded books, ironing and tea cups; the minutiae of his everyday life. He decided that it was better with his eyes closed, alone with Holly.

He thought about last night. Was Holly that funny? She certainly made him laugh, and she was definitely gorgeous; he had already framed in his mind's eye that picture of her as he left the bedroom. She was clever too; maybe too clever for him. He could tell she would see straight through any pretence; so best not to bother. He had a life he would have to extricate himself from, before he could realise the hoped for future with Holly, but he couldn't wait to see her tomorrow.

Collins was warm and content now. Sleep was tugging at him, but he didn't want to let go of the picture plastered to the front of his eyelids: Holly, with sheet covering too little, but now too much of her beautifully proportioned body; the sadness of her brown eyes, wanting and waiting.

Janet set down a mug of tea on the bedside table by his head. She ran her fingers through his hair, and he thought of doing the same to Holly, and how those ringlets would struggle to be so easily parted.

"You better make the best of these lie-ins. It won't be the same when the baby comes." Janet's words were a distant echo from another world.

"No more staying out all night when there's a new-born to be fed and changed."

Collins yearned to sleep, but now he could no longer ignore the words Janet kept repeating. "Baby", "our baby".

Now he was wide-awake, and hesitantly responded. The words "you're pregnant?" dribbled from his lips.

"Yes, we're having a baby!" Janet yelped with joy and hugged him.

He held her and thought of Holly. He thought of Holly curled up in that bed just a few hundred yards away, her dark curls falling on the pillow where his own head had been so recently. He thought of her with the bed-sheet wrapped around her knees and breasts, as he turned to catch one last look at her, before he left the room. And that is what it turned out to be, one last look.

Collins saw that image now. It felt a lifetime away. It was a lifetime: Jamie's lifetime. The future he had briefly glimpsed with Holly was not to be, and instead he knuckled down: to work and fatherhood and married life. Except that knuckling down was underpinned by a resentment that something had been lost, something had been stolen from him; a story he told himself that made his occasional flings, tawdry drink-fuelled couplings, acceptable. He told himself he was stuck in a marriage that had been doomed from the start; he was doing his best to hold things together, to be a decent dad and to provide for his family. If he didn't come home on the odd Friday night it was just balancing the books; getting a little something back for all he had put in.

That was until two years ago when he decided he couldn't do it any more. It had become, as he grandly put it to Janet, "untenable". He realised he had spent twelve years chasing the euphoric high he had found with Holly; only to find himself ever more bitter, increasingly depending on alcohol to get through the week, and in an ongoing emotional battle with Janet, in which they had exhausted each other's reserves of hope and happiness.

Collins looked at the balance sheet again, and wondered whether this dry, lonely life he had made for himself was the payback for the poor behaviour and poor decisions that had gone before.

As for Holly, she had disappeared. He thought he had glimpsed her so many times over the years, only to be disappointed. She came to his mind less often now, but she never entirely left him, even if he knew she had become ever more idealised in the years since their night together. Collins thought again about Tara. Might she come to occupy Holly's place? Could she be his second chance?

He determined to get up and get on. One foot in front of the other, small steps in the right direction. One day at a time. He might yet find redemption lay at the end of the road.

MONDAY 14TH MAY

8am

Collins was keen to make an early start in the office. He had spent half the weekend running in the hills. One foot in front of the other, he told himself, as he pounded relentlessly on, building mile on mile. Now Monday had arrived and he wanted to start to turn up the heat on Alex Chilcott, and after what Tara had told him, he wanted to convince Dave Andrews of the urgency of the situation. For all he had thought about work and the Chilcotts over the weekend, he was also eager for the week to start again so that he could see Tara, having also spent too much of the last few days thinking about her.

Stan Bowles was the only one there when Collins arrived.

"Just us early birds, eh Stan?"

"Morning Tommo." Bowles' earthy baritone resonated with pleasure, as he welcomed his favourite colleague through the door, hoping to share some early morning banter. Bowles also had some news he was keen to impart.

"This early bird's got a nice little worm for you." Bowles paused, knowing that he had tantalised Collins with this bait.

"Your man Mr Chilcott's been knocking the missus about again. Call came in about ten-thirty Friday night. Hell of a racket according the guy who rang it in; sounded like he was killing her. No sign of Chilcott when the response team went around, and the missus was saying nothing of course."

"He managed to get himself out of the house when the police came round then? Not bad for an agoraphobic. Do we know who called it in?" Collins replied, feigning only a passing interest in the identity of the caller.

"No they didn't say who they were; a neighbour presumably. The mobile number was withheld, but no doubt it could be traced if needs be."

"Don't worry for now. I'll let you know if it's going to be important to trace the caller." Collins knew that he was taking a chance by making the call, and that there was a possibility that it might be traced back to him, but he wasn't going to be the one to advertise the fact he had been outside the Chilcotts' on Friday night.

"Another thing Tom, the officer who checked on the kids in the house said the oldest boy, Daniel, seemed to have blood spots on his bed cover. Mum said it was a nose bleed. Here you go. It's all in the incident report."

At that moment Collins saw Tara Sharma approaching the glass office doors. He could feel his heart start to pick up pace. He had thought too much about her over the last seventy-two hours. Now he was to engage with the real woman, not the one in his head, he felt anxious that it might all just have been wishful thinking. Collins steadied himself, as she walked towards his desk.

"Morning," she said, with a small smile, and kept walking without any additional pleasantries, or enquiries to give Collins encouragement that their relationship was now on a new footing.

Collins felt crestfallen. She had resumed the polished, untouchable, professional persona he had come to know over the previous year. He had hoped something would be different between them now, and he kicked himself for having let his imagination race away with itself.

Before heading up to the Gartside, Collins wanted a conversation with Dave Andrews. He closed the door behind him as he entered Andrews' office.

"Chilcott's been at it again," he said, challenging his boss to react.

Andrews looked up from a report he had been scribbling on, "what, in the park?" He said it with a degree of indifference which disappointed Collins.

"No, beating Carol up again. It must happen all the time, it's just that people have got fed up with reporting it. That level of domestic abuse is enough for us to start proceedings on its own."

"Evidence, evidence, evidence. I'm sure you're right, Tom, but at the moment it's hearsay, occasional calls, which no doubt aren't corroborated by anyone in the house. We've got to have more; legal have been clear about that."

"We'll have a dead body before long. Carol's, most likely, but god knows what that man is capable of. Two women killed every week by their partner across the country, and plenty of men who take their kids with them at the same time. I don't want blood on my hands Dave. Do you?" Collins looked hard into Andrews' eyes.

"Of course not, Tom. We all want to make sure those kids are safe, and we want to do everything we can for their mum, but, if she's saying nothing, there's only so much we can do for her, and she's making it more difficult to protect her kids."

Andrews was his calm self; choosing to ignore the implicit accusation from Collins that he was complicit in the suffering of the Chilcott family.

"I've been looking at some of Chilcott's previous offences, and he's not just a flasher, he's a rapist. I know you saw the statement that Tara Sharma gave, and that won't be the only woman Chilcott's done that to. You've had the evidence Dave; you've just sat on it." Collins was leaning across the desk towards Andrews now and glaring, eyeball-to-eyeball.

This time Andrews wasn't ignoring the challenge.

"It was her perception. It wasn't enough to run a trial in the crown court, CPS were certain about that, and it wouldn't have been enough for us in the family court to get the kids removed. They were put on CP plans following that incident." Andrews' voice remained level and unwavering.

"Tom, I can see this case has shaken you up. Don't do anything silly, not at the Chilcotts' and not anywhere else." Andrews paused and straightened in his chair.

"You've had a good career. We've supported you through the forensics training, and you're a senior social worker now. We know you've had your ups and downs. I don't want you jeopardising everything now by going on one of your crusades. Do it properly and you'll get the full support of the department."

Collins said nothing, unsure if this was a threat from Andrews, or just a piece of sound advice. He continued to look hard into Andrews' face, trying to weigh up whether he really wanted evidence to get the Chilcott kids out of that home, or if perhaps it had it gone beyond that. Were Andrews and the Director, Frazer Campbell, too implicated to want the truth to come out? Collins breathed deeply to compose himself. He needed to get out of Andrews' office to try to make sense of the situation.

"One more thing, Tom. I've had a report that you were up at Janet's on Friday night and she had to call the police to get rid of you?"

If Collins had been unsure of his position before, with this latest revelation, he was now thrown into turmoil. Janet had actually called the police, and as a result he, like Alex Chilcott, was on the system as a result of a domestic incident.

"Jesus, Dave, all I did was try to have a conversation with Jamie. I didn't do anything wrong. There's no injunction. I didn't threaten her. I wasn't abusive. I wasn't even rude."

"She says that having caused an unpleasant scene, when she asked you to leave, you sat in your car outside, and only moved on when she called the police and you heard the sound of sirens. She says she felt harassed and alarmed by your behaviour, which as you know, is entering the realms of a criminal offence."

"That's not how it was Dave. You know me. I detest abusers and men who try to control women. She's the one with the power. I've got nothing."

"Tom, it doesn't look good. There's no action being taken on this occasion, but you're on thin ice. Take it easy. As I said, you could end up throwing away your career the way you're going at the moment."

"Don't worry Dave, I'll stay well away from her, and I'll be the consummate professional in my dealings with the Chilcotts."

With that Collins left Andrews' office and walked, ashen-faced, passed Tara Sharma, Stan Bowles and the rest of his colleagues, without stopping. As he accelerated out of the car park, Tara Sharma stood at the third floor window watching him go, wondering at the content of what had obviously been a heated exchange with Dave Andrews.

10.30am

Collins was reeling from his impromptu meeting with Andrews. He couldn't start to make sense of what was happening to him. As he drove he kept asking himself if he was really the scary estranged husband, with the anger management problem, that Janet was suggesting. Was he sufficiently in control of himself to know? And if he wasn't sure about how he was conducting himself in his personal life, was he in the right mental state to be dealing with matters as serious as the abuse being perpetrated by Alex Chilcott? Before he had made any headway with these questions he found himself approaching the towers of the Gartside.

He had planned to spend time on the estate checking in on a few of his current clients, including Lisa Johnson, mother of Mickey, the boy who had made the allegation against his father. Like Carol Chilcott she wasn't having any of it, and was standing by her husband. Collins had also pencilled in another chat with Carol before he had his late afternoon session with Daniel. With time to kill before his first appointment he found himself outside of Parkside Point. He looked up at the 1960s tower block, one of the three that appeared to have been deposited by an alien architect in the heart of the rolling countryside. The low rise flats and maisonettes of the rest of the estate seemed an afterthought to these colossal structures.

As Collins stared out of his car window, he thought about the return of Damon Hartley. It was twelve years since he had seen him, and in that time he had heard nothing of his progress. Yet Damon had never completely left his mind. As all social workers know, there are a handful of cases which never really leave you. Damon was one of his.

He recalled the first time he had met Damon, when he had gone to his house in the shadow of the tower blocks, on the east side of the estate. Collins was there to get information to write Damon's first court report. Fifteen year old Damon was up for 'TWOCking': Taking Without Consent. He had been caught driving back to the estate, in a car stolen in Town. In the vehicle with him were Paul Price and Stevie Dignan, both of whom were known to Collins for persistent crime to support their burgeoning teenage drug habits. While this was the first time Damon had been caught, if he was hanging out with those two, Collins was pretty sure it wasn't his first offence.

Collins remembered being taken aback by his first encounter with Damon. He was a sparky, charismatic, risk taker, who didn't want help or sympathy; he just wanted to be allowed to get on and take his chances. Damon was also brazen in his attitude to the law and any attempt to rein him in. His first exchange with Collins concluded with Damon telling him, "whatever it is you think you're going to do to change me, you won't, so don't bother."

Collins remembered the sad look that Cathy, his mother, wore as she shook her head and wearily agreed. "You won't change him you know. He'll do exactly what he wants to do. Right now what he wants to do is piss about with his arsehole mates, getting stoned and getting nicked."

This was the first time Collins had come across a young person who told him straight that he was wasting his time and he needn't bother. Just as Damon was convinced he would fail; Collins was equally convinced that he would succeed, and even more determined as a result of the challenge thrown down by Damon.

At first Damon was as good as his word, and was almost impossible to engage in anything constructive that Collins planned for him. He would miss their meetings or turn up stoned. Collins realised after a couple of months that the only time when Damon seemed at all likely to attend appointments, and be in a state to participate, was if he was promised a game of football. So that was what they did once a week on Gartside Park. Damon had obviously been a gifted player as a younger boy, but had abruptly stopped playing when his coach died when Damon had just turned thirteen. It was to this that Cathy traced the start of his troublesome behaviour. Having already lost contact with his father, it appeared this bereavement was too much for Damon to take. Not that he would admit anything of the sort of course. He was just having a blast with his mates.

Over time his defences started to come down, and gradually, almost imperceptibly at first, they slowly built a relationship, which provided a window on to another path for Damon; one which wasn't just about stealing, taking drugs and getting arrested. The regular football was often supplemented by irregular call outs to police stations, or to the accident and emergency department at the hospital. Collins had numerous reasons to hastily visit the superstore in Town to buy a coat or a top for Damon: when his clothes had been nicked, or lost, or held by police as evidence. Collins made it his business to be there when Damon needed him.

Despite their blossoming relationship, Damon's behaviour didn't get much better in their first year of working together. Damon was using cocaine and ketamine with his mates, and had started to dabble in smoking heroin by the time Collins met him. He carried on using, and carried on stealing, so that he could use some more.

It took a year, but, finally, Damon admitted he wanted to stop. Collins remembered picking him up, looking dishevelled, having spent yet another night in a police cell.

"I'm done with this shit Tom".

"What, until next weekend Damon?" Collins answered casually, not wanting to seem too exultant that Damon had for the first time decided it was time to change.

"You know I know my own mind. I sat freezing in that cell, staring at the graffiti on the wall, and thought, if I don't stop now I'm gonna be looking at a cell wall for the rest of my life. I'm done with it."

Collins knew it was an important moment, an awakening for Damon, he had waited a long time to see. It didn't mean he would change but these were the green shoots that made change possible.

The next year saw slip ups and stumbles, but there were more steps forward than back. Collins helped Damon to get an apprenticeship at a car mechanics in Town, and to get a move off the estate for him and his mum. He remembered his pride, and Damon's, the day he got his first pay packet, with a bonus from the boss for the effort he had put in. He waved a £20 note at Collins with glee.

"On my way to my first million now Tommy."

Two years on from meeting the angry, lost boy, who swore he could not be helped, Collins knew it was time to say goodbye. He hoped, after their work together, Damon now had a fair chance of making a success of his life, without him at his back.

He said farewell to Damon in the way which would become his sign off to his successful graduates.

"It's been a pleasure working with you, go well, and I don't want to see you again."

Damon knew, that if it came to needing help from Collins, he could always get in touch, but the idea was, if possible, to move on with a normal life away from social workers and police.

Collins got out of his car and looked up at the tenth floor of Parkside Point, wondering what he would find when he knocked on Damon's door, curious as to what had happened to bring him back here to deal drugs to teenagers. Collins was pleasantly surprised to find the lift up to Damon's flat worked and that, unlike the last time he was in it, there was no stench of urine. This time the smell was cannabis. Collins guessed skunk by its pungent aroma.

It was with some trepidation that he knocked on number forty-two. He realised that this anxiety was borne out of the expectation that his own story, of his potency at turning around the lives of troubled teenagers, was about to be shown up for what it was: a story. A story that suited him and his colleagues to tell themselves, but one that didn't often bear the scrutiny of time, and the tests of a harsh world.

Collins' knock provoked movement in the flat, but not an answer. He knew well enough that an unexpected morning knock on the door of a flat like Damon's would cause a degree of concern. It could be the police, council, social services, DWP, or any number of representatives of official-dom. Drugs and their paraphernalia needed to be hidden, roach filled ashtrays emptied, and any inhabitants who weren't supposed to be there would need to hide in the bedroom. Collins never expected a front door to be opened quickly.

Eventually it did open, and there he was, Damon Hartley, the man. Collins had prepared himself for the fact that it wouldn't be the scrawny, pubescent teenager he had said goodbye to twelve years earlier, but he hadn't bargained on the effect that the intervening years would have had on Damon. Collins was presented with a face which looked nearer forty years old than approaching thirty. Lines had gouged their way into his forehead and cheeks, giving his face the look of a weather-beaten cliff. Damon's skin looked damaged, as if recovering from having been scoured by an industrial cleaning machine, which had opened his pores and burst blood vessels on his nose and cheeks. His grey eyes lacked the mischievous sparkle, that had got him into, and away from, many a scrape, but they still had an intensity, which reminded Collins of the headstrong fifteen year old he had first met.

They stared at each other for what may only have been a moment, but felt an eternity, as each man weighed up the other's journey over the previous decade. Damon broke the silence.

"I wondered when you'd come."

Damon ushered him in, and Collins surveyed the flat, taking in as much data as possible, to inform an ad hoc assessment.

From what he could see the place was tidy enough, it was clean and it didn't present, on the surface, as the drug den Collins feared he would find.

"What's been happening Damon?" Collins opened, trying to be as non-accusatory as he could manage in the circumstances.

"Life, mate, life's been happening." Damon paused and looked into Collins' expectant face. He knew he would need to go on.

"I finished my apprenticeship. I was all set up for a permanent job at the garage when my mum got sick. I looked after her for a year through her cancer. I watched her as she slowly slipped away, and it just ate me up. I just felt so empty when she was gone and so alone."

He looked down at his twitching hands, as he continued.

"That's when I got back on the drugs. Pills at first to get me out of it, and before long I was taking coke to make me feel alive again. I've wound up with a crack and a heroin habit and hit rock bottom about four years ago. I ended up robbing a taxi driver, and getting a five year stretch. I've only been out nine months. The council stuck me up here after I'd done me time in a homeless hostel."

Damon's head dropped again in the manner of a penitent looking for forgiveness.

"And? What are you doing with yourself up here?" Collins couldn't help but feel for Damon, the pain and the shame were evident in his story, but this was tempered by the information he had that Damon was dealing to school kids.

"I stayed clean in prison, and so far I've stayed off the gear since I've been out."

"The reason I know you're here, Damon, is because the police say this is a regular haunt for teenagers, a place where they come to buy drugs." Collins could feel his anger rising. Anger for the time he had wasted on Damon, and anger for the fact he was giving him a sob story, while pushing drugs on vulnerable children, like Daniel. He also knew from bitter experience that most of the addicts who had told him they were, "off the gear", weren't.

"I'll give it to you straight Tom, there's a few kids that come up here sometimes, when they're supposed to be at school. They're not going to stay in school anyway; whether I let them in or not. I figure they're safer in here than they would be on the street." Damon opened his palms out to indicate he was giving Collins the whole truth. He could see Collins was unmoved, and he would need to do more to persuade him.

"Do they take drugs? Yes, they sometimes smoke some weed, but that's it. I don't sell it to them, and I don't let any other drugs in the house."

"Come on Damon, how does that make it okay? They're out of school, and they're up here getting stoned. How's that going to help their future? That's just the first steps to ending up like you have."

Collins knew that would hurt. For Collins it was personal, like a father berating his errant son, whose actions have shamed them both. Damon was slow to reply, struggling to retain some composure in the face of his mentor's admonishment.

"I know I'm not exactly a role model, but I reckon I've kept those kids off harder drugs, got them to think about their future, and kept them from going completely off the rails. Isn't that what you and all those drug counsellors call harm reduction?"

Collins remained on the attack. "Come on Damon, I don't know if you're kidding yourself, but you're not kidding me."

"I mean it Tom. These kids have got nothing. Homes they're not safe in, schools that don't want them there, and if they didn't come here, they'd be in a hell of a lot more bother. I'm genuinely trying to help in my own way. It's not like there's any youth workers left any more to do it."

Collins remained sceptical of Damon's explanation, but he also knew that the Damon of old wasn't a liar. Maybe he was trying to get clean and help the next generation stay on the straight and narrow. Collins was at least willing to countenance the possibility now. In doing so he was also providing balm for his own disappointment at what he had thought, until now, was Damon's complete fall from grace.

Even if Damon was telling the truth, Collins wasn't convinced that sheltering with a recovering addict was the intervention that these kids needed. He was about to question him about one boy in particular, when Damon beat him to it.

"Take that kid Dan you've just picked up. You can tell he's petrified at home, and if he didn't come here, he'd be doing aerosols down the park and looking for any other shit he could put in his body to get out of it. He's vulnerable, he'd be preyed upon by all sorts. As if things aren't bad enough for the poor kid. At least he's safe when he's here, and at least he might open up to someone like me."

"And has he opened up to you?" Collins' interest was aroused now. "Has he told you why he's petrified?"

"He won't say what it is, other than his old man's a bastard. As you know he's not the most outgoing, but he does talk a little bit, and I reckon with a bit of time and patience he'll say a lot more." Collins could feel himself being won over again by Damon.

"Time and patience, that was always your way Tom, and it does work. It worked for me. You were always there for me when I needed you, and I learnt to trust you in the end." Damon was now looking Collins squarely in the eye.

"I know I fucked up, but you gave me a chance for a different life. I still want that life. Maybe I'm just taking the long route to get there."

For the first time Collins saw Damon's boyish grin, that he remembered so well. He had now put aside his doubts, and was firmly back in Damon's corner; willing him to come out on top, despite the hand that life had dealt him.

"I'm sorry about your mum Damon. I wish I'd been there for you then."

Damon continued to smile, but now more ruefully. "I wasn't your problem anymore. There's always the next load of kids who need your help."

"You're right, there's always more kids." Collins returned to the particular kid who was the reason for his visit.

"I'm really worried about Daniel, and I don't think we've got the time to patiently build a relationship. Let's just say, I think his old man is a worse bastard than you imagine. Something bad is going to happen in that house soon; I can just feel it."

"I can help, Tom. Like you helped me."

"I might need you to, Damon. For now though, don't let on to Dan that we've had this chat."

Collins' phone had been persistently vibrating since he had been in the flat, and he now reluctantly interrupted his reunion with his former charge to see who wanted him. It was Tara Sharma but he let it ring out.

"Just see what you can find out from Dan, and I'll be in touch."

Collins knew it was time to be moving on. Damon held the front door open, and Collins went to shake his hand. To his surprise, Damon pulled him in close and hugged him.

"I never said thank you. You know, typical teenager. I'm getting there, just taking the long road. Thank you, Tom."

In the lift down, Collins smelt the cannabis and smiled to himself, "harm reduction, cheeky bugger," but he accepted that Damon's method probably had more chance of succeeding with Daniel than his own.

Back in the car he rang Tara. "I was just worried about how your conversation with Dave went," she said. "You didn't look good when you walked out of his office."

"It was a tough conversation," he replied. "I don't know if he's covering up, or just too cautious to take the Chilcott case to court. He still says I need more evidence." Collins neglected to share the details of his incident with Janet, or the fact that Andrews had a police report about it.

"Let me know how I can help," Sharma said, before ringing off.

Collins was glad she had rung, glad that she saw herself as an ally, but also disappointed that a working alliance seemed to be as far as it was going to go.

11.45am

Collins made his way up to Gartside Gardens to speak to Carol, while the kids were still at school. When she eventually answered the door, Carol didn't want to let him in.

"I did my interview for your report, I've told you all you need to know, you've got no reason to come in. The kids aren't on child protection plans, so I don't have to let you in." Carol fixed Collins with a determined stare.

"Carol, you know the system well enough. My assessment may well recommend that the children are placed on child protection plans and, as you say, you'll need to cooperate fully then. Being obstructive now won't help the situation, and won't help the children."

Collins knew he was walking a tightrope between trying to build a relationship with Carol, and the need to raise the stakes, so she could understand the seriousness of the situation.

"You've got no reason to put them on a plan, and I'll tell the conference that."

Collins realised that reason and gentle persuasion were not going to budge Carol Chilcott. He returned her stare and spelled out his position to her. "The outcome of this may not be a plan Carol, it may be immediate court proceedings to take your children into care."

There it was, he had said it, and Carol knew from the way he said it, that Collins was determined to make it happen. She held the door tightly, as she knew her legs might go from beneath her at any second. She was under strict instructions from her husband not to let the social worker in, yet she knew that to turn him away would further antagonise Collins, and increase the risk of losing her children. Hobson's choice, violence from her husband, or the force of the state.

Carol desperately computed her options. She was stuck between two foes: to oblige one, would invite the wrath of the other.

Think, girl, think. He's bluffing, they can't take the kids. They've got nothing, nothing more than they've ever had. Breathe, keep breathing.

"You've got no hope of that. You've got no reason to take them into care," Carol parried.

"We have yet another incident reported to the police of a serious disturbance here on Friday night, where a witness says they heard screams, following a violent argument." Collins was going to continue but was interrupted by Carol's denial.

"It was nothing like that," she countered.

"Then there's the escalating worries about the children, particularly Daniel's physical and mental well-being." Collins hadn't intended to start reeling off the list of concerns when he came up here, but he now felt it was time to accelerate his investigation. "In addition there are obviously serious concerns about your husband's behaviour inside and outside of the home. Frankly Carol, you are not providing an environment which is safe for your children, or where they are ever likely to thrive."

Jesus, he's serious. Al will be picking all this up from behind the door. "I'll kill you all before I let them take them away", that's what he'll say, and that's what he'll do. Give the social worker something to get him off your doorstep at least.

Carol stared furiously at Collins, all the while desperate to devise a strategy to placate both the social worker and her listening husband.

Buy some time to think of a way out of this. Dan, let him see Dan.

"You've got no business saying that. You're adding two and two and making five. My kids are all right, they're good kids. I thought you wanted to spend time with Daniel anyway. He's here. Why don't you do that? You'll see he's a good kid. Nothing wrong with him."

"So he didn't make it to school again today then?" Collins realised that, after his fraught start to the day, he hadn't checked if Daniel had got to school.

"No, he's had a few nose bleeds over the weekend, so I kept him off to be safe. I'm sure he'd be all right to go out with you for a while."

"Okay Carol, send him out, but you've heard what I've said. It's in your interest to cooperate with me, to make sure we can come to the best decisions for your children. You've probably realised I'm not going to be fobbed off. So have a think about what that means for you."

Collins made sure his delivery was clear and authoritative. He needed Carol to understand that the stakes had been raised, and the ball was in her court if she wanted to keep her children.

"I'll be back to see you on Friday at midday, and before I go today I'll have your mobile number please." Carol shrugged and turned to get her son.

As Collins waited for Daniel to appear, he considered whether he was just another bully in Carol Chilcott's life. Care and control was his business, but in Carol's case, it was the control which was now the dominant feature.

Upstairs Carol was struggling to persuade Daniel to go and meet with Collins.

"He's a dickhead. I don't want to go out with a social worker," he said, from his prone position on his bed.

"You said he was all right last week. So what's changed?" Carol asked, but got only a shrug from her son.

"You've got to go out with him, or else it will just make it worse for all of us. They'll put you in care, or at least they'll try, and god knows what your dad will do then."

Daniel stared at his shoes; avoiding his mother's imploring eyes.

"Please Dan, for me?"

He signalled his willingness by zipping up his hooded top and rising slowly from the bed.

Collins welcomed Daniel with the same enthusiasm he had shown on their first meeting, and hoped that they could build on their tentative start of the previous week. He was disappointed that Dan seemed even more withdrawn than before.

135

"Hi Dan, good to see you. Are we going to go for a spin then?"

Daniel shrugged, but followed Collins down the path towards his car.

Collins decided to drive them into Town, knowing that you could often get the most from kids like Daniel just sitting alongside them, keeping it casual, without the pressure of being face-to-face. Collins ran through the list of likely topics which might engage Daniel: school, music, friends, his little brother and sisters. The trouble was, if a child doesn't want to talk, it can make it tough going. And Daniel really didn't want to talk.

Collins thought he saw a flicker, saw him tense up in the seat next to him, when he asked about his weekend. In the absence of small talk, Collins waded into deeper waters.

"It must be horrible Dan, hearing the violence; hearing what your dad does to your mum? I can't imagine what it must be like to live with that." Collins could see that Daniel was struggling to stay still, and was looking increasingly uncomfortable. "Was that what it was like on Friday night?"

Finally Daniel cracked. Still looking at the dashboard in front of him, he hissed at Collins: "You'd know all about Friday, wouldn't you?"

They were just arriving at the Coronation Recreation Ground in Town, which Collins had planned as their destination. He pulled up at the edge of the football field, and switched off the car's engine. Collins didn't know if Daniel knew he had been there on Friday night, and he didn't want to admit to it too readily if that wasn't what Daniel meant. He chose his words carefully.

"Yes, I know there was another incident with your dad being violent to your mum. I'm not a police officer, Dan, but I did make sure there were police on hand if it kicked off, and I know they got there quickly and calmed things down."

Collins was glad to be able to claim a hand in stopping the violence escalating, without admitting to being outside the house, but he felt shabby in not being able to be straight with Daniel; especially as he was the one asking for a trusting, honest relationship.

It clearly wasn't a good enough account for Daniel. "Bullshit," he muttered, and then returned to silently staring out of the car window.

"Come on let's have a kick around," Collins suggested, to break the silence. "I've got trainers and a ball in the back, and I've dressed down especially." By this he meant he had swapped his suit for black jeans and his own hooded top. "I'll go in goal if you like?"

As Collins put his trainers on, sitting against the open boot of his car, he was reminded of the afternoons that he had played with Damon. He knew he had enjoyed it every bit as much as the boy. Whether racing each other to a loose ball, or competing to see who could do the most keepy-ups: in the fresh air, getting muddy, having a laugh. In the hurly burly of his working week, between courts and police stations, reports and statutory contacts, this was an oasis of un-matched joy, when he could do the things he enjoyed most; building a relationship with a wayward kid and, of course, playing football.

Collins juggled the ball from foot to foot and kicked it in Daniel's direction. Daniel looked back at him and then down at the ball, as it came to a stop just in front of him. He kicked it hard in the opposite direction to Collins, and turned to walk back towards the car. Collins tried to hide his disappointment. Maybe football wouldn't be the dynamo that powered their relationship. He fetched the ball and ran after Daniel.

"All right Dan, I get it, you don't want to play football with me. That's fine. Let's get a coke and have a sit down."

As before, in spite of his clear reluctance to engage with Collins, Daniel was willing to take up the offer of a drink and sweets. Collins went to get supplies from the nearby cafe.

They sat on the bench nearest to Collins' car, each opening the ring pulls on their drinks in turn.

"You may not have wanted to play with me, but that's a hell of kick you've got on you. You really should give it a go."

Daniel had once again retreated to his silent thoughts, unwilling to acknowledge Collins' comments, much less reply to them.

"It's fine. I know it's hard. You don't trust me, and why should you? But you will in time. Ask your mate Damon, he'll vouch for me."

Daniel continued to feign indifference, but Collins sensed his acknowledgement that they both knew Damon Hartley would be of interest.

"He was like you in many ways. Louder, I admit, but he was angry and lost and didn't trust anyone. Except maybe his mum. Sound familiar?" Still no response from Daniel.

"Damon didn't have a violent dad at home though, not any more, at least. That's what worries me Dan. I think you and your mum, and brother, and sisters are in real danger. I can't just let it carry on. You're going to have to help me to change it, before one of you gets seriously hurt, or worse."

Daniel carried on looking across the empty football pitch. Collins had finished what he needed to say. He knew Daniel had listened intently, and would be weighing up if, when, and how, he could say anything about his dad, and what went on behind those closed doors. Collins didn't expect it would be today, but it would come out. His worry was that time was running out and Daniel's disclosure might not come soon enough.

Having left a minute for his speech to fully land, and sensing that Daniel was not about to pour his heart out, Collins jumped up from the bench. He flicked the ball that had been between his feet on to his right foot, then his knee and on to his head. He stood in front of Daniel, nodding the ball repeatedly on his head, and then on alternate feet.

"Now you probably think I'm just showing off," he said, with the ball still in the air, "but this is actually part of an important life skill. Ask Damon. If you can juggle a football, you're never far from happiness. You've always got a friend in a football."

Daniel had stopped staring into the distance and was focused on Collins now.

"People might let you down, a football never will."

As he said it, the ball escaped his control, and rolled down the path towards the café. Collins laughed, acknowledging he had fallen short of his own grandiose statement.

As he looked up, to where the ball had rolled, he saw his other boy, Jamie. He was amongst a group of his friends, in their St Christopher's blazers, getting their lunch hour snacks. He could see Jamie had been watching him from outside the cafe. Collins walked towards him, pleased to get a chance to speak to him, away from his mother.

"Hello son, my juggling skills are a bit rusty," he said, with an apologetic smile.

He knew the reference would remind Jamie of the many hours the two of them had spent together practising keepy-ups. The hours in which Collins had patiently worked with his son, to take him from a small boy with no control over a ball, week on week, season on season, until he was the brilliant young star of Corton Juniors; who could out-perform his dad in any skills contest.

Jamie scowled at him.

"You haven't been at football the last few weeks?" Collins knew that Jamie hadn't been, because he had turned up to watch him from a distance, only to be disappointed. Collins sensed Jamie's absence from football was a means of punishing his absent father.

"You've got the County Cup final coming up. Don't miss out on that son. Don't think about me. Think about yourself. You'll always be gutted if you miss out on a final."

Jamie continued to look at his father dismissively. He was fighting the urge to respond but couldn't stop himself.

"It's not about you. Not everything is about you."

He flicked the ball up with his left foot and volleyed it with his right, back over his father's head, to bounce in front of Daniel, who was watching with interest from the bench.

"Have a good game," Jamie shouted, with all the venom he could muster, as he turned to walk away.

Collins struggled to breathe. No woman had ever had the power to crush his heart the way this thirteen year old boy could. It turned out, in setting himself free from Janet, he had lost the most important thing in his life. He struggled to think it was a price worth paying.

Collins dragged himself dejectedly back to where Daniel was sitting and picked the ball up. "Maybe another time, eh Dan?"

Daniel met Collins' eyes now, not in defiance, as he had a few minutes earlier, but with understanding. Daniel gave a small, gentle smile, as if acknowledging that Collins' life wasn't all he had imagined it to be. Like him, Collins was vulnerable and hurting; the injured boy wanted to let the wounded man know that he recognised his pain.

The silence on the way back to Gartside was an easier one than before. Collins didn't feel the need to keep pressing conversation on Daniel, he had said what he needed to say, for today. More importantly, his relationship with Daniel seemed to have been salvaged by the incident with Jamie.

By the time they were back on the Gartside the atmosphere had become more tense, as they got near to Daniel's home. When Collins dropped Daniel in Gartside Gardens, he felt a forbidding weight in his stomach. It was as if Alex Chilcott's menace was seeping out, under the front door, and on to the estate; tainting the summer breeze with his malign presence.

"You don't need to go in, Dan. If you tell me you're scared of what goes on in there, I'll get you somewhere else to stay, where you'll be safe."

Daniel looked at his fidgeting hands in his lap.

Collins waited, sensing that the floodgates could be about to open. He could feel the boy wrestling with his responsibilities towards his mother and siblings; yet drawn to the idea of being free of the burden of that abusive house.

Daniel finally turned to Collins and gave another tentative smile. "I'll see you," he said quietly, as he exited the passenger seat and made for his front door.

Collins sat outside wondering what sort of reception Daniel was getting on his return. Was he being quizzed by Carol, or threatened by his father? Or had he been able to quietly take himself to his room, to be alone with his thoughts and his aerosol cans? Collins decided he needed help to accelerate progress on the Chilcott case. He could only think of one person who might be able to assist, so he headed across the estate to the tower blocks.

2.15pm

"Damon, it's Tom again, can I come up for a chat?" Collins put his mouth close to the intercom at the front door of Parkside Point.

"I'm just coming down mate, stay there," came the crackly response from the tenth floor.

Collins sat on the wall at the base of the tower block. His mood was starting to respond to the warmth and promise of the early summer sun. The connection he had made with Daniel provided some relief from the sadness he felt whenever he thought about Jamie. Now, having had an hour to process his latest encounter with his son, he was more determined than ever to find a way to re-connect.

Five minutes later Damon appeared. To Collins' surprise, he was accompanied by a willowy, auburn haired woman, in a flowing patterned skirt, who looked about thirty years old.

"Tom, Nicky, Nicky, Tom," Damon said by way of introduction. Nicky shared a slightly shy smile. Collins shot Damon an enquiring look, with eyebrows raised. Damon replied with a little nod, by way of confirmation, that Nicky was his significant other. "We're just off to the health clinic," Damon explained.

"I won't keep you. Could you give us two minutes Nicky?"

Nicky sat on the wall, while Collins and Damon walked around the block.

"Looks like a nice girl. Been seeing her long?"

"We met on the drugs programme I did when I got out. She's clean too. She's been good for me. We've been good for each other."

"Clean, as long as you don't count the weed, eh?" Collins offered by way of gentle challenge.

"Better that than methadone, and definitely better than crack or smack. Like I say, harm reduction. Not strictly in accordance with the programme, but it seems to be working for us."

"As long as you're sure you're not kidding yourself," Collins said, with an air of acceptance. He knew there were many ways to get over, or at least get on with, an addiction, and it wasn't for him to say what was going to work for Damon and Nicky.

"Damon, you said you wanted to help with Daniel. He's almost ready to talk, but just can't make himself tell me anything. He's terrified in the house, but he's frightened of what will happen if he speaks. I think he might talk to you."

Damon wasn't sure. "He knows that I know you, so he'll guess that I'm going to pass on anything he tells me, so he'd be in the same position as if he's told you. Which means he's not likely to talk."

"He's close, Damon, very close and I think it will be different with you. Easier because he knows you've been in a similar place. Maybe do something different with him instead of cotching in your flat all day though, eh?" Collins gave a wink to Damon, to show he hadn't fully bought into his youth work methodology.

"What? Football?" Damon replied with a glint in his eye, both in acknowledgement that it was what had done the trick for him, but also as a gentle jibe at Collins' own limited repertoire.

"You'll do it your way, my faithful assistant, you always did. Whatever you do, just get something I can use to nail Alex Chilcott, and to get those kids safe. And by the way, I think that boy could be a decent player with some expert tuition. You might be just the man."

"Football it is then," grinned Damon. "I'll try and catch up with him tomorrow."

TUESDAY 15TH MAY

10.30am

Carol Chilcott sat at the kitchen table, fingers quietly drumming on the formica surface. She faced the closed front room door, from where she could hear the muffled TV sound of sirens and a gunshot following a police chase. Cops and robbers, heroes and villains, goodies and baddies, all day and all night. She knew which ones her husband identified with, as he sat brooding, snarling, with his roll-up pursed between his lips.

Carol's mind turned óver, in a desperate attempt to settle on a direction. She felt the walls of the kitchen crowding in to crush her. This had been her prison home since Daniel had been born, and now, one way or another, her time was almost done. She winced as she tried to take in a calming gulp of air. Her tender ribs reminded her

147

of the pummelling they had received the previous night: "don't scream bitch, or you'll have the filth around again." She wasn't even allowed to make a sound now when he assaulted her.

Sunday had been some relief. The chair against the bedroom door handle had done its job. He sloped away with typical threats, "I'm coming back for you" whispered menacingly through the door and "it will be worse when I get in there." She had heard the backdoor slam, and knew he was off out to do whatever he did, in the park or on the estate.

She thought that last night might be the end of her. He was raging without any identifiable cause, other than his general hatred of women. "You're all slags, all women, all slags", "dirty whores", "come here bitch, you thief, you fucking thief." Carol knew what was coming next and didn't know whether she would survive another drowning.

Each time now he was more out of control. He used to be cruel, but at least measured; meting out punishment in even doses. She had even kidded herself that she had made a space for her and the children, in which she could insulate them all, and manage his abuse. Now his violence was reckless, a man possessed, reaching the end of his road.

She did survive Monday night, just. Bloodied, bruised and choking on lungs filling with water. She survived, but she didn't know how much longer she could stay alive.

Carol closed her eyes. The constant conversation she had been having with herself, since Collins' visit yesterday, continued unabated, but now in pictures. The kitchen walls were replaced by the walls of a maze. Each way she fled her pathway was blocked, and all the time, behind her, she could feel that presence; that malevolent force, pursuing her to her end.

He's going to kill you. Maybe today, maybe tomorrow, maybe next week. It will happen. Don't tell yourself you can manage this, because you can't.

She could hear her heart pounding, as she considered her options. She thought about fleeing, she thought about calling the police when she was taking the kids to school. She thought about Collins.

Could you trust him?

The idea of telling Collins what was going on had never seriously crossed Carol's mind. She trembled as she tried to assemble an escape plan. She hadn't ever contemplated telling a social worker what her life was really like. If she shared the reality of her brutal existence with Collins, she would have to pray that he didn't let her down. If he did, she knew she would be dead, along with her children.

This would be a leap of faith, the like of which she had never made before, with the exception being, of course, the faith she had put in Alex when she was sixteen years old.

Look where that got you.

Carol was pulled out of her fantasy by a roar of "tea" from the front room, and she was brought back to the confines of her kitchen cell.

11am

While Carol Chilcott tried to devise a route to safety, her son had made his routine disappearance from school premises, and headed back on his bike to meet Damon at Gartside Park.

Daniel knew what Damon was up to. His new fitness regime was a poor cover for doing Collins' work for him.

"Yeah, I'll meet you down the park tomorrow. You can fuck off if you think I'm running anywhere though," he had said to Damon, when he had taken refuge in the flat the previous afternoon.

Daniel didn't mind what Damon was up to, he was happy to be with him, even if Damon now had an ulterior motive. Apart from his mum, Damon was about the only one Daniel ever spoke to, and he felt safe enough with him to know he wouldn't try to get him to say anything he wasn't ready to share.

Damon sat waiting patiently at the park gates for the arrival of his young charge. Eventually he saw him approaching on his shabby bicycle. Skidding to a halt, Daniel scoffed at Damon's attempt at sports attire.

"Fuck me, Damo, those tracky bottoms haven't been out in about twenty years. You look like some paedo PE teacher from last century."

"It's not what you look like, it's what you can do on the ball," Damon said, producing a football from his rucksack, in the manner of an amateur magician.

"Behold the life changing orb."

"Fuck-sake Damo, you even sound like that fucking social worker."

"I probably sound like him, Danny Boy, because he spent hundreds of hours with me, trying to stop me becoming the arsehole I eventually became. But no more. I'm once again heeding the words of the wise Mr Collins. I've got clean, I'm going to get fit and life is going to be sweet. I'd advise you to do the same."

"I just need a joint mate," Daniel said wearily.

"Plenty of time for that, once we've finished our session. I should warn you, I won't be joining you in a smoke. Clean means properly clean now. For today at least, and we'll see what tomorrow brings."

Despite Daniel's protests, he found Damon's enthusiasm infectious. After night on night of horror at home, Daniel loved the easy freedom of being with an adult he could trust.

"Let's start with a bit of pass and move, and see where we get to."

It wasn't a question. Daniel was half of this game whether he liked it or not. While at first a reluctant participant, he soon got into the swing of it.

"You've got two choices when you receive a ball. A live touch, or a dead touch. Go on, hit it at me," Damon shouted.

Daniel hit the ball hard at Damon from ten yards away. Although he hadn't kicked a ball in a dozen years, Damon stopped it instantly with his left foot and rolled it back.

"That's the dead touch. That's when you've got time and space to stop it, and look up for the next pass. Now hit me again."

Daniel again found Damon with a firm right footed pass. This time Damon took it on the move, pushing the ball a yard in front of him as he received it, before hitting it back.

"And that's the live touch, for when you've got a player up your arse. Let's have a go at both of those. You've got to shout 'dead' or 'alive' when you hit it, to tell me which you want, and I'll do the same for you."

Apart from the occasional break, in which one or both of them would be bent over wheezing and spluttering, they kicked the ball to each other for twenty minutes, all the time moving across the field. Damon's assured touch was in contrast to the boy's, which was clunky in comparison; the ball often deflecting away when he was supposed to kill it. Damon was impressed that Daniel persevered, and got better as time went on.

In the end the passing disintegrated into tackling each other, with Damon rehashing step-overs and body swerves he had perfected many years earlier with Tom Collins. Their game ended when Daniel got fed up at being left behind by Damon's shimmies, and resorted to kicking him up in the air. Damon lay in a heap on the ground, as Daniel ran away with the ball at his feet, laughing joyously.

"You little bastard," Damon shouted at him, picking grass off his lips. He couldn't help bursting into a broad grin at the cheek of the boy. "Help me up, you little shit."

Daniel offered Damon a hand, but as the older man went to grab it, he withdrew it swiftly, leaving Damon to topple backwards to the floor again; provoking more laughter from the boy, and ultimately from the supine Damon. He dragged himself up and over to the bench where he had left his rucksack, from which he produced two bottles of Lucozade.

"Here you go: the athlete's choice," Damon said, offering a bottle to Daniel.

"The drink of kings" Daniel replied.

"Who's sounding like their social worker now?" Damon chided the boy.

"He does have that effect though. Most of what I know that's important, I learnt from him. I spent the first year thinking I was taking him for a ride, but before I realised it, he'd got in here." Damon pointed to his temple. He paused and looked ruefully across the empty football pitch.

"I was on the up. I'd turned things around, and it would have been different if my mum hadn't got sick. I was set for something a lot better than drugs and prison."

He paused as he thought back to the tortuous path his life had taken.

"But it's never too late. I'm not giving up on that dream, and I've got him to thank for making me believe things could be different."

Damon's words had set Daniel thinking about his own mother, and the perilous situation she was in.

"I wouldn't want to live without my mum. I bet you were in bits."

"Yeah, I was," Damon replied. He paused, before gently steering the conversation in the direction Collins needed from him.

"Is that what worries you Dan? You think you might have to live without your mum?"

"Yeah. It's one of the things." Daniel thought some more before making his admission. "Yeah, it's the worst thing."

"What you worried about? Being taken into care or something else?"

Daniel fell silent.

"It's all right mate. I'm not going to pressure you. If you want to tell me, I'm here. If you don't, I'm still here for you."

Damon knew Daniel well enough, and he remembered sufficient of what he had been like at the same age, to know when to stop probing. By now Daniel was lighting a joint he had produced from his school bag.

"It's all yours Danny Boy. Blaze away if you want to, but I'm a mean, clean, fitness machine from here on."

As Daniel sought the comfort provided in cannabis, Damon reflected on his football career that got away, and gave Daniel some encouragement.

"You're a decent player, Dan. You could get in a team. You'd enjoy it."

Daniel snorted at the idea. The thought of the structure, the team mates, the camaraderie, the normality. It was all such a distant world.

"I need some proper fucking drugs to imagine that's ever going to happen."

"You can choose these things. They're not just for other people, Dan. You can have the life you want. You've got to believe that, or else you're just stuck with your shitty lot. There's got to be more than what you're handed down by your parents, or school, or all those people who think you're nothing, because you come from Gartside. Don't just accept it, Dan. That's what they want, that's why things don't change."

"He taught you that too, didn't he?"

"Yeah that and a lot of football drills" Damon said, laughing. As he finished the sentence, he looked into Daniel's face and held his eye.

"It's your life Dan, it's there to be lived, your choice, dead or alive."

As they made their way along the path out of the park, and back on to the estate, they passed a group of four boys, a year or two older than Daniel. They leant against their bikes by the peeling, black, iron railings of the park gates, watching the footballers approach. Daniel put his head down to avoid eye contact, but Damon greeted them warmly.

"Afternoon fellas, you lot didn't fancy school today either?"

"Study leave Damo," the tallest of them, a sickly looking, stick thin, ginger lad, replied with a sarcastic smirk.

"You'll have your books in those carrier bags then will you, Streak? Along with those tinnies? I suppose you need those to calm your nerves before the exams?"

"We're down here to keep watch Damo. That pervert's been out again." As he said it, Streak shot a glance in Daniel's direction.

Damon was keen to know more, but didn't want to be having this conversation in front of Daniel.

"Okay boys, good luck with that. I'll catch up with you later Streak. You can let me know how you get on."

9.10pm

Collins saw the missed call from Damon as he left the gym. He had spent the day trying to get on top of all the casework he had piling up, but all the time he had the Chilcotts on his shoulder, and in the pit of his stomach. He kept finding himself wondering how Damon was getting on with Daniel, and if Carol would be able to keep her husband at bay for a bit longer.

"What you got for me Damon?" he enquired with a casual air, which belied the knot of anxiety at his core. "Did he give you anything?"

"It was a good start, but I got nothing new from Dan. You're right though, he is on the edge of telling. We've got a fitness regime started. We'll do it again tomorrow, and see what he comes out with."

"Don't tell me, is it a football-based fitness regime?"

"Piss off, you're just jealous you're not the one he wants to play with," Damon fired back jovially. "You're right though, we might make a player of that kid."

"He might not be playing anything if we don't get him to talk, and get him out of that house," Collins replied. "Let me know how you get on tomorrow. I think we're running out of time though Damon."

"Tom, one more thing you might be interested in," Damon threw in before the call ended.

"Go on," replied Collins.

"Some of the kids I know from the estate say that there's been an attack in the park, Sunday night. The details are a bit sketchy, but they reckon a man has tried to rape a girl as she's taken the cut through off the last bus."

"I've heard nothing about that. Did she report it?"

"No, she's petrified apparently. They said she's taken to her bed, and hasn't spoken to anyone but her mum, and won't even speak to her now. The word is getting around the estate, and people are pointing the finger at Alex Chilcott again."

"He's not the only sex offender on the estate Damon. He's probably not even the only sex offender on his road," Collins replied, but immediately reminded himself this was Alex Chilcott they were talking about. "I'm sure they're right to put his name in the frame though. Do you know who the girl is?"

"Yeah" Damon paused. "It's Stevie's little girl, Greta."

Stevie Dignan had been one of the terrible threesome, along with Damon and Paul, who Collins had supervised in his youth offending days, when he had first come to the patch. Of those three likely lads, it was Damon who was faring best. Paul was still inside, doing another long stretch for robbery, the latest in an ever more desperate cycle of drug-fuelled crime, which showed no sign of abating. As for Stevie, he was dead at eighteen years old, his brain fried from too much acid, mixed with ketamine, and a host of prescription drugs he nicked from his mum. One day it got too much, and he jumped from a balcony on the eighth floor of Hillside Point, directly across from where Damon was now living. He didn't live long enough to see Greta take her first steps.

Collins had seen Greta around the estate over the years; kept an eye out for her and her mum, Charlie. He imagined that one day Charlie and Greta might officially be his problem, but, up until now, they were just on his informal radar.

"Shit, poor kid. She hasn't had much luck. Thanks Damon, that's helpful. I'll see what the cops make of it."

Collins rang the duty inspector and shared the intelligence he had picked up about the attack on Greta. He was glad to find it was Gill Thompson on shift. He had worked with her on a number of tough cases over the years, and she was pretty reliable. Collins suggested they put an extra patrol on Gartside for the night. He also reminded her of the marker on the Chilcotts' and encouraged her to get an officer to do a doorstep call.

Thompson replied to his request with gentle sarcasm, "No problem Tom, why don't we just put an officer on the door of eighty-four Gartside Gardens all day and night, like ten Downing Street? I've got four cars covering the whole area tonight, that's Town and the villages, and we've already had three other domestics, not to mention all the other calls."

159

"I know Gill, I get it, but believe me we will be putting an officer on the door twenty-four-seven and a load of tape around the house, if we don't keep a lid on it. This one is ready to blow."

"Trust me, it will be defensible decision-making within the limits of the resources at my disposal." She rehearsed the line, which people like her and Collins needed to have ready, whether for the domestic homicide investigation or serious case review, in the aftermath of the tragedies that inevitably scarred their working lives.

"Don't worry, I hear you Tom. I'll do my best."

WEDNESDAY 16TH MAY

8.30am

Collins woke early, eager to use his new information to force the Chilcott case over the line with his bosses. As soon as he was able, he planned to go up to the Gartside to try to learn more about the latest attack, and find a way to get Greta to make a statement that might identify her attacker.

He waited, until he knew Andrews would be in, to give him the heads up that there had been another attack.

Andrews was quick to pick up Collins' call. "Tom, I'm glad you called in."

"Dave, there's been another sex assault on Gartside. A kid I know was the victim. She hasn't told the police yet. I'm not saying it's Chilcott, but there's got to be a good chance."

"Tom, slow down. I'm glad you rang, because I need you to come in." Collins recognised a formality in Andrews' voice which perturbed him, but he ploughed on regardless.

"Dave, listen to me. This is important new information that needs to be investigated. I need to go up to Gartside to get the girl to make a statement."

"Tom, you listen to me. I need you here in my office at 9.30. I'll see you then," and the call was over.

Collins was concerned by Andrews' tone, and the fact he felt the need to issue such a categorical instruction. This was the first conversation they had had since he had been warned by Andrews to stay away from Janet's. Nothing had happened since to inflame the situation, so why would Andrews' stance have hardened? He anxiously turned it over in his mind on the short drive into the office.

Andrews had said nine-thirty, so Collins had ten minutes to update team mates on the Chilcotts and the Gartside developments, before he had to face his boss. He motioned for the three available colleagues in the office to gather around his desk. Tara Sharma, Stan Bowles and Cathy Creswick listened as he gave his assessment of the gravity of the situation in the Chilcott house, and the news that there had been another attack, which may well have been the work of Alex Chilcott.

"We need to get those kids out as soon as, and if possible their mother too. I'm not sure she'll play ball though. I'm going to go up to the Gartside to see if I can move things along with the girl, and have one last go with Carol," Collins explained.

"Where's the boss and the Director on this?" Bowles asked, intuitively picking up that they were not in the same place as Collins.

"They're cautious," he said, shooting a glance at Sharma.

"Probably because you're trying to do the police's job for them Tom," Cathy chimed in. "You're convinced Alex Chilcott is some psycho-monster, but you've got nothing to prove it, only this speculation. All the while, there are dozens of other kids in worse situations, who need to be protected, while you're off playing football with the Chilcott boy."

Collins stared angrily at Creswick.

"Sometimes I don't know why you do this job Cathy? It's not about having an open and shut case, beyond reasonable doubt. This is social work, it's the balance of probability, it's hard evidence but it's also gut instinct."

The anger he felt at having to standby and allow Alex Chilcott's abuse to continue was now being directed towards Creswick. Collins was spitting the words out.

"It's about knowing people. I know the Chilcotts, and I can tell you it is well beyond any balance of probability, that man is a psychopath and those children are suffering."

Collins and Creswick eye-balled each other, leaving Tara to fill the silence.

"Cathy, he's right, Alex Chilcott is a dangerous man, and we need to help Tom get those kids out."

Collins had more to say, but he saw Andrews' door had opened, and his boss was beckoning him in. Tara Sharma gave him a sympathetic smile and mouthed, "good luck".

Within seconds of entering the room, Collins knew that this would be a most formal encounter. There had been none of the normal pleasantries that are used to oil the wheels of the working week; acknowledgements and enquiries about the humdrum, the common human concerns of work, and weather, and family. They don't seem important until they aren't there. Without these little sentences things soon turn cold.

It was that chill that Collins felt as he walked into the office. His concern was amplified when he saw that sat next to Andrews was the department's Head of Human Resources, Greg Tudor. Collins knew it was ominous enough to be summoned into the office to meet his boss without explanation but, to find Tudor at his side, felt disastrous. In his mid-forties, Tudor's lean frame and the remains of his boyish good looks were in marked contrast to Andrews, who sat two feet to his left. Tudor was a spectral presence who floated around the department, turning up unexpectedly, usually delivering bad news to some unfortunate employee. Before a word had been uttered, Collins knew that a calamity was about to befall him.

Time seemed to slow, as Collins experienced the unfolding scene one frame at a time.

"Sit down please, Tom."

As Andrews began to speak, in his familiar hushed but resonant tone, Collins saw his lips and tongue carefully craft every word, as they were propelled forcefully in his direction.

"I have to inform you, that I have received a serious allegation regarding your conduct."

Andrews' words didn't tumble forth, but were thoughtfully prepared, chiselled methodically, for clarity and effect. As the magnitude of the charge was revealed, the words thumped from Collins' head, to heart, to lungs. His body felt like it was being assaulted by a force that he could not see, but which streamed towards him, filling him up and shaking his core.

"I have taken advice from the Director and from the HR department, who agree that this allegation, if proven, would amount to gross misconduct."

The force of those two words, gross misconduct, when first delivered, took what breath Collins had left in him away.

"You will be suspended on full pay, for an initial period of two weeks, while an independent investigation into the matter is undertaken."

"At this time I can only tell you that the complaint relates to your conduct, particularly, but not exclusively, in the

Chilcott case. We have received a letter detailing what amounts to inappropriate behaviour directed by you towards Daniel Chilcott. We also know that you were at the Chilcott home at 11pm last Friday night, as your phone was used to make a call to the police from that location, regarding a domestic incident. This was the same evening in which police were also called as a result of your harassment of your estranged wife. I am also aware from my own dealings with you that you appear to have something of an obsession with the Chilcott case, which supports the suggestion that you are not in a fit state to be in work at the moment, while this situation is fully investigated."

Sixty seconds. It couldn't have taken much longer to deliver those few short sentences. Collins experienced it like an epic poem, laying bare his fatal flaws and caricaturing, what he had thought of as his noble deeds, as compulsive delusions. In those few short seconds, everything Collins had envisaged for his future was thrown into the air, and he had no idea where it would land.

The initial assault concluded, elastic time sprung from slow-motion to gather a pace, propelling the exchanges that followed, one into another. Was it ten more minutes he was in that room? Perhaps twenty? Collins didn't know. He maintained his composure, despite the panic which gripped his body. His mind jumped from one explanation to another, to try to account for this unexpected turn of events, as he did his best to respond to the charge laid before him.

"I admit, I was worried about the Chilcotts, and found myself outside last Friday night, when Alex Chilcott started kicking off again. I was only there because nobody else was doing anything. I went up there just to check, and it's a good job I did. That's not gross misconduct, that's just a duty of care, and I haven't done anything else out of line in the Chilcott case. And as for…"

"Tom, I must ask you to stop there," Tudor interrupted, in his clipped Home Counties accent, polished by an expensive education. "These are matters for the investigation, and you will have your chance to give your account."

Collins ignored him and spoke directly to his boss. "Dave I've already explained to you what happened with Janet. I don't know what the hell this other allegation is about, but we all know it's in the nature of our business. People make complaints to deflect from their own wrong-doing. Can I see this letter?"

"No, I can't show you it at this time, Tom, but I can tell you this appears to have come from one of your colleagues," Andrews replied, almost apologetically.

"Tom, taking it all together, it really is for the best if you take some time out, while we get to the bottom of this."

A colleague? This was a further blow. Collins was struggling now to retain his calm demeanour. He looked hard into Andrews' eyes.

"Dave, you're not suggesting I take some time out for the sake of my well-being, you're suspending me on the grounds of gross misconduct, for which I could be sacked."

Tudor interjected again. "Tom, suspension is a neutral act, it does not indicate any blame," he said, with the stress on the 'not'. "We need to investigate the allegations and, in this case, it isn't appropriate for you to be in work while we do so."

"It doesn't feel like a neutral act," Collins snapped back at Tudor, before turning again to Andrews.

"You say I'm obsessed with the Chilcotts, but that family is a tragedy waiting to happen, and it will happen soon. You take me off the case and who's going to get in there and stop it?"

"Don't worry, we will re-allocate your cases while you're off," Andrews replied flatly.

"Like I say, who's going to get on top of the Chilcott case, just like that, and get to grips with Alex Chilcott?"

"It will be re-allocated."

"Who to? Who Dave? Tell me who's going to get in there and keep those kids safe?" Collins was now speaking rapidly, in a demanding tone.

"I think the Chilcotts are going to be looked after by Cathy Creswick in your absence." Andrews couldn't conceal a hint of embarrassment, as he conveyed this news.

Suddenly Collins felt he had his blinkers removed, and was able to survey the whole of the terrain around him. Andrews didn't want to do anything about the Chilcotts, and giving the case to Creswick would ensure that nothing was done. This complaint was perfect ammunition, to put alongside other circumstantial evidence, as a means to get him out of the way.

"Brilliant, you want to do nothing, so you're getting me off the case, and putting Cathy on it. That works fine for you doesn't it? Unless of course Alex Chilcott murders his wife. It works fine, if you don't care that you're leaving a predatory sex offender to roam Gartside Park at night; and it works fine, if you don't give a damn about the Chilcott children." Collins paused. Having delivered his charge he rode back from the precipice he was lurching towards.

"That's not you Dave." Collins' fear for his own future had reduced now when put against the implications of leaving Alex Chilcott to continue his abuse unhindered.

"Is that really what you want?" Collins half accused and half pleaded.

Tudor again tried to draw them back to the formalities of the suspension meeting.

"Tom, you may wish to consult your union or a solicitor. Your suspension starts with immediate effect. Please ensure that during the suspension period you have no contact with colleagues, or any of your clients, and that you do not enter any council premises without prior permission."

"All right I hear you." Collins looked at Tudor briefly, nodding to confirm he understood the rules of his suspension, as he sought to continue his dialogue with his manager. Before he could do so, Andrews added further emphasis to the instruction.

"And Tom, stay away from Gartside, and especially from the Chilcotts."

Collins glared at him. "You know this is bullshit, Dave. I don't know why you think you need to do this. I don't know what you're frightened of?"

Collins had gone to say, "I don't know what you're hiding?" but thought better of it. He had his suspicions about Andrews, but he didn't need to air them just now.

With that, Collins got up and left the office. He tried to retain his normal confident gait, while feeling like he had been knee-capped. The short walk back to his desk, passing colleagues, who were now shrouded in suspicion, felt like a marathon. One of them had complained about his 'inappropriate behaviour towards Daniel Chilcott'. What did that mean? What were they suggesting?

Collins looked at the photo of Jamie on his desk, and wondered if he would be receiving this in a cardboard box, with his other personal effects in a few weeks' time, when they decided he was indeed guilty of gross misconduct. He hastily shot a glance at the colleagues dotted around the office. Each was assiduously going about their normal business, but he knew all of them would be wondering what had gone on in Andrews' office. Cathy Creswick had her head down in a file, which appeared to be of gripping importance, as she never for a moment looked up. She was already Collins' prime suspect as the letter writer.

He took what he knew might be his only chance to probe her before his period in exile started.

"Cathy, I understand you're going to be asked to cover the Chilcott case for the short-term?"

"That's news to me Tom. Are you giving it up?" she replied, in what sounded like a tone of genuine enquiry.

He examined her face for clues to her prior knowledge of why he wouldn't be working the case. She was inscrutable.

"You'll need to talk to Andrews about that, but if you're caretaking you really need to get to see Carol and the kids as soon as. It's a very volatile situation."

"So you keep saying, but so are all my other cases. You've been up there enough in the last week, and you've got the response car keeping a watch over them. I'm sure they can wait for another social work visit until next week."

"Thanks Cathy, thanks for all your help," the bitterness in Collins' voice was evident, but so was his resignation. He knew his fears weren't shared by Creswick, and she wouldn't be the person who was going to make the difference in the Chilcott case.

Collins looked around the office as he tidied his desk. He didn't know if or when he would be back here, and he already felt a keen sense of loss. As he walked towards the office door, and passed Tara Sharma, she looked up at him with a puzzled expression. Collins gave a strangled excuse for a smile and kept walking.

10.30am

Collins drove towards home in a daze. Nothing had prepared him for the encounter with Andrews, and finding himself so unexpectedly removed from work, ripped away from the world which had held him through all his recent troubles. "Suspension", "gross misconduct", those shame-steeped words reverberated around his body, infecting his very marrow. He was deemed unfit to do his job, unsafe to remain in work, while his conduct was being investigated.

With each second the ramifications became clearer. Losing his job would mean losing his career, with no obvious prospect of a ready-made alternative. With his job would go the money for the flat, the mortgage on what used to be the family home, the payments on the new car. Not yet a mile from the office, Collins was already staring at a very different, much reduced, future for himself. And then there was Collins' other "obsession". What of Alex Chilcott? The unrestrained offender, terrorising his home and neighbourhood. What could Collins do about him now? Nothing, if he was going to follow the instructions just given to him by Dave Andrews.

Collins' numbed brain struggled to hold together the strands of his tortuous fall. Had he really done anything which equated to gross misconduct? He had trodden a thin line but, surely, nothing which so affronted his profession's code? He knew it was the complaint which had tipped the balance, and Collins was sure that this was just trouble-making from an embittered colleague. The only person he could think could do this was Cathy Creswick, but even for her this was out of character. She was plain speaking, blunt in the extreme, and no fan of Collins' methods, but a letter of complaint? That didn't feel like her way of doing things. But if not Creswick, then who?

The darker thought, which had hovered on the horizon of Collins' mind in the previous week, started to take a clearer form. He had repeatedly had cause to ask himself why Andrews was so reticent to take action in the Chilcott case. Was there something he was hiding? Was he worried that Collins was about to crack the case, and expose Andrews' failings, and perhaps those of the Director, Frazer Campbell? Was he getting too close to a secret the department didn't want aired? Time to get him off the case, and the letter could be the perfect device to make that happen.

As this train of thought gathered pace, Collins was shaken by its implications. If the letter had been manufactured, then there must really be something for Andrews to hide. If he was being fitted up, the prospect of him losing his job became all the more real.

Collins arrived at his apartment block and sat staring at the pear tree blossom overhanging his parking space. A pair of tortoiseshell butterflies busily flitted from one flower stem to another, ignoring the pollen laden bumble bees who were busy at their work. Collins stared at them unseeing, while his mind grappled with its own heavy load.

He sat paralysed in his driver's seat, not knowing what to do next. Every way he felt compelled to go led to a dead end. No colleagues to speak to, no wife, no son, nothing to be done about Alex Chilcott. At every turn his way was barred. He could ignore the instructions he had been given, but to be caught flouting the rules would only aggravate his situation. He was on his own, both lonely and alone, and staring into the abyss.

Collins had an overwhelming desire to have a drink. A drink that could, for a time, make this pain stop. He could smell Irish whiskey and taste its numbing warmth. He turned on the engine again, setting his sights on the nearest off-licence. The only path open to him was to get smashed and hope, when he came round, the world had somehow righted itself. Like a hooked salmon, which had fought with all its mite, twisting and turning and thrashing to be free, he was now overwhelmed and exhausted. He was ready to be reeled in.

At that moment his work phone started to vibrate. It was Tara Sharma. He so wanted to speak to Tara, wanted to confide in her, wanted someone to share his pain, but he had expressly been told to have no contact. The phone vibrated for a third and then a fourth time.

On the fifth vibration he picked it up.

"Tara."

"Tom what's happened? We've just been told you're not going to be in work for at least the next two weeks?" Sharma's voice was full of concern.

"Yes Tara, I've been suspended. Did they also tell you not to contact me?"

"Yes, but I'll take my chances."

"Well I shouldn't be answering the phone to you, and the consequences of us being caught communicating are probably a lot worse for me than you," Collins replied.

"Sorry but I needed to let you know I'm here, if you need me. Whatever they're investigating has got to be rubbish." She paused. "Hasn't it Tom?" He sensed she needed reassurance on this before they could move on.

"Total rubbish, Tara, believe me. I'm being stitched up by someone."

"That's what worried me. I'm here for you," she said, having received the confirmation she was eager to hear. "I'll text you my personal number."

"Thanks Tara. Really, thank you. I needed you to call me. I'll send you my own number too. Best use that for now."

For the first time since leaving the office, Collins found himself fighting back tears. "I've got to work out what's happening to me, and what I can do about it, but, yes, please do send your number; I could do with your help."

"You're not on your own Tom. You know that don't you? It's not just me, there's a whole team of people who are going to make sure you come through this and out the other side." With that she put the phone down.

Collins turned off the engine and made his way, with heavy legs, up the stairs to his flat. He poured himself a pint of water, and went and laid on his bed. He recognised that Sharma's call had averted a disaster. He was close to the edge, close to throwing himself headlong over the ledge, and she had pulled him back. He would get through this. Somehow, he would get through this.

The tears he had felt welling in the car were still close to the surface. He lay breathing deeply, propped up on his pillows, staring at his blank bedroom wall. "You'll get through this", he repeated to himself, as a teardrop rolled slowly down his cheek.

Collins didn't know how long he had lain in a semi-coma-tose state, staring at his bedroom wall. When he roused himself he only knew that it was time to get out. He planted both feet on the floor, in a deliberate fashion, and pushed himself up to standing. If he was going to get through this without resorting to booze, and wallowing in his own despair, he needed to keep active and get out of his flat. He pulled on his running shoes, shorts and t-shirt, and headed for the hills.

At first he felt stiff and ill-equipped to take on a hill run. His limbs were leaden, as if he had already spent the morning running, but he knew it was the emotional energy he had expended that was weighing him down. Resolutely, Collins ploughed on, until he found some rhythm, and in that rhythm he found solace. The path was already starting to take on its hard summer character. No longer the slog through muddy puddles, on rutted bridle paths, Collins had become accustomed to over the last six months. He began to find a spring to his step, which he hadn't imagined would be there today.

Having ascended gradually for forty five minutes, he emerged from the last of the shaded thickets of the hillside, on to the Ridge, which over looked the district. Down to his right was the sprawl of Queenstown, with its ever burgeoning skyline of new office blocks and apartments. The houses and shops became less dense as the town merged with the surrounding countryside, until there were just the occasional farmhouse enclaves, surrounded by fields of every shade of green, along the valley floor. As the ground rose again, on the other side of the valley, a swathe of rape seed had been planted, painting the fields a vivid yellow in the afternoon sunlight. Between Town and the distant hills lay the sprawl of the Gartside, dominated by its three concrete giants.

All this was Collins' patch. He felt a pang for all that was now denied to him, which was matched by a renewed determination to get back what was his, and to put right his troubles. He commenced his descent with the outline of a plan starting to take shape, and his spirits somewhat lifted.

8.15pm

"What news, Bertie?" Collins opened his call to Damon with a deliberately bright tone. He had realised he was at liberty to have contact with Damon, who hadn't been his client for over a decade, and Damon could continue to keep an eye on Daniel. This was one route Collins thought was still legitimately open to him.

Damon distantly remembered that the reference Collins was making to a historical figure, Bertie Smalls, the original supergrass. Collins had told him all about Bertie Smalls' loose tongue and they had joked about Damon being a 'Bertie', in his younger years, when he would inadvertently drop his mates in it, when telling Collins of his weekend exploits.

"Yesterday I was your trusted assistant and now I'm just a common grass, cheers." Damon replied in equally upbeat fashion.

Collins cut to the chase. "Did you see Dan today?"

"Yes, we're getting there." Damon paused for dramatic effect. "His first touch is definitely better," he said, with a little chuckle.

"Come on, Damon, did he say anything about his dad?" A slight impatience was already creeping into Collins' voice.

"He says he's a bastard who knocks his mum around the whole time."

"Okay, I think we've established that already," Collins interrupted. "Did he give you anything new?"

"He said he's cruel, but he didn't go into any detail. I got the sense it's a nightmare living in that house, but no, nothing specific. He did take his hoody off for the first time though, which must have taken a lot of guts for him, because he's been cutting himself. He said it's the only thing that makes him feel better when he's at home."

"I'm not surprised, poor little sod. Well done for getting that much out of him. I think we're nearly there. Will you have another go tomorrow?"

"Surely you've got enough to take those kids into care by now?" Damon expressed surprise that they still needed more evidence.

"You'd think so, wouldn't you Damon", Collins replied, before deciding it was time he let Damon in on his own news. "Unfortunately things just got a lot more complicated. I'm off the Chilcott case. In fact I'm not going to be in work for a little while. There's been a complaint about me, which they're investigating."

"Bloody hell Tom, they're about fifteen years too late if they don't like the way you go about things. I'm sorry, that's bad news for you and for Dan."

"I don't think it will come to anything," Collins said, with a confidence which he didn't entirely own. "But I'll need you to keep an extra close eye on him until I'm back on the case."

"I'm seeing Dan tomorrow. What if he decides to tell all then though, what do I do with it?"

"If he does, just let me know what he says, and we'll decide what we do from there."

"No problem, Tom. You can trust me."

"Thanks Damon, you're doing a good job and, yes, I do trust you." As he put the phone down, the irony that he now had more faith in a multiply convicted addict than in his boss and some of his colleagues, was not lost on Collins.

Exhausted from the emotional energy he had spent, in addition to the physical outlay from running ten miles up and down the hillside to the Ridge, Collins was pleased to feel the draw of an early night, and to be able to lay the day to rest. His brain still turned over the events, their causes and their implications, but with an increasingly weary repetition, that drew him towards sleep.

THURSDAY 17TH MAY

3.35am

Collins woke with a jolt in the darkness. A look at his phone confirmed he had only had half a night's sleep. He didn't know if it was a noise outside that had pulled him out of sleep, or, whether it was his unconscious mind's refusal to deal alone with the weight of jumbled facts and fears, crashing one into another, around his head and all over his fretting body.

Immediately he became aware of a dull ache in the centre of his chest. A solid leaden weight, crushing his heart and lungs. The feelings came first, and then the events of the previous day crowded into his conscious mind. He knew, from that moment, returning to sleep would be impossible, as his brain was now active and on the hunt for reasons, a plausible narrative that would give shape to the mosaic that was still a mass of fragments in his mind.

He lay staring at his bedroom ceiling. Collins had never felt so set adrift from all he knew, and all he cared about. His family were becoming ever more distant, and the job, which defined him and shaped his whole identity, was hanging by a thread, dependent upon the outcome of an investigation he feared may be rigged against him.

As he lay turning uncomfortably in his bed, he tried to plot a route towards redemption. The idea he had started to develop as he ran down from the Ridge was rudimentary. As a starting point he hoped that Damon could garner sufficient information from Daniel to demonstrate his concern with Alex Chilcott was more than just a solo obsession. That would be a start in countering the allegations that were ranged against him. He also knew his case would be more compelling if he could get Greta to give a statement about her attack, particularly if the attacker fitted Alex Chilcott's description. Lying there he realised there were plenty of hurdles to overcome to make this plan a reality, not least because he now had no legitimate means of any formal engagement with Greta and her mother. Behind all this was also the recognition it may not matter what evidence he could produce, if his suspension was the result of a cover-up by his bosses.

He weighed up his options. He could go and try to speak to Charlie and Greta himself, but in doing so, and going to the Gartside on a fishing expedition, expressly against orders, he would be risking his career. He could ask Damon to go and speak to Charlie, to see if he could encourage her daughter to give a statement to the police. Damon knew Charlie from of old, but Collins wasn't confident that this approach would be successful and, even if it were, getting Greta to give a statement to some faceless police officer wasn't necessarily going to connect the dots to Alex Chilcott.

What Collins really wanted to do was to ask Tara Sharma to go and speak with Greta. She had said she wanted to help, but even as the thought became clear in Collins' mind, he recoiled from it. Tara Sharma, the consummate professional, would she really be willing to kick off a clandestine police investigation? Yet Collins knew that he had to ask Tara. It was his best hope of stopping further harm being perpetrated by Alex Chilcott, and at the same time represented the best chance of moving him closer to a return to work.

What was it that was causing him to resist then? Collins admitted to himself he didn't want to ask for help. He was the skilled helper, the rescuer, the one who came to the aid of those in need. To ask for help would mean he was one of them now. The stigma of suspension didn't just mean he could no longer do the things he could do yesterday morning, worse than that, he couldn't be the person he was yesterday morning.

He concluded his internal debate. If he was to get out of this mess, and at the same time help Daniel out of his, he would have to throw himself upon the kindness of others, starting with Tara Sharma.

8.30am

Collins left it until a respectable time to call Tara. He had already sat for too long looking at the new entry in his phone's contacts: 'Tara Own'. In spite of his dire circumstances, he couldn't help feeling a small tingle when he saw her personal number in his phone. If he had to be rescued, then he couldn't think of anyone he would prefer to be rescued by than Tara.

"Tom, I'm so glad you rang. How are you?" He was heartened by her warm reception.

"I'm okay. I was a bit shell-shocked yesterday, but I'm getting my head around it. Like you said, I'll get through this and out the other side. It's just a bit tough when you're in the middle of it. I'm feeling pretty powerless."

When he had thought about what he was going to say, Collins wasn't sure how much vulnerability to expose to Tara. He wasn't one for baring the contents of his heart and soul, but now he was finding it hard to hold back.

"I really need your help Tara. I don't think I can get out of this mess without you."

"I said I was going to help if I could, so I'm glad to know I can. I knew you were someone I could trust, that's why I told you about my experience with Alex Chilcott. I don't know what you're supposed to have done wrong, but I trust you, and I'll do what you need me to do."

Sharma's tone was assured and, true to type, she didn't plan to sit on the fence.

Again Tara had brought Collins to the edge of tears. He felt such pathetic gratitude; that he wasn't on his own, that he had her unconditional support, and that he was held by the powerful grip of Tara Sharma's trust.

Collins laid out the charges against him, as he understood them from Andrews, and told her about his intelligence regarding the latest sex attack in Gartside Park. Collins was genuinely perplexed, and recognised he was losing any semblance of objectivity. He wanted Sharma's view of whether he was the fall guy in a cover up, or if he was just the unfortunate victim of a set of circumstances that could befall anyone in his line of work. He also wanted her honest opinion as to whether his conduct had been seriously beyond the pale.

Sharma wasn't quick to reach any definitive conclusions. After testing out various perspectives and lines of enquiry with Collins, she slowly came to a view.

"Tom, you're definitely unorthodox and, with all that's been going on for you in your personal life, you may have made some dubious decisions. That said, you do what you do out of passion, you do it for the right reasons, and we need to get you back to work as soon as possible."

"I'm glad you think so Tara," Collins replied.

"I don't know if there's a cover up. Maybe we'll find out in time, maybe we won't, but like you, I just want to do the right thing. That means going up to the Gartside and talking to that little girl to find out what happened to her, and what help she needs. If it turns out it was Chilcott who attacked her, we'll crucify the bastard this time, and get his kids safe while we're about it."

Sharma had settled on a course of action and was definite about what needed to happen next.

"Let's follow our instincts and get this sorted, and you just might find you get your job back in the process."

Collins had always admired Tara's professionalism; her ability to marry a deep passion in her work with clear-eyed analysis of how to get a job done. Today he was in complete awe of her ability to untangle the complex threads of an investigation, with such precision, and to coolly determine the action that was required. He hadn't needed to ask her to go and see Greta, and to follow the trail to Alex Chilcott, if that was where it led. Tara knew what she needed to do in this situation, and there was no one going to stop her, not Andrews, not the Director and, least of all, any fear of Alex Chilcott.

10.15am

"Who's this?"

When Collins rang Greta's mum, Charlie, he wasn't surprised by the defensive tone when she picked up. He had got her number through Damon, in order to pave the way for Sharma's visit.

"Charlie, it's Tom Collins. You remember me, don't you?"

"Oh yeah, what do want?"

Collins could imagine the thoughts ricocheting around Charlie's head, on realising it was a social worker on the phone. Was the fact her daughter had been attacked evidence she was a bad mother? On top of all the hurt that had been done to Greta, was this now a matter for social services to start crawling over?

"Charlie, I heard that something bad has happened to Greta?"

"Yeah, maybe. Depends what you mean."

Charlie clearly didn't know whether she should be honest with Collins. From what she knew of him he seemed a decent bloke, but she was wary this conversation might embroil her and her daughter in a whole new world of pain.

"Charlie, I've got a colleague, Tara, who would like to come and talk to Greta about what happened. At this point she just wants to know if she needs any help, if there's anything we can do for her. She also needs a description of the man who attacked her. This isn't a social services investigation into you or Greta, this is about getting her help, and catching the man who did this."

"Greta doesn't want to talk to anyone about it," Charlie replied.

"Charlie, just give Tara a chance. Greta might feel better for speaking to someone. Just let her try. If Greta really doesn't want to say anything, she doesn't have to. It's really important, if she's able to tell us anything, because there's a dangerous sex offender out there, who we need to catch before he hurts someone else."

Charlie was silent on the other end of the line. Collins took this as good enough.

"Charlie, Tara will be up to you by midday. Take care of that little girl of yours. I really hope we're able to be of some help to her."

He sent a text to Tara's phone to tell her she was good to go.

11.45am

After two rounds of Tara Sharma ringing the doorbell, Charlie poked her tear-stained face around the front door. At barely thirty years old, she was acquiring the battle lines of a mother who has fought to bring up a child with little support, and now had to re-double her efforts to rein in her wilful teenager. Having spent fourteen years striving to protect her only child, for her to return home traumatised after a sexual assault, meant that Charlie herself was a second victim of the attacker.

Charlie wearily acknowledged her visitor through the half-opened door.

"I think you're wasting your time, she's not in a good way. She won't want to talk to you."

"Hi Charlie, just let me have a go, eh?" Tara smiled encouragingly.

Charlie reluctantly showed her in, and pointed up to the top of the stairs of the maisonette. "First door on the right."

Sharma knocked softly. "Greta, can I come in?" There was no noise from the other side of the door. Tara waited a few moments.

"Okay Greta, I'm going to come in."

In the small bedroom, bedecked with posters of super models, who Tara recognised, and rap artists, who she didn't, the police officer found Greta curled up in bed under a duvet. She was clearly awake, as her eyes were open, and fixed at a point on the wall in front of her, but she made no movement when Sharma entered the room. Tara carefully moved some clothing from the chair by Greta's dressing table and sat down.

"Hi Greta, I'm Tara. I'm a police officer on the child protection team. Can I talk to you about what happened on Sunday night?"

Greta said nothing, still staring, without recognition of the question she had been asked, or the fact that there was a stranger sitting in her room.

"Greta, this isn't a formal interview, you might want to do that in time, but for now, I'm worried about you, and I'm worried because I think there is someone dangerous out there who needs to be stopped." Tara spoke softly trying not to unduly pressurise Greta.

"Greta, I've got an idea what happened to you, so tell me if I'm right?" Still no acknowledgement from Greta.

"You were coming home off the last bus through Gartside Park and someone has come at you. A man has come at you, and tried to sexually assault you, but you've got away? Is that what happened Greta?"

Greta closed her eyes, as if revolted by the picture that was now in front of her, looming from the bedroom wall, but still she said nothing. Sharma shifted her chair closer, pushing her face forward near to the girl's.

"Greta, I can't put words in your mouth but I think I might know what you're seeing in front of you now, what you're trying to get out of your mind, but keeps coming back. I see it too." Sharma spoke slowly, deliberately, revisiting again the night she had been confronted by Alex Chilcott.

"After five years, I still see him coming at me, see his eyes, see what he's got in his hand. In Gartside Park, Greta. I know what he wants to do to me. I see him still, but I'm not frightened any more. I just hate him. Hate him and want to destroy him."

Greta opened her eyes again and met Sharma's. Falteringly she found words. "Hangman's Hollow. He came out of nowhere, and he's dragged me down into Hangman's Hollow." Sharma could see that it was a huge effort for Greta to get the words out; the duvet rising as she struggled to take in sufficient air to finish her sentence.

"Well done Greta, take it slowly, in your own time."

"He's pushed me on my back, and shone a torch in my face, and said 'don't make a sound' and he's pointed the torch at this big knife he's got, and he's said it again, really vicious, 'not a sound bitch', and he's put the knife towards my face." From her hesitant start the words were now gushing forth in a torrent.

"Okay Greta, you're doing well. What happened then?"

"He said 'take your knickers off'. I was just saying 'no', 'no', 'please don't', but he's waved the knife at my face again and I've had to take my knickers off. I've started to do it, and he's just staring at me, and he's shouted 'slowly, do it slowly'. I put them on the ground and he's picked them up, and held them against his face, and he's got this horrible smile. It's evil. That's when I've seen his eyes in the torchlight. It was like looking at the devil."

Both the police officer and the young girl were now seeing those eyes again. Sharma moved towards Greta and took her hand. "What happened next Greta?"

"He started to unbuckle his trousers, and he's still smiling, as he pulls his pants down, and then there's this noise from a bunch of lads coming back from Town, shouting and singing, just by the Hollow. I screamed and got up and started to run. Because he's got his trousers half down, I was able to get a bit away from him, and I just kept running."

"Greta that must have been terrifying." She held the girl's hand and waited to see if there was any more for her to say. Greta's chest and shoulders rose as silent sobs gripped her. When Tara realised, after a long silence, that Greta was retreating back into frightened isolation, she reached out for her again.

"For men like that it's not about sex, it's about power. Don't let him have any power over you. Take back the power. Let's destroy him. Let's make sure we catch him, and he gets put away for a long time."

Greta swallowed deeply and forced words out between her tears. "Do you think it's the same one who tried it with you in Gartside Park?" Greta said, looking once more into Sharma's eyes.

"Maybe." Sharma's gut felt sure it was, but she also wanted hard evidence. "Did you see what he looked like?"

"A bit. He was big, probably six foot and heavy like. Not fat, but heavy built, and he had a black leather jacket on."

"Was he white, black, Asian?"

"He was white, with dark hair and, like I say, he had those wicked looking eyes, really black."

"Have you seen him before?"

"No, but I'd recognise him. I'd never forget that sick smile and those eyes."

"You've done amazingly well Greta. I think this will be the start of something for us. I'm going to give you all the help I can, and between us we're going to make sure that man rots in prison. Are you okay if we do a proper statement tomorrow?" Greta nodded her assent.

Tara rose to leave the room, and gave Greta's hand a final squeeze. "Girl power, honey. We're in this together." As she reached the door, Sharma turned to Greta. "Did you see what he did with your knickers?"

Greta shook her head. "No, I didn't see, but I just feel like he kept them." That had been Sharma's suspicion too.

"Do you remember what they looked like?"

"Pink. Pink with an angel on the front."

"Well done Greta, I'll see you tomorrow."

12.40pm

As Sharma was leaving Greta's house, on the other side of the estate, a track-suited Damon Hartley was approaching the gates of Gartside Park, where Daniel was sitting, impatiently waiting for him.

"All right Danny Boy, fit to go?" Damon shouted to his young acquaintance. Daniel barely looked up in response.

"What's up Dan, worried I'll embarrass you again with my silky skills?"

Daniel remained seated on the low wall at the entrance to the park. He ignored Damon's attempt at banter and looked up at him inquisitively.

"Did you tell Collins what I told you yesterday?"

"You didn't tell me much that he didn't already know. I told him about your cuts, and how you said things were so bad at home that was the only way you got any relief."

"What's he say to that then?" Daniel's expression suggested he was taking Damon somewhere with this line of enquiry.

"He says we're nearly there. He says he's almost got enough evidence to go to court, and make sure you and your brother and sisters are kept safe. How do you feel about that then Dan?" Damon replied.

Daniel didn't answer immediately. He stood up and the pair started to walk towards the football pitch. Hesitantly, he finally spoke.

"I just want to be with my mum. That's all I've ever wanted. Can Collins make that happen?"

"I don't know Dan, but I know if that's what you want, and it's the best thing for all of you, he'll do his best to make it happen."

Daniel paused, as if on the edge of a diving board, willing himself to find the courage to take the plunge.

"She does want to get out, she told me, but it's impossible to get away from him. He'd kill her, he'd kill all of us. She's got a plan, and she wants Collins to help her. She's going to write it down, and give it to him when he comes tomorrow. She's going to put everything in there, so that he gets put away."

Damon was struggling to make sense of Daniel's revelation. "Why can't she just go to the police, and why has she got to put it in a letter?"

"She says the police would just fuck it up and anyway, it's got to be done in secret, you know, like by arrangement, if she's going to get all the little ones out, and make sure he gets nicked at the same time. She wants Tom to meet her, with us, on Saturday, to get us all away."

"And the letter?"

"She can't just talk to Collins in the house, because the Bastard's behind the door, listening to everything. He knows where she is every minute she's out of the house, and he checks her phone the whole time, so she can't do anything without his knowing."

"Hold on, just one thing at a time Dan." Damon was overwhelmed by the flood of information coming his way. "You're telling me your mum has written all the stuff your dad does down, to give to Tom tomorrow?"

"Yes, all the shit he does to her, and all the times she covered for him, when the police have arrested him for his weird stuff in the park with girls, and all the trophies he collects"

"Trophies, what trophies?"

"I don't know, all the stuff he collects when he goes out at night. Girls' stuff I suppose. I've never seen it but my mum's talked about his 'collection' and 'his trophies'."

"Bloody hell Dan, that's massive. And you say she's written it all down with a plan to make an escape on Saturday?"

"Yeah, we're getting out." Daniel's hesitancy had been replaced now by a mounting sense of elation at the prospect of being unshackled.

Daniel took the ball from Damon and kicked it high into the air. He ran after it as it fell towards the ground, trapping it with a deft first touch, which pushed the ball a yard in front of him.

"Alive!" he shouted across the ground to Damon, with a wide grin, hitting the ball back to his friend and shouting again, "alive!"

2pm

Collins was determined to use his enforced absence from work productively, and turned his mind to all the 'life

196

admin' he wilfully ignored in the course of his normal busy week. He tried to concentrate on bank letters and insurance forms, but found himself repeatedly checking his phone for news from Damon or Tara. The only message he received before lunchtime was from Den, the long-serving manager of Corton Casuals football team:

"Tommo can u play 2nite @ Elm Green, 7.30 KO we r short."

The league season had finished, and Collins didn't normally play in the summertime friendlies. He considered the offer, and whether he would stand up to the emotional challenge of throwing himself into a team game. He decided it was best to keep active; seeing his football mates might take his mind off of his current predicament. Having a game of football to look forward to would at least give some shape to his day.

He texted Den back: "You're in luck, see you there."

Tara was the first of his informants to make contact. She relayed the story that Greta had told her. Tara was sure it was Chilcott, and she was also confident that Greta was going to make a statement.

"Let me see if Damon gets any more out of Dan. I'll call you this afternoon. Are you writing up a formal report today of what Greta told you?" Collins enquired.

"Of course," her sharp reply reminded Collins that Sharma was no rogue cop, "but until she gives a statement, there's not a lot more we can do, except step up patrols on Gartside. I'm in meetings now until three-thirty, I'll call you then." Sharma ended the call abruptly and Collins was reminded that she was still in work and that their contact was clandestine.

Shortly after, it was Damon's turn to call in to update. Collins was astounded by the information that Daniel had given him. "Carol is ready to leave, and to spill the beans on everything her husband has been up to? That's fantastic Damon, well done mate. We're going to get the bastard."

"You could see Dan was so relieved to tell someone and so excited that there's the chance to get away. You've got to keep them with their mum, Tom, he lives for her."

"Bless him. We'd want to keep them together, so long as there's no evidence that she has been involved in their abuse."

"She's the victim Tom, how can she be blamed?"

"It's a thin line sometimes Damon, between victim and abuser, sometimes you can be both. How do you think Alex Chilcott became the man he is? I don't suppose he was born like that. I hear what you're saying though, and obviously, if the kids are going to be safer and happier with her, then that's what should happen. The most important thing, is to get them away from him."

"And how you going to do that when you're suspended?" Damon pointed to the major obstacle now impeding the escape plan.

Collins had forgotten that, as things stood, he wouldn't be the person to go to the Chilcotts' tomorrow, and Cathy Creswick wasn't even planning to fulfil the commitment anyway.

"I'll speak to my boss and see if I can go tomorrow. If not, someone else will have to go."

"It sounds like it's you she's trusting to make this happen. I don't know if she'll go through with it, if it's not you."

"Okay leave it with me Damon, I'll be in touch. Well done mate, you've done amazingly well with Dan."

When Collins got off the phone he decided his only option was to call Andrews to try to persuade him to end his suspension in the light of the new information. He was relieved that Andrews took his call rather than letting it go to voicemail.

"Tom, how are you? I've been thinking about you."

Collins was surprised by Andrews' warm tone. Over the previous day he had caricatured Andrews as a heartless bureaucrat, intent only on protecting his own reputation. He was reminded now that the Dave Andrews he had known over many years was actually a kind and considerate man.

"I'm okay Dave, it's not me you need to be worried about."

"I know, it's the Chilcotts." Andrews said it without any hint of irony, suggesting he now shared Collins' degree of concern.

"I'm guessing that you know the latest, Tom, and I'm not going to even ask how you know. Tara's told me about her conversation with the girl on the estate. Tara is sure it's Chilcott again, and this time he's not just flashing, but pulling a knife and attempting a rape."

"Chilcott was never just a flasher," Collins interrupted his boss. "Tara told you that five years ago."

Emboldened by the fact Andrews was willing to overlook the source of his new knowledge about the case, Collins ploughed on.

"Carol is ready to tell us all about what her husband gets up to, but she wants it to be me, tomorrow. She's putting it in a letter and has a plan to get out. I need to be there."

"Tom, it worries me that you know so much about what Carol Chilcott is planning, given the instructions you were given. Anyhow, you know you can't do that appointment, Tom."

"Why not? You can see the Chilcotts aren't just my misguided obsession; this is life and death. Anything I've done can be understood once you accept that. There isn't any reason for me to be suspended any more."

"There's the complaint Tom. It's serious and it needs proper investigation."

"You haven't even told me what's in it. You'll do your investigation and find nothing. In two weeks' time I'll be back at work, but we'll have missed the one opportunity we've had of Carol Chilcott coming over to our side, after all these years. Anyway, that family haven't got two weeks Dave." Collins paused to allow the magnitude of the situation to register with his boss.

"Tom, I'm not in a position to just unsuspend you, so put that to one side. Is there a way we can get this letter? What if I ask Cathy Creswick to go up there?"

"Not Cathy," Collins immediately replied. He had her as the most likely complainant, and she was much diminished in his eyes as a result, nor did he have any confidence in her ability to gain Carol's trust.

"Tara, is a better bet," he quickly suggested.

"Okay, Tara can do the appointment. On reflection it's probably best if it's a police officer going in this time, given the circumstances."

Now Collins' request had been granted, he reflected on the prospect of Tara going in there alone, to the home of a man they knew was a violent psychopath.

"What's to stop you going in with a police unit and nicking the old man, and getting Carol and the kids to safety?" Collins asked.

"We'd just be taking him in for questioning. Without the girl's statement there wouldn't be a charge, so he'd be out on bail, and we'd have missed our best chance of nailing him. We'd also have to be sure that Carol has actually written this letter. I'd want to see it before we move on Chilcott."

"Does Tara have to go in alone? Couldn't we send her in with someone else?" Collins suggested.

"I think we risk spooking Chilcott if we start looking like we are gearing up for something, and getting heavy handed. It's just one visit. We've done enough over the years to that house, and you never see the old man anyway, not unless you've got half a dozen coppers and an arrest warrant. We'll make sure there's a patrol car nearby in case of trouble."

Again Andrews didn't seem as worried by the situation as Collins.

"All right, will you at least give me permission to talk to Tara, so she knows what she's walking into?" Of course Collins was planning to do this anyway, but would rather do so with his boss's blessing.

"Okay, but keep it to the Chilcott case, nothing else."

"Don't worry, I'll make sure I don't corrupt your sacred investigation," Collins replied, unable to keep the bitterness from his voice.

He thought it was worth one more go at trying to persuade Andrews to give him more detail on the complaint, while he had him on the phone.

"I'm sure, if you just let me see this bloody letter of complaint, I could tell you what's behind it. You wouldn't need to launch a full scale investigation, and I wouldn't need to be suspended." After the conversation the previous day, Collins had been expecting a flat 'no'. He was surprised that instead his request was met only with silence.

"Dave?" He sensed Andrews was weighing up his options.

"Meet me in half an hour at the car park behind the Ridge."

"Will do. Thank you."

Collins' mind raced. Were his prospects about to get better, or a whole lot worse, as a result of this hastily convened rendezvous with his boss, and a chance to see the infamous letter?

2.30pm

Collins was at the meeting place twenty minutes after getting off the phone. As he got out of his air conditioned car, he was struck by the warmth of the mid-afternoon sunshine. He made his way over to the viewing point and marvelled, as ever, at the panoramic scene across the valley and over to the hills, which rose in the distance. As familiar as this sight had become to him, from his frequent runs up and down the Ridge, he never failed to be impressed.

On this early summer's day the scene was glorious. Cyclists carefully navigated dogs and their walkers on the path beneath the viewing point, and newly arrived swallows darted elegantly across the fields below them. He watched a distant aeroplane, which appeared to hang half way to the horizon, waiting to make its descent. A train which looked for all the world like a model, just out of the box, trundled past the Gartside, making its untroubled way along the valley from Town.

The bucolic setting provided a strange backcloth for the drama which was playing out in Collins' head, as he waited for his boss. He filled his lungs with pollen rich air, soaking in the scene, trying his best to remain calm.

"I thought I'd find you taking in the view," Andrews said, appearing from behind him. "We're lucky to have this on our doorstep. Not that most of the people down there appreciate it, or bother coming up here."

"It's the best thing about being off the drink, discovering running and exploring the hills," Collins said, without breaking from his immersion in the view in front of him.

"How long's it been now, Tom?"

"Just short of two years. I could tell you the number of days but that would make me sound a bit sad. It's been a hard couple of years, for lots of reasons, as you know, but I'm proud to have done it."

"So you should be. You weren't the worst drunk I've ever met, you weren't even the worst drunk in the office, but I know you've had your battles, and I'm glad you're winning."

"That's what makes this suspension so hard, Dave. I feel like I've been doing things right, working hard, keeping my nose clean, choosing life and all that. You've given me the hardest case on our books, that nobody has got to grips with for years; I think I'm about to crack it, and suddenly I'm suspended."

For the first time since Andrews arrived, Collins turned and looked him in the eye. "I thought you'd have my back on this one?"

"I'm sorry Tom. The Director said he was taking, what he called, 'a calculated risk', putting you on the Chilcott case. We've been burned over the years by this one. You'll know we've been in court with them before, trying to get a care order, and their barrister made a monkey of me and Campbell, back when he was doing my job. What you won't know was that we got a proper dressing down behind the scenes, from the resident judge, for bringing proceedings with insufficient evidence. It set the department back years in our relationship with the family court."

Andrews had now looked away from Collins and was speaking to the horizon.

"In deciding to go again with the Chilcotts, we needed to have a watertight case. We rate you Tom, that's why we put you on the case, but we also know you don't come risk free. Campbell got nervous when your behaviour started to become erratic. I have had your back Tom, but with that complaint, I couldn't keep him at bay any longer. He wants you off the case and for you to have a cooling off period."

Andrews looked back into Collins' face again. "Nobody wants to sack you Tom, we know you're honest and, by and large, do a bloody good job."

"That feels like pretty cold comfort right now, Dave."

"Tom, there's a serious allegation levelled against you, from one of your colleagues, that needs investigating."

"It all feels a bit convenient. You and the Director are getting cold feet about how I'm running the Chilcott case, and, hey presto, you've got an allegation about me. Are you sure you didn't write it yourself?"

Collins looked directly at Andrews, as he levelled the accusation that he had decided to swallow the previous day.

"For Christ's sake Tom. We're not the FBI and you're not the president of the USA, you're a provincial social worker. Where's these conspiracy theories coming from? Don't be ridiculous."

Collins just glared back at Andrews, unconvinced by his flat denial.

"I was completely taken aback when I received the letter making allegations about you," Andrews continued. "It was the last thing I needed. I wanted you to see this one home. I just needed you to come through with the evidence, and I would have backed you all the way."

"Okay, if not you and Campbell, then who on earth in our department is going to manufacture this complaint about me? I know you've said you're not going to tell me who it is, but whoever they are, do you really believe them? Is it someone whose judgement you would trust one hundred percent? Someone you trust more than me?"

There it was, Collins had thrown the gauntlet down to his boss. Which of his colleagues did he trust more than Collins?

"I don't know who wrote the letter Tom. I said to you, the person doesn't want their identity revealed," he paused, hesitating before finishing the sentence, "it's anonymous."

Andrews threw his hands up in front of his chest, to demonstrate he was as perplexed by the complaint as Collins.

This was a revelation to Collins, he could feel his anger rising at the realisation that he was being investigated on the strength of an anonymous complaint.

"You're joking. I'm suspended because of an anonymous allegation? That wasn't the impression you gave me yesterday. I just hope you've brought the letter up here to show me, because this is a complete crock of shit."

"Tom, I explained to you the suspension wasn't only about the letter. That was just the final straw. But if you're asking me if I trust you, well I'm here because I trust you. I'm telling you things I shouldn't, on the basis that this conversation hasn't happened, and yes, I've brought the letter."

Andrews reached into the inside pocket of his suit and handed Collins a brown envelope. Collins examined the outside of the envelope, before taking out the one sheet inside.

"Is this the original envelope it came in?"

"Yes, that's how it came to me, straight from the Director."

Collins unfolded the A4 typed page to reveal three paragraphs, under the heading 'Formal Complaint'. As he read, his stomach was squeezed ever tighter, until by the time he had finished he felt the whole of his insides had been crushed to the size of a small lump of coal. Having read through the contents once, he immediately returned to the top of the page, to try to make sense of the allegation at a more measured pace.

Frazer Campbell
Director of Children's Services

Formal Complaint

Dear Mr Campbell,

I feel compelled to write to you to highlight the conduct of Tom Collins, who I have the misfortune to have to work alongside. I have felt uncomfortable about Mr Collins's practice in relation to boys who are on his caseload for some time. He has a habit of becoming over familiar and encouraging a degree of dependence. I have always thought he has a concerning lack of boundaries, which is inappropriate for someone undertaking important and sensitive work with vulnerable people. This is obvious in his current work with Daniel Chilcott and Mickey Johnson.

What I had previously considered as poor practice I now believe is actually deeply harmful conduct which has no place in social work or in our department. My reasons for reaching this conclusion stems from Tom Collins's behaviour with Daniel Chilcott, who is an extremely vulnerable fourteen year old. I know that Tom Collins spends a large amount of time with Daniel, when he should be seeing his other clients. My concern regarding his intentions was confirmed when I was in Coronation Recreation Ground and saw them playing football together. Tom Collins kept putting his arm around Daniel while they were playing and then when sitting next to him on a bench he put his hand on his knee and squeezed his leg. This looked like the wrong behaviour for a social worker with a child and I found it upsetting to see a colleague behaving like that. I have no doubt about what I saw.

This letter has been written as soon as I returned home following the incident. I would like Tom Collins behaviour to be fully investigated and for him to be stopped from working with children.

Yours faithfully
A Deeply Concerned Colleague

Collins was appalled to read the description of his behaviour; that someone could have spent their time con-cocting this vile caricature, gone to such lengths to depict his conduct in these grotesque terms. Who did he work with who hated him so much they would want to fabricate this account?

He turned to Andrews and handed him back the letter.

"That's extraordinary Dave. I don't know what to say. It makes me feel sick. You do know it's complete horse shit, don't you?"

"I was very surprised to read it. It's not for a moment how I imagined you behaved with your clients and, like you, I was intrigued to know which of your colleagues might feel the need to write this anonymously. You can see though that we needed to investigate."

"Investigate, yes, but suspend me, no. Come on Dave, someone wants to have a free hit at me, without having to come forward. They're not going to in the course of your investigation and, with nothing else to go on, you'll have to conclude there's no case to answer. In the meantime, I've got the shame of being suspended, and trust me Dave, it does feel shameful."

"It's a serious allegation from a colleague, Tom. HR were clear that it warranted suspension and that was the Director's view."

"We've already established why that would suit him," Collins fired back. "And now you've got the Chilcott case about to blow and I'm not there. Is that really what Campbell wants? This could end up a whole lot worse for everyone than he appreciates. It's not a telling off from a family court judge he needs to worry about; it's facing the press and a serious case review following a tragedy. A tragedy he's got his fingerprints all over."

"I've talked to him already this afternoon Tom. He's not lifting the suspension. We'll make sure we are shoulder to shoulder with the police on this over the next few days. We've lined legal up and we'll be ready to get those kids out at the first opportunity."

"And if Carol wants to meet me as part of her escape plan on Saturday? Am I allowed to do that?"

"Let's just get the statement from the girl who's been attacked, and make sure we get the letter from Carol. We'll make a decision about what next tomorrow."

Andrews placed the envelope back in his pocket and Collins knew their impromptu get together was coming to an end. Collins decided it was best to finish on a positive note and try to be magnanimous.

"Dave, I appreciate you coming out to see me. I realise you didn't have to, and you didn't have to show me the letter. Thank you."

"Tom, it's a messy situation but you'll come through it, and trust me I won't see you hung out to dry."

Andrews turned and made his way back to the car park, while Collins returned to surveying the scene in front of him. His eyes flitted from the towers of Queenstown, beneath which his office nestled and beyond which was his family home, and then back to the nearer towers of the Gartside. This drama was playing out in the few miles separating these pillars of his life, pillars which he now felt were built on shifting sands.

3.40pm

Collins called Tara on his drive home from the Ridge. He was struggling to get the lurid images painted by his accuser out of his head, but knew he needed to focus on making sure Tara was fully briefed, before she faced into the Chilcotts' at midday tomorrow. When he relayed the information from Damon about Carol's plan, Tara immediately volunteered to be the one to fulfil Collins' appointment.

"I was hoping you'd say that, because I've already suggested you're the best person for the job."

He was pleased when she offered to come over to his flat to talk through the plan of action.

"That would be great Tara, there's a whole load of stuff I need to talk to you about. Dave has given me the details of the complaint about me, and I could do with someone to share it with."

Collins had given up any pretence of being in control. He needed a friend to pull him out of the hole he was in, and he was happy that Tara Sharma had volunteered.

Collins flicked his car stereo on. He turned to an old favourite, from where he often sought consolation. The first bars of Nick Cave's 'Into My Arms' kicked in and reminded Collins of his own paradox. Like the singer, he sought the help of an interventionist god he didn't believe in. He allowed himself a meagre smile. Tara Sharma was a close as he would come to divine intervention.

5.30pm

Tara arrived looking her effortlessly elegant self. Before she got there, Collins had hurriedly tried to make the place look more presentable. He realised she was the first woman to come to the flat in the time he had been there. He looked around at the sparse decoration.

"Could do with a woman's touch," he said to himself with a wry smile.

Collins showed her in.

"There's not much to it and I've not been here long."

Tara briefly surveyed the front room and smiled, "minimalist, very male."

He directed her towards the dining table, with its two chairs, that occupied one end of the front room of the flat.

"Tea?"

"Just a water please."

"Is your body such a temple that you don't take in any toxins at all?" He asked in a gently mocking tone.

She gave a little shrug. "I think I've put enough crap in my body for a lifetime, but don't worry I'm still no saint."

An old song went through his mind, "don't drink, don't smoke, what do you do?" but he thought best not to trot it out, not yet anyway.

Collins recounted the detail of what he had gleaned from Damon's time with Daniel, and Tara told him exactly what Greta had described to her about her attack.

"Are we sure we don't just want it to be Chilcott? There's plenty of other sex offenders on the Gartside and across our patch. It's not even his style pulling a knife," Collins offered by way of challenge.

"Trust me Tom, he's well capable of pulling a knife, and all the evidence suggests his behaviour is becoming ever more volatile. But that's not what convinces me, it was her description. When she was describing him, it was like we were both looking at the same person."

"Maybe you were seeing Chilcott as you saw him five years ago, she might have been seeing someone different."

Tara tried to hide her frustration.

"I know what you're saying, Tom. I know about flakey witnesses and flakey evidence; that's not me."

She saw the chance to turn Collins' own words on him.

"As you say yourself, sometimes you've got to listen to your gut, whether you're a cop or social worker. I know who that girl saw, and I know it was Alex Chilcott." Sharma said it in her most authoritative tone.

"Okay Tara, you know I have to ask those questions, you would too because you're a good police officer. Believe me, I trust your judgement completely."

Sharma seemed content to accept Collins' acquiescence. He turned his attention to the anticipated sequence of events.

"If all goes well with Greta's statement, the evidence will be there to charge Chilcott, maybe by tomorrow evening, if we can hurry things along. Have you arranged an ABE interview for her?"

"Yeah, Cathy Creswick is going to do it with me." They shared a look in recognition of the irony of this.

"It will be fine; she's competent, just not passionate," Tara said. Collins held his tongue.

"You don't have to go to the Chilcotts' tomorrow, you know. If he's brought in and charged, we could get the letter from Carol then. I'll let her know that I can't be there and –"

Tara cut him short.

"Tom, you know one of us has to do the appointment with Carol. CPS probably won't be willing or ready to

215

charge tomorrow, and maybe not even any time soon. She will have worked herself to such a pitch; to let her down would be unforgivable. And what are you going to tell her? 'Hold tight Carol, the Old Bill will be round for your husband at some unspecified date in the future?' I'm going to go in, get the letter, let her know we're good to go with the plan, and get out." Tara sounded confident and certain of her ability, qualities that Collins increasingly felt he lacked.

"Okay, I'll text Carol in the morning at school drop-off time to say that it will be you and not me. That will be the safest way to get a message to her. She can delete it before her husband checks her phone. The less time she has to fret on the change of plan the better."

Collins pictured Tara in the Chilcott house, and shuddered at the prospect of her being sucked into to the oppressive pall. It didn't feel the right place for a woman like Tara, but then nor was it the right place for four children and their long suffering mother.

"When you're in the house, be aware that he's behind the door trying to hear the conversation, so you're going to have to be very smart to get in and out with the letter, without arousing any additional suspicion."

She gave him a look of mild disappointment, "Tom?"

"Yes, I know, this is what you're trained for, this is what you're good at. I'm sorry, I just feel it should be me."

"What is it, a woman going into to do a man's job? Or is it more personal than that Tom? Is it that you need to be in control?" She looked hard at him; he felt she was looking inside him.

"You wouldn't have thought twice about going into the house yourself tomorrow, but you struggle to imagine anyone else could do it. What does that say about you Tom?"

Hard as her assessment was, she managed to deliver it with kindness. Not for the first time, Tara had forced Collins to examine his interior and ask himself if he really knew who he was.

"You're right Tara, I'm sorry. You'll do a great job. I just find it hard being a passenger."

"You're not a passenger, you're just having to play a different role. Don't worry, you're not the only man in the world that likes to be in control."

Collins knew that Sharma's reference encompassed both the men at the extreme end of the spectrum, the ones like Chilcott who were the source of much of their work, and the men like him, the ordinary, everyday patriarchs. He knew he had plenty of work to do on himself but also recognised he was struggling to let go just yet.

Having made her point, Tara thought it was time to move the conversation on.

"So what else have you found out about why you're suspended?"

"Andrews showed me the complaint. It's horrible."

Collins was struggling to relay the sickening description of his actions.

"It makes me out to be someone who grooms the boys on my caseload. It even says they saw me touching Daniel inappropriately in Coronation Rec. It's definitely an internal job from the case details they've given, but there's no name on it, it's anonymous."

Sharma took a minute to process this new information.

"Really Tom? I just can't see it being one of your colleagues. Everyone on the team thinks you do a good job. I know you have your run-ins with Cathy, but she doesn't think that about you, and if she did, there's no way she would do it anonymously. She'd have said it to your face."

"Okay then, what about in the wider department?"

Collins had already asked himself this question many times in the preceding day, and with renewed vigour since seeing the letter, but had drawn a blank. He couldn't think of anyone with either the motive, or the detail the letter contained. Sharma reached the same conclusion.

"It's possible, but it's a bit implausible."

"That's what I think," confirmed Collins.

"But if it's not a supposedly aggrieved colleague, then does that point to Andrews and Campbell?" Sharma said it hesitantly, aware of the significance of this suggestion.

Collins was still processing his meeting with Andrews on the Ridge, and tried to recall for Sharma why he felt content in the conclusion he wasn't the victim of a departmental cover up.

"I put it to Andrews straight, that this was very convenient for him and the Director right now. He denied it, said he wanted Chilcott nailed and backed me to do it. When this complaint came in, it tipped Campbell over the edge, and he got cold feet. I know it's not definitive, but if we're listening to gut feelings now, I think Andrews was being straight with me."

"Where's that leave you, Tom? Someone's written that letter."

They both paused to consider the options.

Ever the police officer, Sharma returned to question their original assumptions.

"I take it the letter came in the internal post? That's why you're so sure it was an inside job."

Collins had noted the stamp and the postmark on the envelope Andrews had given to him, but having read the contents, he had dismissed the relevance of it having come through the Royal Mail.

"No it was posted from Town on Monday, but if you saw the case detail, it would have to be someone on the team. The letter said it was written when they got home after seeing me at the park with Daniel."

"Was there anything in the letter apart from mentioning Daniel and the Chilcotts?" Sharma asked.

"There was a reference to Mickey Johnson," Collins replied.

"Who lives near the Chilcotts and goes to St Christopher's with Daniel, I'm guessing?" Sharma interjected.

"So who are the people who know the detail of your work on the Chilcott case, outside of the team, and could know you're also working with Mickey Johnson?"

Sharma's mind had raced ahead, and she was now leading Collins to the destination at which she had already arrived.

"The Chilcotts, primarily."

As Collins said it, the lights went on for him.

"The Chilcotts? Who Dan? Carol? Alex? It was written in a fairly polished style. From what I've seen of Dan and Carol, I couldn't see them writing it. Who knows if Alex can write like that, but he would have to have got the information from Dan, or at least Carol." Collins paused again.

"What would that mean? That they're all in it together?"

Both Collins and Sharma were furiously trying to establish a firm footing with this latest theory. Was it true that the letter came from the Chilcott house? If so, what were the implications for Carol's escape plan, and the letter she was supposed to have written to give to Collins tomorrow? Maybe this was part of an entirely different plan that Alex

Chilcott was cooking up. There was no second letter. The only letter was the one that he had already written to the Director, to get Collins suspended. The letter that Carol was supposed to have written was just bait.

Collins considered what this meant for Daniel.

"Does this mean that Dan is part of their scheme as well?"

Again Sharma had already thought this through.

"Not necessarily. Daniel doesn't need to know the letter his mum is supposed to be writing is a hoax. In fact, it's probably better for their plan if he doesn't."

Given that Collins already knew that Carol had repeatedly lied for her husband, and that Alex Chilcott had a complete grip on everyone, and everything, that went on in the household, this had to be an explanation to be taken seriously. The implications rapidly became apparent to Collins; he was being played by Alex Chilcott.

"So what about the meeting tomorrow? What does Alex Chilcott expect to get from that, now he's got me out of the way?"

As he said it, a new horror arose in Collins' mind, one he barely wanted to consider. Could Chilcott have envisaged it would be Tara who would be coming to his doorstep? Was this a fulfilment of a long held desire? He wrestled with sharing this thought with Sharma but again she was already there.

"Is there any way that Chilcott could know there's a good chance it will be me, who's going to be turning up tomorrow, in your absence?" she said hesitantly.

Collins considered it. "You know what that estate is like, people know you're on the team. Carol might know and could have told him."

He thought some more.

"And you did drop that note in for me last week. He could have seen you then. I know that Carol did. It may be that getting me suspended is his main prize, you turning up, well…"

Collins paused without finishing his sentence, not sure that he really wanted to share what he thought was in the mind of a psychopath.

Sharma filled the gap he had left.

"If he's just trying to cover his tracks and create a diversion by getting you suspended, then why the need to manufacture the idea that Carol is about to leave, and that she's got this letter to handover, spilling the beans on him?"

Collins concluded his previous line of thought.

"Maybe he's finished covering his tracks, maybe he wants to get caught now, or he's got so mad he just doesn't care anymore. We know his behaviour has become more extreme: pulling knives on girls in the park, beating Carol up every other night. Getting you in house might be what he's working up to."

He paused again but knew, what was in his mind was also in Sharma's. "This might be his final act."

They sat in silence as they contemplated this new and horrifying conclusion. Characteristically, it was Sharma who brought them back down the path to where they started.

"Tom, we've come a long way from thinking it was Cathy Creswick, or one of your other colleagues, who wrote the letter. We've got to keep a number of possibilities in mind at the same time, and not get fixed on one as the only answer."

Even as she said it, Collins knew that she, like him, felt the chill presence of Alex Chilcott in the room with them, pulling their strings, and distorting their thoughts.

"Okay, but with the possibility Chilcott has engineered you coming to the house tomorrow, we've definitely got to make sure there's a response car close by and you need to make sure you've got all the protective equipment you can get your hands on."

Collins was unnerved. He thought about his own role in proceedings tomorrow and made a request to Sharma.

"You know I said I felt like a passenger? Well, maybe I could literally be a passenger. How about I come up with you and lay low in the car." As he said this he reflected on her earlier challenge.

"It's not about control." Collins struggled to explain his desperate need to somehow be part of the action tomorrow.

"I've just got it this far, you know, I've been involved all along. I just want to be there," he almost pleaded.

Then he made a further admission.

"I want to be there for you as much as me."

His eyes lowered towards the floor as he came out with it. He didn't know exactly what he meant, as he was working largely off emotion now, rather than reason, but he knew, if Tara was going into that house, he wanted to be close by.

Sharma shook her head and raised her eyebrows in despair.

"You're suspended, remember Tom? You want to get me suspended too by taking you up there? You need to trust me to do this. It's the best way, the only way."

Collins knew she wouldn't have let him come, but had needed to ask. He reluctantly accepted her decision, knowing that further debate would be futile, as her mind was set. Instead he concentrated on what he could do.

"Like I said, I'll text Carol in the morning. Whether she's on our side or his, we'll just have to continue to act like we're going along with the plan to get her out."

Sharma looked at her watch. "I need to be going, Tom. Body Pump at 7.30."

"Of course it is," he smiled, "got to keep the temple in tip-top shape."

"And you? Not running or gym-ing this evening, you fitness freak?"

It was only then that Collins remembered, he was supposed to be playing football.

"Damn, I completely forgot. I've agreed to be play in a football match tonight. It's the last thing on earth I feel like doing right now."

"Go on, go, what else you going to do, apart from drive yourself mad thinking about the Chilcotts, and suspension, and all the stuff, which ultimately, is just work? Go and see your mates and have a laugh."

"'Just work', that's rich coming from you."

He raised his eyebrows to suggest that Sharma was the last person who would consider what they did was "just work".

"Maybe you're right, what harm can it do?" he conceded.

As Sharma turned towards the front door, Collins asked her the question, which had played on his mind, since their lime and soda the previous week.

"Tara, was it drink with you too?"

"It was lots of things, Tom. Drink, drugs, and an abusive relationship. I needed to get clean from all of them. Once I had, I joined the police. So yes, you're right, this isn't just work for me either."

7.15pm

Collins got to the Elm Green ground late but that wasn't unusual for him. He was often late for matches. He liked to make them think he wasn't bothered, as if football was just a bit of fun, but he cared, just as much as his team mates cared, which was far too much. This in spite of the fact they were all too old for it to matter at all.

As he entered the narrow corridor that led to the dilapidated Elm Green changing rooms, he was struck by that peculiar smell and sound of ageing men preparing to play football. The pungent air in the passage was thick with Deepheat and Tiger Balm. Cutting through it was the familiar squabble over the best bits of kit.

"Fuck off, I always wear the number nine."

"Yeah, coz it's the only one that fits you, you fat bastard."

The decibels rose as he pushed against the half-open door.

Walking into the changing room was an extraordinary assault on almost every one of the senses. This was amateur football in the raw, literally.

A dozen men, aged between thirty-five and fifty, in various states of undress, were crowded into the tiny dressing room. Only Den McKay stood out, looking every bit the football manager: full length coat with his 'DM' initials on his breast, on top of shiny tracksuit bottoms. Stumpy, naked but for a jockstrap, overhung by a sagging belly, sat squashed in a corner, concentrating on rolling a second-to-last cigarette before the game. Lloydy, Dodge and Sammy were huddled around Den, as he relayed the game plan, and determined who would get the bad news they were not in the starting line-up. Jonesy sat in just his underpants and a pair of long football socks. He was in no hurry to put a shirt on, knowing that he would be the unlucky one, who would have to stand on the line in the semi-darkness for at least the first half; watching as the rest of his team mates ran themselves to a standstill.

As he entered the changing room, Collins was smothered by a wave of affectionate abuse.

"Tommo, you wanker! Fucking hell, are we that desperate?" It was Smudger, Collins' longstanding strike partner.

"Yes you are," he replied, slapping palms with his abuser.

"I hear you haven't scored since the last time I played, when I set you up for that tap-in," Collins shouted at Smudger.

Keen to leave him in no doubt of his value to the team, he added, "If I remember rightly, I got two that day."

"Yeah, the last one went in off your arse though," shouted Scouse, from the far corner of the dressing room.

"Tom Collins, the man with the golden arsehole. Welcome back sunshine." Georgie gave him an avuncular pat on the backside, entitled as he was, being the elder statesman of the team.

They were referring to a fortuitous ricochet from a corner that went in off Collins' rear to win the game the last time he played. Collins had a well-worn retort for them.

"As Freddy Flintoff used to say, 'It takes a big 'ammer'", he left a theatrical pause to allow his team mates to catch up:

"To knock in a big nail!" replied a chorus of voices.

Den broke away from his nuanced tactical debate, in order to greet him.

"Here he is, Shergar. Arse the same size and he's seen about as often!"

Den was pleased with that. He turned to the players to whom he had been outlining his vision to see if they had appreciated his wit. He continued to ensure maximum effect.

"Arse like a shire horse, that boy, but that's how I like my centre forwards."

They all knew what was coming next but let him complete a familiar gag, "and my women!" He was already snorting to himself, before he had finished the punch line.

"Fat bottomed girls. We've had a few of them, eh chaps?" Den was now on a roll and in his element. He couldn't stop his hands from shooting out to fondle an imaginary and sizeable backside in front of him.

"Corrr, those were the days, eh Dickie?" Den slapped the shoulder of his friend of twenty years, David "Dickie"

Hart. "Back when we were men, before we had our knackers nailed to the kitchen table by the old trouble and strife."

Den was never happier than when he was with his 'boys', in the dressing room before a match. It was then that the smut and innuendo would flood out, as he re-lived a largely invented past of womanising, high-rolling and high jinks. In his own eyes he was a suburban Simon Cowell. To his players he was the lovable, laughable, rogue who held their disparate team together.

Collins looked to carry on the topic of his late winner with Smudger and Georgie, while Den continued his reminiscence with Dickie and anyone else he could draw in.

"There was nothing lucky about that goal. It was a predatory finish. A sniffer's goal," Collins offered.

This was enough to get Den's attention again.

"That's you all over Tommo, nothing if not a sniffer" he roared, before concluding in music hall fashion, "you dirty, lucky git you."

Then returning to his familiar football manager's bark.

"Now get your tools in a pair of shorts, and get out there, and stick another one in the net, and I don't give a monkey's what bit of you it comes off."

The jokes continued in the dressing room until, in ones and twos, the lads filtered out into the floodlit night. Collins was left fiddling with shin pads and tie-ups, with only

Jonesy for company. Jonesy's parting words betrayed the seriousness with which these ageing players still treated their football.

"5-3-2? Wingbacks on a pitch this size? Den must be mad, it's all very well getting up there, but they ain't gonna get back, are they?"

He stared at Collins angrily, daring him to offer an alternative view, before returning to another well-worn theme.

"And why am I sub? I'm here every week, and if we've got too many, it's always me that's sub. If we lose to Elm Green because of his stupid tactics, that's it, I'm turning it in."

It was often 'it' for Jonesy, but after a tantrum and a week's sulk he's always back. Terrified of missing out, of leaving football behind, or more precisely, of football leaving him behind. So he was there at forty-five years old and no doubt he would still be turning out somewhere, for someone, at sixty. Collins just hoped it wasn't the same team he was on.

Sitting alone in the quiet of the deserted changing room, Collins mused on his current circumstances, and felt the relief of being back amongst these straightforward, funny, down-to-earth men; excluding Jonesy of course, the scapegoat that every team needed. It felt good to be back amongst football folk. He knew, if he told them about his personal misfortune, they would find it hilarious, but they would also be sure to do their best to take care of him.

Collins made his way from the gloom of the dressing room to the sharp, white lights of the pitch. Elm Green were always competitive, but Casuals usually had a bit too much class for them. Despite widening girths and slowing legs, there were some players on his side of genuine quality. Smudger could hit a ball so cleanly with his left foot it whistled as it sliced through the air. At fifty years old, Georgie's reading of a game was still so impeccable, he was always a step ahead of men half his age. Then there was little Sammy, who could mesmerise with a shuffle and a feint. Old Charlie, one of the Casuals' few regular supporters, purred at Sammy's mastery of a ball and, as if watching Fred Astaire, would coo, "oh, he's got lovely feet that boy". 'That boy' was forty-eight years old on his last birthday, but Collins had to agree with Charlie, he did have lovely feet.

Tonight, though, the team didn't seem to click, and Collins felt like the worst offender. He just couldn't seem to get into the game. When he went looking for the ball short, a defender nicked it off his toes. When he went long, the sweeper was there before him. He had played in enough games like this to know you have to persevere, keep going and your luck will change. Gaps will appear as the game goes on, and chances will start to come. Tonight his head wasn't on it. The harder he tried, the more frustrated he got. He saw Jonesy on the line, looking imploringly at Den, hoping to get a piece of the action. After half an hour Collins decided he could have it, it wasn't his night. He peeled off his shirt, and told Jonesy to get on in his place.

Den shouted from behind him, as Collins made his way towards the dressing room.

"Tommo. What's up? Where you going?"

Suddenly Collins felt drained. He felt ridiculous. He kept walking without answering.

He asked himself what on earth he had been thinking. What was he doing on a football pitch going through this charade? His head was a mess; his life was a mess. He berated himself for his stupidity in thinking he could just treat this evening like any other, and turn up for a game of football. Now he just wanted to get clean and get home.

8.05pm

Collins pushed the dressing room door behind him, and pulled his kit off. Barely half-an-hour earlier he had sat here full of expectation, back as part of a team, with his mates. Now he felt alone, disconsolate and dejected.

He pulled off his underpants, letting them drop to the floor as he rummaged in his bag for a towel. He heard the creak of the door opening behind him but continued his search. It was his right to be naked in the dressing room, and anyone who trespassed in this un-holy place should know what to expect.

Glancing casually over his shoulder, Collins found a small, blond boy, seated next to the door. Seven, or perhaps eight years old, he sat wide eyed, with a huge grin.

"Oh, hello. What are you laughing about?" Collins said, suddenly feeling self-conscious, as he sought his towel with increased urgency.

"Your team's losing," replied the boy, his grin broadening further.

"We'll win" Collins countered. Thankful to at last put his hand on his towel; he quickly wrapped it around his waist.

"Don't you want to be out there watching the game?" Collins suggested to the boy.

"No. I think I'll stay in here with you," he said, stretching his legs out on the bench, in a manner that suggested he was in for the long haul. This was starting to become a problem. Collins didn't feel at all at ease about progressing to have a shower, with this child in attendance.

He didn't know what to say to get him out, but thought he should make conversation, to try to find an excuse to get rid of him.

"So what's your name?" As soon as Collins had said it, he felt he had made the situation worse. It sounded like he was trying to befriend the boy.

"Billy," he replied, making himself even more comfortable on his bench. Collins' unease was in complete contrast to the matter-of-fact way the child was dealing with the more-than-half-naked adult he had encountered.

"No one knows I'm in here" he continued. "My dad's playing football and I'm hiding from the other kids."

"Oh God" Collins mumbled under his breath. He thought of the boy's dad thundering through the door at any moment to rescue his child, when he discovered he had been lured into the changing room.

"What's your name?" the boy asked.

"Jim", Collins said, absent-mindedly. He wasn't sure why he lied, but thought, in his somewhat distracted state, that this might help to stop the boy getting too familiar. Maybe there wasn't a good explanation, but he had just said it, and now he was Jim.

The initial mild discomfort Collins had experienced, in being surprised by the appearance of the small boy, had now been replaced by a more pressing anxiety. He hardly needed years of social work experience to know this was not a good position to find himself in, particularly at a time when he was suspended as a result of lurid accusations about his relationships with young boys. This was a situation he wanted to get out of, quickly, but the kid wasn't making things any easier.

"They'll never find me in here," he said.

"No Billy, they will. This is a terrible place to hide. Go behind the main stand, and hide under all the old nets and stuff. Quick, I think they're not far away."

To his relief Billy took the bait.

"Yeah, I will, I've made a den under there that they don't know about."

As Collins ushered him out, his towel fell to the floor. Fortunately Billy had run off before catching sight of anything which might have troubled him in later life. Collins stood in the middle of the silent dressing room; so grateful to be alone once more.

Akin to most washing facilities in leaky, creaky, lower league football venues, the water dripped reluctantly, rather than burst forth in the manner of the modern power shower, but he was glad of the modest soaking. Collins struck the classic pose of the troubled man, allowing the water to trickle down his back, as he stood still, stooped, with hand on neck. He smiled at this most ridiculous development. As if things weren't bad enough with all that was going on at work and in his personal life. He had foolishly decided to play football, stupidly got upset about playing so poorly, and then got himself embroiled with a small boy in the changing room. Collins had a strong word with himself, with instructions to buck his ideas up.

And then the lights went out.

The changing room and showers were in total darkness, save for the shimmer of the floodlights through the cracked skylight window.

"Come on, turn the bloody light on," Collins shouted from the shower. He presumed it was one of his team mates, playing around in what, by now, must have been the half-time break.

"It's me, Billy," came an excited voice through the gloom.

"They were getting close to the den, so I came back here. If we stay in the dark, they'll never guess anyone's in here."

"Oh Christ," Collins groaned. Again he fumbled for his towel but couldn't locate it in the dark.

"Billy, turn the light on and get out. I need to get changed." Irritation was for the first time evident in his voice.

"Can't we just hide in here together?" Billy pleaded. He was loving this adventure as much as Collins was hating it.

"No, you've got to get out." Collins didn't want to be rude to the boy, but this was now getting serious.

"Turn the light on and go," he said, in his most authoritative tone.

For the first time there was an element of hesitation in Billy's voice.

"I can't, the light switch is on the outside, and there's no door handle on this side. Well there is, but it doesn't work. I think we might be stuck in here."

Again the situation had taken a substantial turn for the worse. What was to be done? Collins stood in the shower and considered his options. He was locked in a changing room, in the dark, wet and naked, with a small boy for company; and he thought tonight would be a bit of light relief from his current travails.

"You're not frightened of the dark are you Jim?"

From Billy's voice, Collins could tell he was close by now, and this propelled him into action.

"No Billy, I'm frightened of your dad and his team mates coming in and shoving my bollocks down my throat."

He didn't say it, of course, but it was what he was thinking. What he actually said was:

"Billy, find me a towel from someone's bag, while I find a way to get the door open."

Collins gingerly picked his way towards where he thought the changing room door must be. He remembered now, having played at Elm Green before, that there was a long-standing problem with this door, which was normally left ajar.

He found the door and the knob, which turned easily, too easily, disconnected as it was from the locking mechanism. His knowledge of mechanics was scant, but he knew in his current predicament, still wet, still naked and in the dark, there was absolutely nothing he was going to do to promote a better working of the lock that stood between him and safety.

Billy, at least, had been able to locate a towel. The problem was, it was little more than a hand towel. It is the curse of the real footballers' wives that they will never let their husbands leave home with a good-sized, fluffy bath towel. What ageing footballers take with them to games is a threadbare, handkerchief-sized, piece of material, that would no longer be given house room, even in the dog's basket, were it not for the need for a football towel. The underwear that is worn during games is often of a similar ilk, but, just now, Collins would have taken any sort of underwear as a blessing.

His eyes were starting to adjust to the gloom of the changing room. He wasn't going to get out of the door, and the only windows were tiny openings below the ceiling, with bars to ward off the many opportunist thieves, who supported their drug habits from such sporting facilities.

The shouts from the pitch had stopped, so Collins guessed it was half-time. As his team had not returned to the changing room, he presumed they were just going to have a five minute blow at the side of the pitch, and turn straight round for the second half; just time for a slice of orange, or a cigarette. This meant that Billy's dad would, at this moment, almost certainly be starting his half-time search for his boy.

Collins looked up at the skylight that protruded from the flat roof. This represented his single hope of getting out of there quickly. If he could just manage to reach it, get it open, and pull himself out. He knew this proposition contained a number of big 'ifs'.

Collins stretched to his full height, but was still a foot short of the sky-light. He had to do so with one hand trying to retain the towel in position around his waist. He wondered if there was a chair he could move to climb up on? But even as he considered this, he thought of emerging up onto the roof, having probably lost his towel in the process. He pictured the smattering of spectators, slack jawed, as he appeared in their eye line. He could see calls for an armed response unit to shoot down the naked marauder. There was, he supposed, the option of groping around in the dark of the changing room, in the hope of finding either his own clothes, or someone else's he could fit into. Before this thought could settle, a better one had arrived. He could send the boy up there. Collins didn't need to think for long before reaching into the darkness and finding Billy's shoulder.

He tried his best to summon a commanding tone, that belied his anxious state.

"Billy you're going to have to climb out the sky-light, then crawl down the drainpipe, and open the door for me."

"Great. This is fun isn't it?" Billy's excited response slightly assuaged Collins' guilt at sending a small child out on to the roof.

"Yes Billy, great fun. Now let's get you up on my shoulders."

This, he could see, was the most hazardous part of the whole operation. He would have to struggle to keep the face flannel of a towel wrapped around his waist, while he lifted Billy up. As difficult as it was, Collins would just have to press on and lift the boy on to his shoulders, talking him through the tricky business of opening the sky-light. He knew there was every prospect of losing the towel and leaving his genitalia to wave in front of him and, critically, in front of the changing room door, if someone, such as Billy's father, came looking for the absent child.

Years of sage social work advice went through his mind, "never touch children unnecessarily, always make sure their parents or another adult are present if you need to do so… don't have close physical contact with children when you're practically naked in a dark changing room." He didn't recall that the text books had felt the need to include that final instruction.

"Here goes Billy."

Collins hoisted him up, and Billy clambered to stand on his shoulders. Mud from the soles of his trainers squelched against Collins' still damp skin.

There was a shout from the corridor outside.

"Billy? Billy?"

It was his dad. Collins felt physically sick at the prospect of the boy's father crashing through the door at any moment.

"Quick Billy." Collins encouraged, now in desperation.

Fortunately Billy didn't respond to his father's call, preferring instead the excitement of his game with his new friend. He fiddled with the catch of the skylight and then, thankfully for Collins, declared: "It's open, I think I can get through."

"Good, Billy, just go."

Collins watched with relief as Billy disappeared through the small gap he had created. Even this moment's respite was lost to a new fear that he had put the child in peril by sending him out on to the roof.

"Wait Billy. You've got to be really careful."

"Don't worry, I've been up here loads of times," and he was off. Collins heard his feet scampering above his head, and then the creak of the drainpipe at the end of the building, as he lowered himself down. Seconds later, the light came back on.

Collins tightened the small towel around his middle as the door opened, and Billy's beaming smile filled the doorway. Seemingly, his dad was continuing his search elsewhere.

"We did it!" he yelped.

"We did Billy. Good lad, now run along and find your dad while I get dressed."

Billy disappeared back down the corridor, planning his next adventure, while Collins pulled his clothes on hurriedly; keen at last to cover up his body, which seemed to have been exposed and unprotected for too long. When he was dressed he sat with his back against the dressing room wall, giving himself a chance to let his panic subside.

He tried to put his bizarre night into some perspective. How had he got himself entangled in such a freakish scrape, with a small boy, in a changing room, now of all times? The incident had passed with, as far as he could tell, no harm done. He smiled to himself, and decided that all he could do was try to make the best of the evening. Rather than slink off home, he would do the decent thing, and go and give his mates some encouragement from the touchline.

9.45pm

Casuals won 2-1. To Collins' genuine delight Smudger poached a late winner. Collins stayed behind for a celebratory pint of orange squash and, by the time he had finished it, he had shared with his team mates the news of his suspension from work, as a result of the anonymous allegation. He left the detail deliberately ambiguous, describing it as a complaint of having "inappropriate relationships at work".

"Rat up a drainpipe! If it's not dead, he'll shag it! That's my boy, Tommo!" roared Den.

He was enraptured by the whole saga. Den believed that everyone else on the team was as much of a womaniser as he himself dreamed of being, and treated them accordingly. Collins inwardly winced at how wildly Den had misconstrued the nature of the allegation against him, but didn't feel inclined to correct him. He was glad to be able to bring Den such joy with his pitiful tale.

Den slapped Dickie's shoulder, "once a crumpeteer…? Eh Dickie?"

"Always a crumpeteer!" Dickie responded enthusiastically, knowing that he and Den were now perfectly set for a wander down memory lane.

Smudger said it was all blindingly obvious.

"There's some bird who can't get any, who you've given the cold shoulder to. It's some bitter woman in your office, she'll have made the complaint."

Den and Dickie were now embarking on a nostalgic meander and were keen that others should join them.

"What about that night Ronny Brown ran out of dough playing cards at Smokey's, and he used dirty pictures of his wife as his stake? I was trying to lose; Dickie here has never tried harder to win a game of cards in his life."

But they had all heard this story enough times. Tonight the rest of Collins' team mates were concentrating on trying to untangle his complex story.

"No Smudger," chipped in Macca, "it's someone he's knobbed. Have you shagged anyone in your office and then given her the knock back?"

The explanations were revealing, even if Collins thought they were well wide of the mark. The obvious explanation for any ill to befall a man was the vexatious ways of women.

Jonesy used it as an excuse to scratch an old itch.

"No mate, it's your ex-missus. Trust me, they're always looking to do you over." Jonesy was speaking from the heart here. Five years down the line, he was still horribly embittered about the terms of his divorce.

"It can't be mate. There was work stuff in that letter that she couldn't have known about."

"I'm telling you, it's your ex."

Jonesy was glaring now, with the same anger Collins had seen when he had been told he was the substitute; an anger which normally boiled over for one reason or another at football on a weekly basis. Collins was by now looking to change the subject; feeling that he didn't want to go down the rabbit hole of Jonesy's anger towards women.

"Jonesy, it can't be. Let it go."

Jonesy was insistent and pulled Collins by the arm, away from the main conversation.

"Listen to me. It's got to be your missus. You know your Janet and my ex Marie are thick as thieves. Janet's made no secret, she's gonna make things as hard for you as she possibly can."

"Jonesy, how do you know this stuff? You don't even talk to Marie."

"I talk to her brother, who keeps me in the know," Jonesy said, tapping the side of his nose.

"Jonesy, like I say, there were details in there she couldn't possibly have known. I can't see how it could be her."

"You'd be surprised mate. Your works not so secret. People see you up on Gartside, and about Town, and they talk. I don't know what was in the letter, but I'll give you a pound to a penny it was something your ex has cooked up."

They returned to the wider gathering with Collins pondering Jonesy's hypothesis. Jonesy was always quick to blame the 'ex', be that his or anyone else's, but Collins couldn't completely discount the possibility that it was Janet. She was the one person who had an obvious motive and, following the incident on the doorstep last Friday, the timing would fit. He decided he would run it past Tara to see if it put a different complexion on her impending visit to the Chilcotts.

The conversation amongst Collins' team mates had moved on from his misfortune, and they were back to talking football. He was glad to be surrounded again by these men, who he had known for more than a decade. In many respects their rough edges fitted the stereotype of the ageing footballer: opinionated, foul mouthed and always bracingly honest. There were, though, depths and shades, which a casual observer might miss: the vegetarian, the tee-totaller, and the avowed pacifist. Their views could rarely be taken for granted. While the pervasive culture may have been one of un-examined sexism, they were open to challenge on this, as with most other things. Collins normally made it his business to provide what they called his 'right on' perspective, but tonight, while he knew he should, he didn't have the energy left for such an argument.

For all their bluster, Collins saw those depths in his team mates this evening as, after the initial jesting, there was a real concern to make sure that he was coping with his situation. It had been a topsy-turvy night, but now he felt that Tara had been right, coming out to the match had been good for him.

Collins was debating whether he should stay for one more drink, now that he was becoming increasingly comfortable in the warm blanket of male camaraderie. Just then his fair-haired little friend, Billy, popped up at his side, at the centre of the tight-knit group of men.

"Jim, can we play that game in the dark, in the changing room, when you come here again?"

All fell silent as Collins' team mates looked quizzically at the innocent in their midst. Before Collins could say a word, Billy added, "Make sure you've got your clothes on next time though."

With that he skipped off towards the door and his father's waiting car, turning to wave as he exited, with a shout of, "see you next time, Jim."

At that moment Den was just completing a re-telling for Dickie of the ever-embellished 'Bucking Bronco' anecdote, regarding an erstwhile team mate, Bronco Blackwood. He finished with a familiar crescendo, "and the copper's torch has picked him out, sunk to the nuts, arse going like the clappers!" When his guffaws had subsided, he turned to find the rest of the team staring open mouthed at Collins.

Scouse spoke for them all, as he enquired, "Jim? Who the fuck's Jim?"

Collins shrugged, palms upturned in front of him. "You might find this story even harder to believe than my last one. I'll get a round in," he said, turning to the bar.

10.30pm

The last of the day's light was disappearing, as Collins got back in his car at the Elm Green ground. He knew it was late to be ringing Tara, but given what lay ahead of her tomorrow, he thought she would rather speak now than leave it until the morning. She answered immediately, as if she had been expecting his call.

"Tom, are you ringing to tell me you scored?" There was a warmth to her voice that made Collins glad he had decided to call.

"No, I was rubbish, but it was a laugh, and good to see the lads again. Thanks for pushing me to get out tonight."

"Sounds like more fun than Body Pump." She waited, not sure if this was just a social call, or if Collins had any pressing reason to phone.

"One of my team mates, Jonesy, is sure the letter was written by my ex-wife."

"I think, actually, she's still your wife, Tom."

Collins was interested that Tara thought to make this distinction. It suggested it might be important to her.

"Yes okay, my wife, Janet. She's friends with Jonesy's ex and he says, he has it on good authority, that Janet was planning something like this. I can't see how she could know about current casework though."

"Remember Tom, you said there are only two names mentioned, Daniel Chilcott and Mickey Johnson. Could she have got those names from anywhere?"

"Perhaps, I guess, particularly if she has made it her place to find out. Thinking about it, Dan and Mickey both go to St Christopher's, the same secondary as my son Jamie. There's a link there I suppose."

"Well then, we've got to consider it's possible she's the letter writer," Tara concluded.

"Where does that leave us with Alex Chilcott then?" Collins reviewed the various permutations once again.

"It's also still possible he's the letter writer", Sharma replied. "Like I said, we've got to keep an open mind. Don't put all your money on one horse, and don't completely discount any of them."

With that, Tara decided it was enough speculation for one night.

"I'm going to get some beauty sleep. It's a big day tomorrow. Night."

"Night".

Ending the call Collins indulged himself in the thought that he was going home to Tara's, rather than his own empty flat. He felt wide awake after his rollercoaster evening at Elm Green, and his mind was now fully focused on Tara's "big day".

As he drove towards home, he turned over scenarios in his mind. At this moment Alex Chilcott was probably inflicting some unspeakable pain and humiliation on his wife. Tomorrow, if she was able, she would open the door to Tara to draw her into that pain and with what result? This was Collins' life, his work, and from now he was to be an impotent bystander; tucked safely away at home, while this sad drama reached its crescendo.

Collins pulled up outside his flat, determined on a course he knew risked ruining his career, but one he felt compelled to pursue.

11.00pm

Collins was only inside for two minutes, picking up a hat and zip-up hoody, before he was back in the car and on his way to the Gartside. As he drove towards the towers, he diverted away from the precinct, where he calculated that a police response car would likely be stationed. He suspected that, even if they didn't recognise his car, they would note the number plate, and that could cause a further complication he didn't need.

Collins wove his way through the back of the estate towards Gartside Gardens. The streets were empty, save for the occasional late night dog walker and a few kids on bikes. He thought he recognised Streak, the lanky ginger lad, who seemed to be the boss of the estate's street corners, with a couple of his mates. They looked like they were on patrol. No doubt they had the same idea that had brought Collins up to the Gartside; to make sure Chilcott wasn't free to roam the streets and park without being challenged.

Collins' plan was not much more sophisticated than that. He would watch the Chilcott house, and if Carol was taking another beating, he would put a stop to it. He knew he couldn't ring the police, as his number would be traced, and being found up here, at this time of night at the Chilcotts', might be enough to get him sacked. He couldn't even run to summons the response car, as this too would ruin his chance of maintaining anonymity. So, if he couldn't involve the police, he would have to intervene himself. He didn't know what that would entail. He would have to cross that bridge when he came to it.

Having got within one road of Gartside Gardens, Collins drew the car to a halt. This was as close as he could get in the vehicle, and he would need to go the rest of the way on foot. He pulled on his hoody and zipped it up as far as it would go over his face, pulling his hat down, so only his eyes and nose were visible.

As he moved along the deserted streets he realised he now fitted the profile of the lone predatory male, for whom the estate was on alert. He walked with his head down, hoping not to meet another pedestrian, or worse, a passing police car. He had already had an unfortunate scrape with Billy in the changing room tonight, which could have further imperilled his career, and the last thing he needed now was to be hauled in by the police, suspected of being the Gartside rapist.

As he approached the entrance to Gartside Gardens, he saw car lights rounding the bend in front of him. He had an urge to hide, in case it was the police, but he knew this was a dangerous course of action; lest he be spotted and found lurking in someone's shrubbery. He kept walking and prayed to go un-noticed.

To Collins' relief it was a white transit van which swept by without slowing down.

He continued down Gartside Gardens. All was quiet, with many houses already in darkness, and others barely lit. Occasional flashes of light came from screens inside rooms with curtains open. As he approached number eighty-four, he was unsurprised to see the only light was from the television in the front room. He slowed a little, to see if there was anything unusual, any noise to suggest an assault was taking place, or was about to. Nothing, just the muted glow of the screen from behind the grey net curtains.

Collins carried on walking to the end of the cul-de-sac. He had already pictured for himself the spot he would take up, at the back of the house, midway down the alley that ran behind Gartside Gardens, out towards the park. There were railings that Collins thought he could perch on, close enough to watch over the Chilcott house, but also out of sight of most passers-by.

When Collins arrived at his intended spot he was pleased to find he had a clear view of the house, and was away from the immediate glare of any street lights. He was also perfectly appointed, should Chilcott decide to take himself out the back gate. Now all he could do was wait and listen.

The temperature was starting to drop off under the clear sky, and Collins was glad of the extra layers he had put on which, while intended as disguise, were going to be of benefit for his vigil. The back of the house was in darkness. Collins could only pick out the outline of the bedroom windows, and the top of the back door over the back fence. The house was quiet, as was the whole of this part of the estate, save only for the noise of the occasional car on the main road.

Collins wondered if he had come too late. Carol may already be upstairs, nursing her new wounds, while Chilcott had returned to brooding in front of the TV. He stared into the gloom, not knowing what was happening inside, and not knowing what, if anything, he would be called upon to do. Collins knew he shouldn't be here, but also knew he could not be anywhere else.

11.30pm

At that moment Carol Chilcott was lying, duvet pressed under her chin, staring at the peeling paint on her bedroom ceiling. Tonight Alex had been quiet, more so than usual, to the point of muteness. The normal threats and slurs were absent; he just stared numbly at his giant screen. He ate his dinner alone in front of the TV, flicking repeatedly through his old newspapers, to alight on the stories that engaged his maladjusted imagination. Carol left him undisturbed, busying herself in the kitchen or the kids' rooms.

While helping Crystal with her homework, Carol could see how her daughter focused on her shaking hands. Crystal took her mother's left hand and held it tight. Carol could see the pity in her daughter's eyes. She hated herself for what she had let happen to them all.

Carol sensed that Alex was building to some act of terrible brutality; worse than those that had come before. She pulled the duvet tighter up to her chin. She assumed she would be the victim, but also knew it need not end with her. For the thousandth time that day she asked herself if she was doing the right thing. She had stayed so long, and tried so hard, to find a space for herself and the children in the shadow of Alex's cruelty, but now she knew it was coming to an end.

She was jolted from her internal debate by the sound of Alex's heavy footsteps rapidly ascending the stairs. The door crashed open, and there he was, already at the apex of incandescent rage.

"Get up you bitch. I know what you're up to. I know what you're up to."

Carol clung tighter to the duvet, but knew this was no protection against what was coming next.

"Up! Up!"

He ripped the cover from her and grabbed a handful of her long brown hair in his right hand.

"Up!"

Chilcott used the back of his free hand to swipe Carol across the face with full force. Her head swung to the right, but was jerked back upright by the grip that he had on her hair. He dragged her from the bed, across the floor towards the bedroom door.

"You conniving bitch. Think I trust you? Think I trust you with that social worker? I'm gonna end you. I'm gonna end you, tonight."

He dragged her into the bathroom and turned the taps on full.

"This time I'm doing it properly. I should have done this a long time ago. Instead of letting you play me along. You've been playing me. No more, this is it."

Blood had by now filled Carol's mouth, and her hair felt like it would all, finally, be pulled from her head. Despite the pain, she felt a moment of clarity. So this was how it would finish. She had done everything to placate Alex, to cover-up for him, to soak up his hatred, and now it would finally be over. He was a sick man, whose sickness she could not contain. She had done everything he had ever asked of her, but it was never enough, in the face of his all-consuming hatred and paranoia.

The water gushed from the taps and Carol knew her time had come. He raised her up by her hair, over the edge of the bath; ready to plunge her into the cold water for the last time. He brought his face close to hers and spat his last words into her face:

"You made me do this."

Carol closed her eyes and waited to die.

11.35pm

Daniel jumped up from his bed, pulling his bowie knife out from under his pillow. He couldn't listen to this torture again.

How many nights had he lain there and heard squeals of pain; torrents of foul abuse, followed by his mum retching and sobbing? Every time now it seemed to be worse, and every time he lay there, fearing it was her last. How many nights had he castigated himself for failing to intervene, to offer some protection, to at least be a buffer for some of the blows that rained down on her?

You'd rather cut yourself than face that cunt wouldn't you?

Not this time.

This is when it all changes.

Daniel held the eight inch blade in front of his face. He fought to steady his hand. He saw his reflection in the blade. His features were fixed in furious determination.

Do it! This time do it!

Daniel stepped towards his bedroom door, set on stopping his mother's misery and ending his father's life.

11.36pm

A crash on the front door brought Carol back into the room, and halted Alex at the moment he was about to thrust her head under the water.

Reaching for the handle to open his bedroom door, Daniel froze in his tracks.

"Get out here now, Chilcott." A man's voice shouted through the letterbox.

Alex Chilcott was motionless. He continued to hold tight to Carol's hair; her frozen features giving her the look of a head which had already been decapitated. Finally he let go, causing Carol to slump to the bathroom floor.

"Come on Chilcott, the police are coming for you. Get out here." The voice was loud. Loud enough to wake the whole road.

Chilcott cursed, "Who the fuck?"

Carol tried to make sense of what was happening around her. She had been prepared to die and now, somehow, she was still alive. She heard another bang on the door and the voice shouting into her hallway.

"Come on you nonce, you rapist, you wife beater. Come out and face the neighbours."

That voice. It was Collins.

She took the chance to scramble past her husband and back to the bedroom, where she wedged the chair beneath the door handle. She hunched herself on the of the edge of the bed, against the back wall. She had escaped death but what now?

She was paralysed by the decision in front of her. She wanted to force herself down the stairs, and go to Collins, but she was rooted to the bed.

Breathe girl, breathe. You can do this. Walk down the stairs and out that front door. Give in to it. Surrender.

The problem was, even an act of surrender was itself an action: it needed commitment, resolution and propulsion, and all she had was a traumatised inertia; having been grafted to this place, and to Alex Chilcott, for as long as should could remember. She wanted to scamper down the stairs and run outside, but she was welded the house's very fabric: one of its permanent fixtures, cemented in place.

Carole kept trying to breathe deeply; to suck in air, to soothe her febrile mind and still her shaking limbs. She knew now, without any doubt, that given his chance, he would kill her. With the police on their way she would have a final opportunity to get out. She wrapped her arms around her knees and sat shaking; shaking at the thought of finally telling all, and shaking at the thought of what her husband would then do.

Breathe and think. Breathe and think. You can do this. If you don't do this now, you won't get another chance.

She heard the wail of approaching sirens. This was her chance.

Come on girl. Do it. Do it.

From outside the bedroom door came a familiar growl.

"One word. Just one word out of line and I'll burn this house down, with you and all your bastard children in it, and if you run, I'll find you. I will find you. Not one word."

11.40pm

Tom Collins continued to batter on the Chilcotts' door, determined to ensure that Alex Chilcott ended his assault, and that there was enough of a disturbance for the neighbours to call the police.

From his vantage point overlooking the back of the house he had seen the upstairs lights going on; heard the muffled roar of Alex Chilcott crashing into the bedroom. He couldn't make out what was happening inside, but he could see and hear enough to know that it had started. He deftly jumped the back fence, and made his way around to the front of the house. He briefly stopped to put his ear to the letterbox, to confirm his belief that the assault had commenced. From inside he could hear the cursing and threats and knew he had to act.

As Collins hammered on the door and shouted through the letterbox, he saw lights going on in the neighbours' houses. Curtains twitched and faces peered out to see what this new disturbance was at the Chilcotts. Collins continued to bang, until he saw the lights upstairs being turned off. Inside the house was quiet now, and he knew that Chilcott had ceased for the moment. A couple appeared from the house next door, the mother cradling an infant. The man, who had hastily put on a pair of trousers, but no top, stared at Collins, trying to decipher whether he was another lunatic, like his neighbour, or if he had some legitimate business at the Chilcotts' door.

"What the fuck are you doing mate? We've got a baby we're trying to get to sleep in here, and I've got to work in the morning."

Collins tried to remain clear and calm.

"Call the police. He's killing her in there. I need you to call the police now."

"I don't want to get involved mate; they're always at it," the man replied dismissively.

"If she dies in there, and she might die in there tonight, and you haven't called the police, you will well and truly be involved. Get in and call the police, and tell me when you've done it. I haven't got a phone, so just do it."

Collins continued to bang on the door and shout, "Come on Chilcott, get out here."

All was quiet in the house.

The neighbour re-appeared, "They're on their way," he begrudgingly mumbled, before turning back into his door. At this Collins took himself off, back around the side of the house, opening the lock on the back gate to let himself out to where he had previously been stationed.

He heard the siren coming from the direction of the precinct, and guessed that Chilcott would be making preparations to leave the house. As the blue lights of the police car entered the road, he saw the back door of the house open.

11.45pm

When he left home that night, Collins had fantasied about finally coming face to face with Alex Chilcott. He had lines prepared; lines he had wanted to deliver to him since he had first entered his tomb-like home. He also knew that it may not just be words that would be needed. He now braced himself for a confrontation with a man he knew traded in sadistic violence. Collins could hear the pounding of his heart, like a powerful engine; not just in his ears but through his bones. His mouth was dry and every sinew tensed for action.

As the back gate opened Collins raised himself to his full height and prepared for war.

At that moment the alley was filled with excitable shouts of a group of boys, attracted by the arrival of the police. It was Streak and his mates. "You two check out the front, us two will make sure he doesn't come out the alley," he heard Streak shout instructions to his comrades.

Chilcott emerged furtively on the threshold of the open gate, turning left to check out the noise at the end of the alley. He appeared to be deciding whether to press on or retreat; listening to the unfamiliar sounds of the vigilante patrol his deeds had summoned forth. Only then did he see Collins, in the shadows, on the far side of the alley.

Collins stood still, staring at Chilcott, processing this embodiment of the monster who had lived in his head, and inhabited so much of his thoughts, over the last week. As he suspected he had a deeply unappealing appearance. Dark hair protruded lankly beneath the black woollen hat he had pulled to his ears; what he could see of his sallow complexion was riveted with pock marks; and his zipped, black leather jacket struggled to hide a heavy paunch.

Chilcott stared back, trying to comprehend why this stranger was posted on his back gate. Weighing his options, he appeared to realise his chances of avoiding the attention of the police would not be helped by a confrontation with this hooded sentry and his group of teenage followers. Collins imagined Chilcott had worked out he was the same stranger who had been banging on his door, but sensed that he hadn't made any other connection to identify him. For Collins' part, he was happy for Chilcott to think of him as a local vigilante.

Collins was also keen to avoid a scene; if he could help it. He gambled on a silent threat, and hoped it would be enough to see Chilcott off. He made a slicing gesture across his own throat, while continuing to stare hard at Chilcott. Chilcott returned his glare, his fury barely kept in check; held back only by his puzzlement at this turn of events, which saw his habitual escape route unexpectedly barred.

Chilcott continued to stare at Collins. Neither man was prepared to stepdown, but equally neither could afford an altercation. Eventually Chilcott drew back his head and propelled his spit towards Chilcott; a globule landing on his shoe. He turned back down his garden path and locked the gate behind him.

Collins breathed deeply, trying to calm himself after the wordless exchange. Mindful of Streak and friends at the end of the alley, Collins edged further into the darkness, hoping they would not make their way to where he was stationed.

He leaned over and silently retched into the shrubbery that surrounded him. His body was reeling from his first encounter with Chilcott. He didn't know if it was adrenalin, or fear, or both. He steadied himself and hoped he could escape the attention of Streak and friends. For now his only option was to stay put and continue his watch.

11.50pm

Carol sat on the marmalade sofa in the front room, while the police officers made their now routine check on the kids upstairs. Making sure all the boxes had been ticked, before they could carry on to their next job. Carol did notice their radio message through to the control room.

"The IC1 resident has left the premises, repeat, he is no longer on the premises."

They seemed to be more bothered by Alex's whereabouts than usual. As they made their way upstairs, she had heard the latch on the back kitchen door click, and knew that he was back. She was surprised he had returned so soon with the police still in the house. Something, or someone, had driven him back inside. Was it Tom Collins she wondered? She knew Alex would wait in the kitchen now, until they were gone. Then what?

Carol had dragged herself to the front door when the police arrived. She had covered her wounded face with her hair, and proceeded to dance her familiar dance with the officers in attendance.

"I've never heard a racket like it. Some lunatic bringing trouble to our door. You want to be investigating him. Causing a riot on our doorstep at this time of night. And those people next door, they're nothing but trouble themselves."

"Al will be back soon, just getting some air. We've all had quite a fright."

They asked their questions, checked on the kids, weighed up the risks, and finally they were gone.

Carol closed the door behind them and took herself back upstairs. On the landing Daniel sat with his arm around Crystal and the twins. They had all been crying, except for Daniel, who sat staring angrily at the wall in front of him, all the while cuddling his siblings.

Carol saw the scabs on the inside of his forearms. Her heart ached for the pain that her eldest had experienced in his short life, and for what all of her poor children had had to endure.

Why can't you do it? Still here. Why can't you? Maybe you are the thick, useless cow he says you are?

Again she told herself she had to be braver. She had to be braver for them.

Tomorrow's another day. I hope.

"Come on you lot, we're in together tonight, all of us."

They all made their way into the twins' room, and Carol and Daniel pushed a chest of drawers against the back of the door. They closed the gap between the two single beds and huddled close to each other. In time, the twins and Crystal's breathing became rhythmical, as they moved into sleep. Carol had never planned to sleep, and knew that Daniel, like her, would be staring at the ceiling, listening for noises downstairs, or on the stairs. She had kept her side of the bargain again and the police had gone. She hoped that Alex would keep his, and they would not be burned, or butchered, in their beds tonight.

Carol felt some small relief when she heard the familiar drone of the TV, penetrating through the floorboards. If he was watching television, she guessed that might be his lot for the night, but she also knew he had entered such an unpredictable phase that nothing was certain. She would remain vigilant.

Daniel knew his mother was awake, and, once the others were asleep, he took his chance to confide in her.

"I was going to kill him tonight. When I heard him dragging you to the bathroom, I had my knife in my hand, and I was going to kill him."

Carol squeezed her son's hand, not knowing whether to thank him or berate him for being on the point of taking a knife to his father. She settled on the one thing she was sure of and whispered in reply, "It's not for you to deal with Dan. I need to do that."

They continued to lie in alert silence, before Daniel raised what he knew would also be on his mother's mind. "That was Tom Collins at the door wasn't it?"

"Yes I think it was," Carol confirmed. She paused still trying to make sense of why he was there, and why he had done what he had done.

"I don't know what it means, or why he acted like that, but thank god he did, or there would have been a murder in this house tonight."

They returned to their watchful silence; both pondering what this latest development meant for their embattled family.

1.30am

It had been nearly two hours since Chilcott had returned into the house. Streak and friends had disappeared from the end of the alley after twenty minutes. Collins had been relieved to see them go, but guessed they would still be on patrol somewhere on the estate. He felt his best course was to stay put and keep his watch.

He had taken one sortie over the gate and back around to the front, to check out which lights were on in the Chilcotts'. The house had returned to darkness, save for the glow of the television. Collins could see the shadows cast from the screen, and thought he could just make out the outline of Chilcott on his leather armchair.

As Collins stared at the lightless back of the house, he couldn't help but see again Chilcott's black eyes, as they had stared at him from beneath his woollen hat. As Tara had said, his eyes were cold, empty wells, which drew from some hellish depths. Collins had always thought that holding people up as either good or evil was over simplistic; that all of us come in multiple shades of light and dark. Having come face to face with Chilcott, and stared into those eyes, he felt he had been in contact with the darkest shade he had yet encountered. Collins suspected some horrible cruelty had been inflicted on Chilcott in his own formative years, but he was far beyond redemption now. All Collins could do was hope he could break the cycle for the Chilcott children.

It had taken an hour for Collins' body to start to come down to something like a state of rest. As he peered into the darkness he felt some pleasure that, thus far, his mission seemed to have been successful. He had stopped Carol being assaulted; involved the police without embroiling himself; and had, with Streak and co, been able to provide some containment for Chilcott until such time as he could be arrested. He remembered the words of his boss,

Dave Andrews, only a few days earlier, "Don't go on one of your crusades Tom". Collins smiled at the thought of what Andrews would make of tonight's crusading. So far he felt vindicated in his decision to breach his employer's ban on coming to the Gartside.

While Collins' body was starting to return to normal; he had a feeling that something had been dislodged in his mind. The roar he had heard from the Chilcotts' house made real the abuse, and seeing Chilcott in the flesh gave Collins an even more vivid sense of his menace. A cocktail of fatigue and anxiety encouraged his mind to drift to other places and other scenes. He saw himself in the early hours of the morning, stumbling through the door of his old home in Carlisle Place, to find Janet sitting brooding in the front room. He remembered angry exchanges when she refused to accept his explanations for coming home drunk again in the middle of the night.

"I didn't expect it to be this late either. It's not often you get a lock-in at the Star these days," he offered as an opener.

When this was rebuffed, it escalated.

"What's it matter to you anyway? What's the difference between twelve and two? What the fuck's it matter?"

For her part Janet was standing firm.

"It's not two, it's nearly three, and the problem is you drink every day, and, whenever you get the chance, you drink yourself senseless."

And now it was really taking off.

"You said you were laying off it, going easy. The only easy thing is you. Easy, weak-willed, pathetic."

And then the push, pushing her away. He didn't want to hear any more. It was only a push.

Collins saw it again now, but this time he replayed the actual tape, not the one he had edited to suit his purposes over the last two years. It wasn't a push. He threw the back of his right hand across her face, and Janet fell backwards over a chair.

Sitting here in the night, watching over the house of a man who lived to persecute his family, Collins shuddered at the recognition that he too was an abuser. He thought about the morning after he had struck Janet. She wouldn't speak to him, and he wearily accepted her cold shoulder. She never mentioned the blow, and if he remembered it at all, it was soon buried. They had had an altercation: six of one and half a dozen of the other. He had pushed her away and she had fallen.

But something changed from there on. The frost, which had for a long time permeated their relationship, had turned into an ice sheet, and had now shattered, taking them apart, on currents which were never to meet. Collins decided he could stay in the relationship no more, and announced he was leaving.

Now he looked back on it, he realised it wasn't any failing of his wife; nor was it a noble mission he was setting out on, as he cut himself free from the ties of his marriage. Now in the early hours, watching over the Chilcotts' home, he realised it was shame that had driven him away. Shame that he couldn't control his drinking, and shame that he had beaten his wife.

With this new knowledge Chilcott re-examined the final stages of his marriage. Was that the only time he had hit Janet? He was sure it was, but he also knew that he was often drunk, and struggled to remember all that had gone on the night before. In addition he had uncovered a layer of self-protection and self-deceit; if there had been other times when he had been violent, he may well have blocked them out.

He racked his brain to see if other incidents would now appear from his un-frozen memory. He saw heated exchanges. He didn't want to see more, but he knew it was there: a hand in the face, a hand across the mouth, pushing, shouting.

A screech of a fox in the park broke Collins away from the scenes he was now re-playing in his mind. He was glad to stop. Tonight he had admitted for the first time that he had his own history of domestic abuse. He was probably right to leave Janet; not for the pious reasons he had given, but because it saved them both from slipping further down the slope of an abusive relationship.

It was now after two in the morning and Collins thought that it might be safe to end his watch. He made his way to the front of the house, and looked into to the living room from only a few feet away. He reckoned that, if Chilcott was still awake, seeing the shadow of Collins outside, in his vigilante guise, would be no bad thing. As far as Collins could tell, from Chilcott's slumped figure, he was asleep.

Collins hastily made his way back to his car. On the way home he pondered what he would tell Tara about his night, and what he would do, while she was paying her midday visit to the Chilcotts.

FRIDAY 18TH MAY

6.15am

Tara Sharma turned over to check her bedside clock one more time, to see if it was a respectable time to get up. She had been awake for over an hour and, even before that, her sleep had been fitful; forced from uneasy dreams to face the dawning light of an uncertain day.

Tara's mind turned over the possibilities that awaited her at the Chilcotts'. It could be just in and out. Get the letter from Carol, then back to base, to put the wheels in motion to get her and the kids out. Sharma wished it would be that simple, but had a strong suspicion that it would not. If Carol had made up the 'escape letter', did that mean it was a trap? Or could it just be part of Alex Chilcott's game, that allowed him to demonstrate he was the one who was in charge?

Tara worked through the worst case scenario. Chilcott wanted her there, in his house, to do what he had wanted to do five years ago. The thought transported her back to that night. What she had wanted to do was spray gas in his eyes and inflict maximum pain. She was reminded of her own words to Greta, "take back the power". If Chilcott was trying to lure her into his trap, she would be ready. It would be her chance to turn the tables and humiliate him, the way he had done to so many others.

This is your moment. Take it. Fuck him up.

She was psyching herself up. Doing the self-talk she had learned in therapy. She knew she could just as easily talk herself down. She could let Chilcott's chilling eyes paralyse her with fear, and start to roll back down the big hill she had forced herself to climb over the last decade. She needed to be able to control herself. If she could do that, she knew she could control Chilcott.

Tara re-visited the work she had put in to therapy. The peeling away of the layers of protection she had built up: the alcohol, the pills, and the unhealthy relationships. All of which she used to avoid facing into the pain of her child-hood, but now she could look back without fear or shame; now she could take strength from her journey.

Tara thought of her beloved mother, Rani, lost to cancer when she was just six years old; only made real to her now from photographs and grainy video. Tara imagined her as a beautiful Hindu princess, who had taken her place with the gods. Tara's place was left behind, the only child in the inadequate care of Kai, her poor, broken father. Tara could barely think of it as a childhood after her mother died, as she increasingly became the carer for her drink-soaked dad. She was seventeen when he finally got put away in a home for incurable alcoholics. Then she was totally alone: no parents, no siblings and no relations to fall back on.

Tara blushed at the thought of her adolescent self: desperate to be one of the good time girls at college, only too pleased by the attention of the bad boys who circled them. She wanted only easy company, people who were too interested in getting blitzed to be bothered about her back story. She knew she was going full-throttle and headed for trouble. Sure enough she found it, in the shape of Pete Dawkins.

Nineteen, leather jacket, a motor bike and all the confidence in the world, that was Pete Dawkins. She saw Pete now, as she first saw him then: unbelievably cool, unbelievably hot. Nearly twenty years on, she could still remember the palpitations she had when he sat her on the seat of his Suzuki, and pushed her summer dress over her knees, leaning in between her thighs, for their first kiss.

Maybe it was all too predictable. A boy on a motorbike who would somehow transport her away from her troubles, expunging her painful past, to live in a constant, heady present. Of course he couldn't wipe the slate clean. How could he?

Pete tried. In his own way, he tried. He said he wanted her to feel alive and be herself. To be free from her past, "What are you scared of? What's holding you back?" he asked

There was so much she could say to that, but it was easier to say nothing, and reach for another drink, or a joint, or any number of pills, and Pete was happy to join her.

She threw herself into him, as if no one else mattered. For Tara there was no one else, so she clung tight to Pete. Unfortunately for her, he was fleeing his own demons. As a result they slipped into ever greater dependency: on each other and on drink and drugs. By the end, their relation-ship had become destructive, as he got more paranoid and possessive, and she more erratic; needing him on the one hand, but also recognising she was being suffocated.

The night he died wasn't the first time they had broken up, but it was the first time they both really thought it was over. He grabbed hold of her hair, on the doorstep of the squat they were sharing, desperate to prevent her going to a party he had warned her away from. Pete was sure she intended to cheat on him.

"What the fuck Pete? Let go, you mental fuck."

She kicked him in the shins and scratched at his face, as he forlornly fought to hold on to her.

"Don't go Tara."

She broke free from his hold, and made her way back into the house to pack a bag.

"That's it Pete. It's over. I'll be back for the rest of my stuff tomorrow, don't be here. I don't ever want to see you again."

She was gone and within two hours Pete's Suzuki had collided with a tree. He died at the scene, his body full of alcohol and amphetamines.

Tara checked her alarm again and it was still not 6.30am. She had by now given up any thought of sleep. Having intended to use her experience of overcoming adversity as fuel to propel her through the day ahead, she was in danger of unpicking old wounds. In doing so she threatened to imperil her new self, and all she had worked so hard to create.

You've been through enough shit to get here. This is who you are now. Strong, confident, powerful.

Say it often enough and you might believe it.

Pete was the only serious relationship she'd ever had. She remembered how she felt that first year after Pete died: guilty, grieving and once more alone. She was always fearful. She didn't want to get close to anyone, because the prospect of it turning bad, or of losing them, was too painful. So she kept her distance. That was until she met Ali.

Ali took all that fear away. As soon as she met her Tara felt safe, and held, and wanted. She had been crazy about Pete, but this was different. She realised that this was what love was.

Ali was older, nearly thirty, and had a blossoming career in publishing. Tara had never really thought about being gay, or straight, or bi. Maybe the damaging end of her relationship with Pete had made her wary of men. Looking back now, she realised that she didn't have the emotional maturity, or insight, to understand her sexuality. She had been drawn to Pete because he met her needs at the time, and then she loved Ali, because she did the same, but so much better.

As Tara thought of her now, she could still easily slip back into the tender warmth of those first years together, despite the trauma which was to follow. Ali made Tara the centre of her world. No week went by without a present, or some visible demonstration of her affection: roses, gig tickets, surprise lunches and dinners. On Tara's birthday, or Christmas, or Valentine's Day, her effort was multiplied tenfold. For the first three years Tara thought she was the luckiest woman on earth. Then things started to change.

Tara recognised that the relationship with Ali had helped her to keep a lid on her drink and drug use. She still took pills when clubbing, but rarely had weekend binges anymore, and her drinking was now on a par with all of their friends. Probably not within government guidelines, but nothing off the scale. Going out drinking and dancing was the first area where Tara and Ali had disagreements. Increasingly Ali would tell Tara they were staying in, or she would cut their nights out with friends short. Ali didn't like it when Tara went out without her and, as it was Ali who usually paid their rent, she could always point to the fact that Tara had it easy at her expense.

Before long Ali was putting her foot down. "You're at art school while I'm out earning, so we can live here, and when I come in, you want to piss off with your scummy student mates." It was easier for Tara to acquiesce than to upset Ali, so she soon dispensed with any thought of evenings out with her college friends.

Giving in didn't mean the matter was finished. In fact it seemed to encourage Ali to draw the circle tighter around Tara. Increasingly she knew all of Tara's movements, and decided who she could and couldn't see. She checked her phone and her bank account. By the end Tara felt she was losing any sense of self, as she had become an adjunct to Ali; able to do only what Ali would allow her to do. Five years into the relationship, at twenty five years old, Tara realised she had been stripped of her identity. She had no family and had become estranged from her friends and estranged from herself. All she had, and all she was, was Ali.

She reminded herself of the strength she had found to break free. In some residual vestige of self, that had not been obliterated, she had found a spark, which, with help, had become a flame, to enable her to navigate a path to a different life.

Ali had pushed her out the door in her nightdress, as a punishment for some minor infringement of the strict house rules, she had by then imposed. Tara sat freezing on the doorstep on a February night, when a passing police car stopped to check on her. Before Ali could usher her back in the door, the female police officer had got her name and slipped Tara her card, insisting that she call her the next day.

"I'm working from 4 o'clock. Tara, I want you to call me then."

There was something in the police officer's manner that made Tara want to call her. It was like she knew; like she understood everything that was happening to Tara.

Tara rang her and that chance encounter was the catalyst that enabled her to leave Ali and strike out on her own once more. This time Tara did it with a purpose, increasingly sure that she could be a functioning, independent adult. Ali didn't make it easy. Tara needed restraining orders and further support from the police to keep her at bay. She also needed weekly counselling to start to reassemble her identity, and to shape a life, which was not dependent on unhealthy substances or unhealthy relationships.

Three years later she had done the work she needed to do to join the police; inspired as she was by her chance encounter with the officer who had changed her life. For the last six years she had been totally dedicated to her profession, making her mark as an up and coming officer, already promoted to the rank of sergeant. In that time she had had nothing resembling a steady or emotionally intimate relationship. When she needed to, she knew where to go to have casual sex, with men or women, who didn't need to know your name or your job.

Now her lonely star appeared to have caught Tom Collins' eye. Tara felt a strong sense of ambivalence: a magnetic pull towards and a powerful push away. Collins was a man she knew was everything she should avoid; a recovering alcoholic in the midst of a messy divorce, someone who people intimated was a womaniser. That said, the more time she spent with him, the more she was drawn in. He was passionate, honest, and surprisingly vulnerable for someone who had a reputation as something of a maverick. This wasn't what Tara was looking for, but it was where she found herself. She wasn't sure whether she wanted a relationship, or if she was capable of maintaining a healthy one, but, for the first time in nine or more years, she felt like she wanted to be part of someone else's life.

Tara brought herself back to the challenge of the day ahead of her. It was time to get up and face whatever it was the Chilcotts would throw at her. She did so reminded that she had come so far. She was no longer that lost and frightened little girl who had blundered her way into her twenties. She was strong, independent and powerful.

Strong, independent and powerful. Go fuck him up, girl.

The self-talk and review of her arduous journey, that had brought her to this place, had served its purpose. She was ready to finish the job Tom Collins had started.

11.00am

It took Collins almost an hour to reach the top of the Ridge from his flat. He was tired from the activity of the night before, and was only running because he couldn't think of any other way to occupy himself, as he waited for Sharma's appointed time at the Chilcotts' to arrive. He had been pacing around his front room and needed to get out.

Collins had been debating with himself what to tell Tara about the night before at the Chilcotts'. What was there that was new and would make any difference to her visit? He decided to say nothing, rather than invite the impression he couldn't control his urge to intervene, despite instructions to the contrary. Acts of omission, often called neglect in Collins' profession; he had neglected to tell Tara the truth about what he had done, and where he had been last night. Perhaps Janet was right, he did want to have his cake and eat it.

His only contact with Tara was a message, confirming that he had sent the text to Carol, and wishing her good luck in her mission to the Chilcotts.

Collins took himself out to the viewing point on the Ridge and looked across to the Gartside. Not long now until Tara would be making her way out of Town towards those towers. He felt a sense of shame that he was keeping a secret from her on such a significant day, yet he told himself that her knowing what he had done would change nothing today. In time he would tell her, but right now, it all felt like an unnecessary complication. She needed to get the visit done and secure the letter. One thing at a time.

As he stared over the fields to the Gartside, a thought which he had known was floating at the back of his mind, bubbled to the front of his consciousness. It was an idea he had tried to fight off, but now started to entertain, as the time of Tara's appointment grew closer. Perhaps his success of the previous night had emboldened him. He was contemplating the idea Tara had dismissed and the one his bosses had strictly prohibited.

He could be there, outside the Chilcotts', at his watch post. The chances were that Tara would pick up the letter and be gone. There was no need for anyone to know he had been there, but, if it did turn nasty, he could at least be on hand. He accepted the conclusion his sub-conscious had clearly already reached; having come face to face with Chilcott, there was no way that Collins was going to sit tight at home, miles away from the action, while Tara faced into that house.

Collins figured that by running he could cover the ground to the Gartside in about forty-five minutes. Being without the car would make him less conspicuous. The idea was fast taking hold. Collins reached into the pocket of his hooded top and found the hat still there from last night. He knew it was no coincidence he had come equipped with his ready-made disguise; this idea had clearly been percolating beneath the surface for some time.

Collins stopped himself and considered how Tara would view his decision to ignore her direction to leave it to her to get the job done. This was a breach of trust. Collins mused on it. What was the greater or lesser evil? If some ill did befall her at the hands of Chilcott, how would he view his inaction then? He told himself that to go was for the greater good, yet, he could still hear his rational brain holding firm, telling him that what he was considering was reckless in the extreme.

He couldn't resist. Couldn't stop himself. The impulsive side of his nature had won out again and he was going to the Gartside.

11.40am

Collins made rapid progress downhill, propelled by the surge of energy unleashed by his decision to go to the Chilcotts'. As he ran past the three vertiginous towers, he felt his stomach contracting, as it had in Andrews' office two days earlier, at the prospect of what lay ahead. Was it really only two days? He thought of all that had happened in that time, all that had changed for himself and Tara, to get them to this point. To where the woman he loved was about to walk in, alone, to the lair of a violent sex offender.

"The woman he loved," that was the first time he had admitted it to himself. Perhaps it was better to say "the woman he wanted to love", because it felt so embryonic, so untested, and would perhaps be unrequited.

This time he approached Gartside Gardens from the park side, so as not to have to pass the front of the house. He realised, as he made his way down the back alley, his perch of the night before would be too visible to occupants of the house in daylight, and he would have to secrete himself away. He lowered his head beneath the height of the fence, as he passed the Chilcotts' back gate. Looking across the alley he saw the bile he had brought up the night before, after his encounter with Chilcott. It reminded him he wasn't the action hero he had imagined, as he had run from the Ridge. He was just a social worker, who suddenly felt out of his element.

Shit. What the hell are you doing here?

Collins realised he was in too deep and the stakes were too high, but he was here now, and Tara was about to knock on that door any minute. He would need to make sure he was ready for whatever came next.

11.55am

As Tara drove past the precinct she saw the squad car positioned as expected. Pulling alongside, she wound down her window and gave her instructions.

"I'm going in at twelve on the dot. You wait at the end of Gartside Gardens. Make sure you're well out of sight of number eighty-four. If I need you, I'll be straight on the radio. If I'm not out by twelve-thirty, there's a problem."

She knew from her briefing at the police station there were other units close by, if they were required, and she had been issued with her full quota of protective equipment.

Tara proceeded to Gartside Gardens, and parked her Polo across the road from number eighty-four. She breathed deeply to try to dispel the nervous tension she felt throughout her body, as she anxiously contemplated what lay ahead. The dispiriting exterior of the house further sapped her enthusiasm for what awaited her inside.

"You can do this," she repeated to herself. "Get in and get out."

She checked her watch. It was twelve. The time had come.

Around the back of the house, Collins had positioned himself on a low wall in the alley behind the Chilcotts' back fence. He heard the knock on the door and knew that Tara was going in. For once the door opened immediately, as if, this time, all had been prepared in advance for the visit. He heard the door being closed and knew that Tara was inside: sucked into the rotting shell of a house, at whose dark centre, Alex Chilcott was waiting.

Collins was left to stare again at the back of the house, this time through a broken fence panel. He viewed a crisp packet caught on the wayward grass below the kitchen window, and wondered how the scene was playing out in the Chilcotts' front room.

12.00pm

Tara Sharma had been in many houses, on the estate and in Town, that had made her stomach turn. Places no human should have to live: the homes of the worst alcoholics, doss houses and crack dens; left to rot, like the addicts who inhabited them. As bad as they were, none of those places had the overwhelming weight of sadness that permeated every corner of the Chilcotts' front room; hanging like an oppressive miasma, clinging to her skin and seeping into her lungs.

Overlaid on the sadness was a pervasive sense of fear. She saw it in Carol's twitching features, and felt it crackling around the room. She looked towards the kitchen door, and could feel the presence on the other side, feel the sinister ooze creeping under the door. Carol's eyes followed Sharma's towards the kitchen, and she gave a small nod, to confirm that Alex was on the other side. Her eyes met Sharma's; in her face the police officer saw pain written on every line. She also saw a plea for help and knew that this was not a set up. Carol wanted her help to get out.

Having done the introductions on the front step, Sharma got down to official business for the benefit of the listening Alex Chilcott.

"So, Mrs Chilcott, as I said, Tom isn't able to be here today, so I've been asked to step in and pick up where he left off."

As she said this, she produced a note pad from her bag and revealed the front page to Carol. She showed the message in bold, 'HAVE YOU GOT THE LETTER?'

"I've got nothing more to say. I've explained everything to that Mr Collins. If he wants to take us to court, he'll have to do it."

As Carol said this, she nodded and pointed to the top of her jeans, indicating the letter was secreted on her person.

"Carol, as I'm sure Tom explained, no one wants to take you to court, or take the children into care, but if you won't work with us, what are we supposed to do? We keep getting reports of abuse in the home and concerns about your husband's behaviour outside of the home. We really haven't got any choice."

Sharma made a beckoning hand signal to Carol, encouraging her to hand the letter over.

A noise from the kitchen startled Carol and she let out a small whimper. Sharma held her hand out, her eyes now urgently beseeching Carol to produce the letter.

"Carol give us what we need, so we know you are taking the children's safety seriously." Sharma continued filling the silence, as Carol was obviously struggling to speak.

Carol managed to find some words.

"I love those kids, surely you people know that? And they love me."

She looked hard into Sharma's eyes as she said it, fumbling beneath her top and the front of her trousers, to produce the letter.

"I love them and they love me, do you get that?"

Now both women had a hand on the letter, and Carol wasn't going to let go until she had an acknowledgement from Sharma that she understood the importance of what she was saying. Carol wanted to make a deal.

"I can assure you Carol, if you demonstrate you can work with us to keep the children safe, then there is no reason why you should be separated from them."

"You promise me?"

"Carol". Sharma didn't know what she could say to make her let go. "Okay but you've got to play your part."

Finally Carol let go of the letter, and Sharma hastily put it on top of the notepad she was still holding.

At that moment the door from the kitchen flew open.

There stood Alex Chilcott, filling the door frame, eyes ablaze and fists clenched. His biceps were taut, as if he had already been pummelling a punch bag in anticipation of this moment. This was the Alex Chilcott that Sharma remembered from Gartside Park, with every bit of menace he had displayed then. Now, though, he had the manic air of a man who was beyond his own control.

"You scheming bitches. I know what you're up to. You dirty, scheming cows. You want to take her and those kids away", he said jabbing a finger in the direction of Sharma's face.

"And you, you stupid, ugly, cunt, think you can go with her," he said turning his frame to loom over his cowering wife.

"It ain't happenin' like that."

Sharma closed her notepad with the letter in it, and moved her hand to her radio.

"Don't touch that!" Alex Chilcott shouted at her. As he did so he produced a six inch hunting knife, which had been tucked in his back pocket.

"Put the radio down."

He took a step forward and extended his arm with the blade in his hand towards Sharma. She threw the radio on the sofa behind her; putting her palms up to demonstrate her cooperation.

"Yeah keep your hands up, where I can see them."

He stared hard into her face, seeming to slowly realise that he and Sharma had met before.

"So it's you. Aren't I the lucky boy? You've come to get what you should have got five years ago."

As he said this his tongue poked out to lick his top lip and he put his free hand on his crotch.

"I bet you still think about that night and what you missed out on. I do."

Chilcott turned to his wife.

"You, I'll deal with you after, you conniving bitch. Get upstairs, while I sort your new friend out."

"I didn't do anything wrong Al, I was just trying to get rid of her," Carol moaned.

"Shut it, bitch, and get upstairs. Make sure you put the locks and chain on the front door on the way up. All of them. I'm watching you."

Carol hurried out the door to the bottom of the stairs, and left Sharma to face Chilcott alone.

Tara gathered herself and stared at Chilcott defiantly.

"There are police officers at the end of your road, who have been told to force their way in her if I'm not straight out. You're going to be arrested, so put the knife down. Don't add any more charges to the list."

"One more won't hurt. Well, not me it won't," Chilcott said, tilting the bulge in his jeans in Tara's direction.

"Anyway I don't think there's police outside about to break the door down. When your boys in blue do eventually come looking for you, it will be too late for you, and that bitch upstairs."

Tara could feel her heart pounding. Every second seemed to last an eternity. She was beyond being able to rationally consider her options, all she could think to do was to try to keep Chilcott talking.

"They'll be here any moment, and you won't have fucked me; because I'm not going to let you, and you won't have killed me, or your wife, or anyone else; because I'm not going to let you do that either."

"Haaa" Chilcott let out a frenzied bellow. She could see the vein on the side of his head protruding and pulsing furiously.

"I don't think you're in a position to stop me. I'll do exactly what I want to do. To you, to her, to them."

He spoke deliberately, certain of his right and his ability to do exactly as he pleased. Chilcott took a step towards her, and started to pull at the buckle of his jeans to loosen his belt.

There was no way that Sharma was going to let him do this to her. One more step towards her and he would be within her striking range. She would rather take her chance, and hope her stab vest protected her, while trying to take him down, than be raped.

Chilcott stopped, as if having re-considered his options.

"No need to rush. Let's have some fun." The tip of his tongue hovered between his front teeth as he deliberated.

"Think I'll tie you up. We'll enjoy it even more that way."

He held the knife closer to Sharma's face and motioned for her to lead the way into the kitchen. He pushed her towards the back kitchen door, with the knife pressed against her back, as he rifled through drawers to get the equipment he needed. Soon enough he had rope, gaffer tape and scissors. Ominously he had also removed pliers, a hammer and a mallet from the drawer. Clearly this was the type of equipment he liked to have close at hand.

Chilcott pushed Tara to the floor, and with his considerable weight on her back, proceeded to tape her wrists together and then her ankles.

"Hope you didn't forget to bring your hand-cuffs. We might get them out later and have some fun. This will have to do for now, to shut you up and stop you doing anything silly."

He went to cut one more strip of tape for her mouth. As he did so, he looked out the kitchen window and saw the vigilante, who had been outside his gate the previous night, scaling his back fence.

12.10pm

Carol put the locks and chain on the door, and made her way up the stairs, as instructed by her husband. She knew that Alex didn't plan to let her, or the police officer, leave the house alive. She knew she needed to do something, but her fear-frozen brain could find no way to safety for her, the police officer, or her son, who awaited her at the top of the stairs.

Daniel was hunched against the landing wall with his head in his hands. He knew his longed for escape with his mother had been thwarted, and now the options had narrowed again for them all. He looked up at his mother as she approached.

"I've got to kill him."

"No son, he'll kill you." Carol said it with certainty. She had a foreboding that this day would end with either her or Daniel dead. Now that looked the way it might be for both of them. She needed to think.

"Come on, think woman," she berated herself.

Carol knew that she would have no chance of opening the double locks and chain on the front door without Alex being alerted. She made her way to her bedroom, and Daniel pushed himself up to follow. The only window in the upstairs of the house that opened, was the four-inch wide panel at the top of her bedroom window frame. There was no climbing out of it, but it was at least an opening to the outside world. She might be able raise the alarm if a passer-by saw her.

Her greatest wish was that Collins had again made it his business to watch the house, as he had the previous night, but she knew this was desperate, wishful thinking.

Carol pushed back the net curtains and forced open the narrow window. She sucked in a lung-full of the scented early summer breeze, which contrasted so starkly with the stale air of the bedroom. She thought she could make out a shape pressed against the hole in the back fence. She waved furiously from her small aperture to get the person's attention.

Collins had been crouched nervously peering through the cracked back fence, trying to hear for the sound of Tara leaving the house, or for the noises from inside, that meant she couldn't. He had heard nothing until the window opened, and he saw Carol's arm waving frantically, and saw her face and Daniel's pushed against the pane, beckoning for help.

He rose from behind the fence.

Immediately they recognised him, even in the hat and hoody he had worn to provide some disguise.

"It's him, it's Collins," Daniel said, hope once more evident in his voice. "That's the top he wears for football. He's come to save us."

Carol pulled her son to her and held him.

"Let's hope so Dan."

They opened the bedroom door and edged out to the landing to listen.

12.15pm

"Come on fucker. Come and try it and I'll kill you as well," Chilcott said, as Collins made his way through the garden towards the kitchen.

Chilcott dragged the now bound Tara to her feet. He slowly turned the key in the back door that led to the garden path, pulling Tara with him to shelter behind the cupboard, adjacent to the back door. His knife was pressed to her throat, with the mallet in his free hand.

"Not a sound now," Chilcott whispered menacingly. "Not a sound."

Tara watched with horror as the door slowly opened, when Collins tried the handle. Chilcott had unlocked the door because he wanted him inside.

As Collins entered the kitchen, Tara shouted, "Tom!". Turning sharply to face her, he saw Chilcott's mallet rapidly approaching the side of his head. Collins managed to get half a hand in front of his face to reduce the full impact of the blow, but, nonetheless, it was enough to immediately fell him, and leave him face down on the kitchen floor in a semi-conscious state.

Chilcott got to work on tying Collins up with rope and tape, dragging him into the front room on a kitchen chair before doing the same with Tara.

In the front room Chilcott surveyed his prey. Sharma's eyes angrily held his stare, while Collins fought to retain consciousness, his head repeatedly lolling forward, only kept on the chair by the rope which tied him to it.

"Well isn't this quite a get together? The vigilante piece of shit turns out to be a social worker who wants to be a fucking hero."

Chilcott snorted with disdain as he looked again at Sharma. "Some hero he turned out to be?"

Chilcott went over to Collins and grabbed a handful of hair in order to pull his head upright.

"Worried about your little friend here, were you? Worried what I might do to her?" Chilcott hissed derisively.

"Well, now you can watch what I'm going to do to her. Watch as I fuck her every which way. Watch her pain and my fucking pleasure, and it will be the last thing you see, because then I'm going to kill you. Then I'm going to fuck her some more and I'm going to kill her too. That's the plan super-hero, so let's get started shall we?"

Chilcott let go of Collins hair, leaving his head to slump forward again.

Tara surveyed the room. Her radio and jacket were only five feet away, but she would need to work her hands free before either would be any good to her. She dug her nails into the tape around her wrists and it yielded a little, enough to encourage her to keep on picking.

Chilcott walked towards the chair on which Tara was tied. He used his knife to flick at the buttons of her shirt, almost grazing her chin with the point of the blade. As he did so, he cut off a button to expose the flash of her black bra.

"This is going to be good," Chilcott said, sneering as he came close to Tara's face and looked leeringly down at her cleavage.

The mania appeared to have subsided, and now Chilcott had assumed a calculating and callous demeanour, taking time to ensure he savoured this fulfilment of the desires he had incubated for so long.

Chilcott stood over Tara with his knife still in his left hand, while he started to work again at the belt of his jeans. She could see the bulge of his crotch close to her face.

"Yeah, this is going to be good," he repeated into her ear. "Going to need to open your legs though." As he said this he cut the tape that bound Tara's ankles together.

At that moment Tara saw the living room door behind Chilcott open. First through the door was Daniel, brandishing his bowie knife, with his mother right behind him.

Chilcott turned and looked incredulously over his shoulder.

"What the fuck is this?" he snarled.

Carol and Daniel kept coming towards the centre of the room. Daniel with his knife in front of him, pointed towards his father.

Carol spoke with a calm determination, which seemed out of place in the midst of the chaotic scene.

"It's finished Alex. You're not doing this to us anymore, and you're not doing it to her, or anyone else. You're a sick, evil man, and it's over."

"Shut it, you silly bitch, I'm just getting started. As for you, you little queer, tied to your mummy's apron strings. Drop the knife before you hurt yourself. Who do you think you are?"

He glared at his wife and son with an intensified menace, "I own you, I will always own you. You're pathetic, you're nothing."

Daniel took a step towards his father. Rather than being terrified, now the moment of this longed for confrontation had finally arrived, he felt strong. He felt alive. The words came loud and clear, as he spat them towards his father's face.

"No, you're nothing. We're free of you. We are going to have a life. A life without you."

Alex Chilcott let out a roar which seemed to summon forth all the demons in hell. A howl filled with hate and rage, which had accumulated over a lifetime. He lunged towards Daniel, intent on plunging his knife into his son's heart. As he did so, the boy jumped out of the way, deflecting his father's knife, unbalancing the older man.

Sharma saw her chance and dug her nails deep into the fraying tape, freeing her tied hands to split apart and wriggling free from the rope around her middle. She leapt towards the sofa and her jacket pocket, pulling out the taser she had been issued that morning. Instantaneously she fired it at Alex Chilcott. As he thrust again towards his son, he jerked to a halt. She continued to pull the trigger to send pulses of electric current through Chilcott's torso, until he folded to the floor.

Daniel stood over the shaking body with his knife still brandished. His eyes were wild now, and his contorted face suggested he hadn't finished with this knife fight.

"No Daniel, don't do it!" Sharma shouted. As she did so, Carol rushed to grab him, pulling him tight to her. They stood holding each other and tears, drawn from a deep well of shared pain, started to steadily flow. Mother held son and son held mother, as they sobbed on each other's shoulders, the knife still clasped in Daniel's right hand.

Sharma cuffed Chilcott and went to the front room window, ripping at the net curtains. She signalled to the officers in the response car, which had just pulled up outside, to get into the house. She carried on tearing down the nets and pushed the windows open, determined to at last get light and air into the room.

Sharma went over to where Collins was bound to the chair. She ripped the tape that secured his arms and legs, and untied the rope. He was now fully conscious but clearly still in pain.

"You okay?" Sharma queried.

"Yeah, I'll live."

He looked up at her as he said it, recognising neither of them could have been certain of that a few minutes earlier.

"I think we got more than we needed. This piece of filth will be inside for a long time," she said looking over to the still twitching body on the floor.

Tara moved to take the knife from Daniel. As she did so she trod on the newspapers, which had been strewn across the floor in the course of the knife fight. A lurid headline about a teenage abduction stood out amongst the open pages. Carol saw where Sharma's eyes had been drawn.

"He kept all the ones that had stories about murders, and rapes, and that stuff," she said managing to stem the flow of her tears. "That was why he collected them."

Carol nodded down at her husband.

"If you go in his back pocket, there's a key. The key opens the little cupboard in the wall behind his armchair. I've never looked in there, never wanted to, but I know it's where he keeps his other collection. I'm sure they'll be plenty to interest you in there."

Sharma reached into Alex Chilcott's back pocket and found a small silver key. As she did so, the response officers entered the room, radios crackling.

"All under control lads. Get this bloke out of here. He's been tasered so follow the protocols. He needs to be arrested for attempted rape, false imprisonment and GBH, and that's just for starters. We're going to need an ambulance too."

Tara pushed the heavy black leather armchair aside to reveal a padlocked door, no more than eighteen inches high, in the living room wall. She undid the padlock and opened the door. Looking inside she could see there was an assortment of female underwear, along with bracelets and rings and other personal effects. She used the aerial on her radio to hook items out into the light. The first piece of underwear she pulled out was a pair of pink knickers with an angel on the front.

"A sex offender's treasure trove. I bet this lot accounts for dozens of unsolved or unreported crimes."

She looked across at Daniel and Carol.

"Well done, both of you. That was so brave. He'll be going to prison for a long, long time. If there's any justice it will be forever, once we've sorted through this little lot."

She looked into each of their shocked faces, and saw what it meant to them both, that their tormentor had finally been caught.

Tara smiled at mother and son, as they continued to cling on to each other.

"You're right, it's over. Time to start living."

1.20pm

Collins and Sharma both sat in the back of the ambulance. Collins was adamant he didn't need to be taken to A&E, but Tara and the paramedics were trying to persuade him otherwise.

Collins' head ached from the mallet's blow but, beyond the pain, he felt he had recovered his wits, and now just wanted to go home and lie down.

"Go with them Tom. You could have a fractured skull for all you know," Tara encouraged him. "I'll come and see you later, when I've downloaded what just happened in there to someone down at the station."

Finally he relented. The thought that she might come and visit him, or maybe pick him up from hospital, was enough inducement to break his resistance. He looked at her apologetically, unsure how the land now lay between them, after his breach of trust, and their shared experience at the hands of Alex Chilcott. That she was willing to come and get him offered some hope that he hadn't totally ruined their relationship.

He turned again to Tara. She looked weary, now that the drama was done, but characteristically she was soldiering on.

"I need to get in touch with Greta too and confirm the arrangements for her interview. The good thing is that it should be a bit easier for her now, knowing that Chilcott will already be charged and on remand, before she has to give evidence."

Collins wanted her to slow down, and admit the significance of what had just happened.

"Give yourself a break Tara. That's scary stuff we've just been through. Don't act like it didn't happen."

She gave him a tired smile and a shrug of the shoulders.

"I will. I will," she said, trying to muster some conviction. "Just some things to tidy up first."

Collins gave up, recognising he wasn't going to get anywhere trying to tell Tara how to manage her life. He also knew he was on thin ice, having ignored her instructions to stay away from the Chilcotts'.

Collins looked at Carol's letter on the trolley in the ambulance next to him. This, together with the trophies in the safe, gave them enough to multiply convict Chilcott of crimes against her, and out on the estate and in the park. Collins was reminded of the other letter, and wanted to know if Tara was any the wiser as to its origin, as a result of their encounter with Chilcott.

"So do you think this whole thing was a trap set for you?" he asked her.

"No, he didn't have a clue who I was at first. He didn't write the letter about you to trap me. Doesn't mean he couldn't have written the letter, but I suppose it makes it less likely, especially as Carol came through with hers."

Collins thought on it.

"It seems I've got some tidying up to do myself," he said, without enthusiasm.

"If Chilcott didn't write the letter about me, my money is on it being Janet. I feel stupid now at not seeing it earlier, as soon as we worked out it wasn't an internal job."

He considered what it all meant for his future.

"For my own satisfaction I'd like confirmation it was her, but proving it might also be the only way I'm ever going to clear my name at work."

"Don't go making things worse for yourself, Tom," Sharma said with a concern he found touching. As she got up to leave the ambulance he said what he had wanted to say since they got out of the Chilcotts'.

"Tara, I'm sorry, I know what you said, but I just couldn't stay away. Sometimes I just can't stop myself... It's something I've got to work on. That was terrifying in there, but you did an amazing job. We've finally got him. You should be really proud of yourself."

"Just finishing off what you'd started."

She turned and gently put her hand on his forearm.

"We could be a good team, just don't ever go behind my back again."

It was a small gesture, but one which filled him with hope there might be something to build on for the future.

7.15pm

Janet opened the door. He was struck by her tan, probably sprayed on, but still effective in giving her a healthy glow. Her clothes looked expensive: tight fitting designer jeans, topped by a shirt with colourful hand-stitched embroidery. Her dark bobbed hair looked as if it had just been cut and dyed. It was the best she had looked in a long time, certainly in the time since they had separated, or in the last bitter years that they were together.

"Five minutes and then you're gone. This had better be good."

He had rung after Tara had dropped him home, having had the all clear from the hospital. Tara had declined the offer to come in, but he had taken heart from her continued interest in his well-being and willingness to collect him. Collins guessed from Janet's agreement to let him come over and speak to her, she must already have been made aware, through her networks, that he had been suspended. He imagined she would want to revel in the moment of his humiliation at her hands, but now he could no longer blame her.

"Can I come in?" Janet reluctantly turned so he could follow her off the doorstep and into the front room.

The room had changed from the last time he was in here, nearly two years ago. Thick new curtains hung on the window, and the sofa and chairs looked like they had not long arrived. The walls had also recently been painted. Collins felt a strange contrast between familiarity, having spent so many years in this house, and novelty as a result of its makeover. He hated that he was now a stranger in what had been his home. It made a mockery of all the years he had spent here. No doubt Janet would say it was him who had made a mockery of all that.

Collins looked at her across the table. Janet was making a statement to the world that she was better now, there were no regrets, no looking back, she was going to seize the day. He was pleased she appeared to be moving on. For such a long time there had been a lifelessness to her eyes, which spoke of a degree of suffering that had numbed her to new pain, but equally to the chance of new joy. Now he could see the spark had returned. He speculated to himself about what might have changed. He knew it was no longer his concern, but took comfort that, who or whatever it was, Janet was clearly on the way back up.

Knowing that the clock was ticking, Collins got straight to the purpose of his visit.

"There's two things I've come to say. The first, is the most important, and it's that I'm sorry. I've never admitted to myself, or to you, how bad things got in the end. I behaved appallingly. I can see it clearly now. The way I treated you makes me feel sick and I am so sorry."

Janet continued to look impassively across the table at him. If this was an unexpected turn of events, she wasn't letting on.

"Okay. It's a start I suppose. It doesn't change the past, doesn't change what you did, but it's a start. What was the other thing?"

"I know you wrote the letter to my work, and I wanted you to know that I don't blame you. Can we draw a line under all this? This being crap to each other? Can we get on with being the best parents to Jamie that we can?"

Janet looked like she wasn't at all surprised by her husband's accusation, but was not about to admit to being the letter writer either.

"I haven't written any letter about you. Christ, I've been tempted but you're not worth it. Do you really think I'm that bothered? I really have left any thoughts of you behind a long time ago."

So she wasn't going to admit it. Collins hadn't wanted to have to lay out the charge, but felt he now had no choice.

"Look, do we really have to go through how I know you wrote it? I've spoken to Jonesy, who says he knows that you and Marie have been planning something like this. There was nothing in that letter that you couldn't have known. At least admit you know I was suspended, because of an anonymous letter?"

"Yes, I've only just found out you're suspended, and I thought it was hilarious, but that doesn't mean I wrote the letter," she snapped back.

Collins was trying to remain passive in the face of Janet's denial. He had come here to apologise and to try to make a fresh start, but now he was finding it hard to moderate his tone.

"Come on Janet, you and your mate have clearly cooked this up together, but it was you who wrote it. I recognise your style, even down to the grammar. Can you just admit it and we can move on?"

Janet wasn't backing down though. In fact she seemed to want to up the ante.

"You come in here with your supposed apology, and then the next minute you're calling me a liar. You've got some front. You of all people. There's only one dishonest creep in this room and it's you. Yes I've dreamed of seeing you humiliated." Janet was gathering steam now and had plenty that she had been wanting to say to Collins for a long time.

"I've dreamed of seeing you made a fool of, just like you made a fool out of me, for all the years we were married. All those stinking, futile years, when you got pissed, and came home when you felt like it. Yes I've written letters. I've written more letters than I could count about you, but I've never sent them. I've got it out of my system, and I left the letters to rot on my hard drive; and do you know why I didn't send any of those letters?"

"Go on then, you may as well tell me for what it's worth."

Her pious act only made Collins more convinced than ever that she had written the letter, but in view of his avowed contrition, he would have to take what she wanted to throw at him.

"I'll tell you why not, because I was too concerned for what it might do to Jamie. If you were sacked or disgraced, you'd probably just crawl off somewhere, and he'd never hear from you again. Unlike you I put my child first. He's been through enough, and didn't need another scandal to turn his world upside down. You'll have to look somewhere else for your letter writer."

Collins could hold back no longer.

"Your child, listen to yourself. How pompous, you supercilious cow. That boy would have been all right if you hadn't poisoned him against me. Other families split up, and it doesn't end up like this, but you couldn't bear that could you? It's not about Jamie, it's not even about me, it's all about you. You can't stand to see me making a life on my own without you, can you?"

His speech was seeped in the bitterness he felt for the position he found himself in.

"Well done. You've made sure that I can't be happy, but you've done it by making sure our son can't be happy either."

"Fuck you, you've brought this on yourself, you're the one who's destroyed this family, not me," Janet fired back.

"You're a fantasist and a liar and the best thing I ever did was leave you."

Now Collins was really struggling to maintain any semblance of self-control. He had come here to try to draw a line under the past, and yet, they were back where they had been two years earlier, tearing each other apart.

"Get out and stay away from here," she was shouting now, and the spark he had seen in her eyes had now become a blaze.

"I'm going, but you know the truth," Collins shouted back, spitting the words across the table.

"Stop!" Jamie screeched from the doorway.

In his hand he held an A4 piece of paper. He walked across to the table and pushed it towards his father.

"I sent it. It was one of mum's, on her computer. I didn't have to change too much, but I sent it."

Collins looked at the sheet of paper. It was the letter. It was the one, an exact copy of what Andrews had shown him two days earlier. To see it here and have it handed to him by his son felt so wrong. It was as if two parallel worlds had become entwined, and the barrier between them breached. Collins looked from the letter to Jamie and then to his mother. He looked for someone to offer some explanation.

All he could manage to utter, as he looked into his son's guileless face, was "why?"

Jamie spoke quietly, but with a composed self-assurance.

"Because I wanted you to feel like I felt when you left. I wanted you to feel as hurt as I did."

His dark brown eyes cut into Collins, as he summoned forth the pain of the last two years.

"When I saw you with that Chilcott boy in the park, saw you laughing and playing football with him, I felt sick after all you'd done to us. That's when I went on mum's computer and found the letter, and added his name and Mickey Johnson's, and some other stuff in there. I thought if mum wouldn't send the letter, then I would."

"The things in there are so awful," Collins said, looking down at the letter.

"Do you really hate me that much?"

He looked up at Jamie as he waited for an answer, but looked down again as he realised what was coming.

"Yes I do hate you. I hate you for what you've done and the way you've treated us."

Collins felt that anvil at the centre of his being once again. Now he no longer felt it as pushing his heart out of its place, but that this heavy lump of metal had replaced his heart completely. Laid bare by his son's raw hurt he stood in front of them now, like the Tin Man, incapable of loving or of being loved.

But then Jamie threw out a lifeline.

"I hate you but I know it's not all hate. You're my dad."

Less assured now, he was starting to struggle to order his thoughts in words.

"I thought, I thought if you felt what you'd made us feel, when you left us behind, that you'd understand. I thought if you were broken down, like we were broken down and had no job, you might need us again."

He paused, struggling to let go of the words he had been holding on to for so long.

"I thought you might come home."

Jamie had grown up so much, he was becoming a mature and confident teenager, yet he still retained the simple childish belief that everything could be made right, everything could be put back together, just as it was.

The silence that followed was heavy with sorrow, alive with hurt. Collins couldn't summon a response that could in any way do justice to Jamie's outpouring. He wanted to defend himself, to try to explain again why it was better for him and Janet to live apart, but such rationalisations felt futile now. Nor could he feel angry any more about the attempt to destroy his reputation and career. Now he knew Jamie had sent the letter, he couldn't really blame him, inspired as he had been by a mix of hurt and hope.

Finally, Collins found some words. Not words of defence or denial, not words that he thought could take the pain away, but words that he hoped would build a bridge to a future which would be a little less painful.

"I do need you. I will always need you. I'm so sorry for the hurt I've caused. I never meant that, believe me."

He looked into Jamie's eyes and, as he averted them, he looked at Janet.

"I didn't think it would be like this. I thought things would be difficult for a while, but that they'd settle down, and we'd be like we used to be, when you were younger. I understand now how difficult it is for that to happen. I really don't know what to do. We can't recreate the past, but we can't go on tearing away at each other like this."

He thought on the situation and tried to find a way forward.

"You've sent your letter now. I've been humiliated. Can we move on from here? Can we put a line under it, and start to be like other families who have a mum and dad who live apart? I've got my flat and you can stay over, we could do family things with your mum if she wants; it doesn't have to be all about the past and what's gone."

Jamie capped off the conversation, capturing the essential dilemma that he and his mother faced, and summed up Collins' hopes of making a workable future with them.

"Yeah, we can play at being a happy family, but we don't know who you are. We don't trust you dad."

Collins didn't know where to go after that. He apologised

to them both again. Said sorry to Jamie if he had thought he had deserted him. He said he would make sure he never felt like that again.

"Please, we can take it slowly and build the trust again. Please give me a chance."

There was little more he could say. He told Jamie that he loved him and left.

FRIDAY 25TH MAY

4.30pm

Collins and Sharma were outside eighty-four Gartside Gardens again, a week after Alex Chilcott had been hauled away in handcuffs, to start what would inevitably be a very long stretch in prison.

Collins was back in work. Andrews had expedited the investigation once it had become clear that Jamie had written the letter. In view of what he described as a "complicated set of circumstances," Andrews was content that Collins be given a verbal warning for disobeying the directive regarding the Chilcotts and the Gartside. Collins felt, once again, Andrews and Campbell had preferred the path which created least fuss, in order to avoid added scrutiny of the Chilcott case, but he was just glad to have his job back.

Despite being fully exonerated in relation to the anonymous allegation, walking back in from suspension was tough. He had been grateful of the warm reception from colleagues, led as expected by Stan Bowles.

"Tommo, I've missed you my boy. This place isn't the same without your charm, and looks, and tea making ability."

Stan raised his empty mug for Collins to fill, as he continued to eulogise.

"Perverts we're coming for you. Tommo is back on the beat!"

Collins was in need of this affirmation, as he was still reeling from the revelation that Jamie had sent the anonymous letter. Despite numerous attempts to call and text, messages to Jamie's phone had been ignored in the intervening week, and Collins carried about his loss like a dull ache.

Now Collins and Sharma were back on the Gartside. He was on the phone to Damon to confirm the details of their new relationship, before sharing this with Carol and Daniel.

"So Damon, you're happy to do the safeguarding course and all the other training and risk assessments that go with being a volunteer with children?"

"Absolutely mate, I'm made up about it. It's like Fagin going legit. A mentor, it sounds properly official. I'll be on the pay roll soon enough."

"Maybe Damon. In time," Collins replied.

"I could do with a proper job with a baby on the way."

"Have you? Congratulations, that's wonderful news."

Collins expressed his delight at hearing Damon was going to be a father, even if this was tempered in his mind by the knowledge of how tough a job it would inevitably be for him. It had been hard enough for Collins, with his steady job and many of the advantages that Damon lacked, but perhaps that wasn't the be all and end all. Damon could well be a far better father than Collins had managed to be.

"Yeah remember we saw you on the way out to the health clinic," Damon explained. "It wasn't a drug test, it was an early pregnancy scan. There's no going back from here. I'm going to have to be squeaky clean, an upstanding member of the community, if I'm going to be a dad and a mentor."

"You'll be great at both, Damon, and I'm sure Daniel will be delighted to be your first official client. See you next week to sign the forms."

Collins ended the call and smiled at Tara.

"Sometimes it's a marathon not a sprint, eh? I think Damon's finally just about there now. How's Greta doing?"

"She'll get there too, no doubt. I think she could do with her own Damon, but until we find one, she'll have to make do with me. Not sure it's my job, but you know what it's like once you make a commitment to a kid, you can't walk away."

He knew exactly what she meant.

Collins looked out at the curtains flapping in the Chilcott's open front room window. "Are they new?" he asked.

"Yeah, we raided the welfare fund to get some bits for the house, and the council have been in to do a deep clean. They'll help Carol to get a move out, if that's what she wants, but, while they're here, we've got to help them make it as different from before as possible."

Before he got out of the car Collins checked the incoming message on his phone and smiled.

Noticing his small grin, Tara probed as to the cause.

"Nice to see you smiling. Care to share?"

"Later. Come on, I've been looking forward to this visit. The start of a new chapter for Carol and Dan and the kids."

Collins realised it was the first time he had got out of the car here with any sense of enthusiasm for what lay ahead. Carol was quick to open the door. From behind her came the sound of the little ones playing in the front room.

"Both of the dynamic duo. I'm honoured. Come in and see my new house."

As Tara passed Carol in the doorway, they gave each other a little hug, bonded as they now were by their shared experience the previous week. Carol had a lightness about her that Collins had never seen before.

"I've just got the twins and Daniel here. Crystal is out playing with friends."

The twins sat on a neat little red sofa. Collins guessed it had been donated by one of his colleagues, or paid for from the welfare fund. The old black leather armchair was gone, as were all of the piles of newspapers, replaced now by toys and pictures of Carol and the children. The fetid cave, that had been the front room, had been transformed by the introduction of natural light from the unmasked windows. The gentle breeze blowing the curtains carried the scent of newly made summer into the room.

Collins wanted to shout with joy, but instead contented himself with smiling benignly, as Carol pointed out all the little improvements she had made in the preceding week. He knew she was eager to demonstrate that, free from her husband, she was a suitable parent, but, nonetheless, she did seem genuinely transformed from the woman who had so resisted his involvement in the previous weeks.

"We best go in the kitchen and leave these two to play," she said, with her pride in the change in her two youngest children evident on her face.

The three of them took a seat at the kitchen table, which had now been covered in a brightly patterned tablecloth, matched by the colourful tea towels hanging by the sink.

"The place looks so different Carol, you've done an amazing job" Collins said.

Carol thought for a minute before answering.

"No, you two did an amazing job, and I know I didn't help you. Thank you for not giving up. You've given us a chance of a life we never would have had."

She looked close to tears as she said it but lost none of her new found joy.

Tara answered for herself and Collins.

"You needed the courage to write that letter Carol, and you and Daniel had the courage to come to our rescue. You're a strong woman. You'll need to stay strong in the coming months and years. What you've all been through is going to take some recovering from, you'll need to use all the help that's on offer."

"And you'll give me a chance to help them get better?" Collins heard anxiety in her voice for the first time.

"A chance to be the mum I wanted to be for them?"

He was quick to offer her reassurance.

"The kids have been through a lot Carol, you all have, but it's obvious that the best way for them to recover is to be with you, and for you all to heal together. I know that's what Daniel wants, and I'm sure it's the same for all of them. If you keep working with us, and show us you can keep them safe, then why would we want your children anywhere else but with you?"

At that moment, Daniel entered the kitchen, looking embarrassed at having intruded. Collins welcomed him warmly.

"Dan, it's so good to see you and in your school uniform. That's every day you've managed to stay there this week. Keep it up, and let me know if there's any problems with the other kids, or with the teachers, and I'm sure we can get them sorted."

In view of his father's very public arrest and remand into custody, the fact that Daniel had made it to school for the week was all the more remarkable.

Daniel blushed slightly and smiled. Collins helped him out.

"Damon has said he would like to be your mentor, Dan. That means he can help you with lots of things, like school, and what you do outside of school, and what you're going to do in the future, and your football skills, of course. How do you like the sound of that?"

Daniel smiled more broadly and nodded, managing to mumble, "great". Collins realised that some of his previous reticence to speak may have been as much teenage shyness as being a selective mute.

"I'll be with you a while too, but hopefully, soon enough, I'll leave you and Damon to it."

Collins felt the need to formally mark this new start.

"Let's shake on it," Collins said, offering Daniel his hand. He smiled, as Daniel gingerly held out his palm.

"To the future?"

"Yeah to the future," Daniel said, feeling an excitement for what that future might hold he had never previously experienced.

5.15pm

Back in the car, Collins and Sharma allowed themselves a congratulatory debrief.

"You've got to savour moments like this. They don't come along too often in our careers."

"Fingers crossed for them all," Tara replied.

They both knew, from bitter experience, the road back from prolonged trauma was fraught with hazards.

"At least they've got a chance now."

"I never imagined it would turn out like this when I first came here a fortnight ago."

As he said it their eyes met, in the shared knowledge it wasn't only the Chilcotts who were going forwards with a new hope.

Tara turned the engine on and they pulled away from Gartside Gardens, making their way past the precinct beneath the three watchful giants.

"What was the message you got that you looked so pleased about before we went into the house?" she asked.

Collins allowed himself another little smile.

"The centre forward of Corton Juniors has invited me to come and watch the County Cup final this evening."

"Fantastic," Tara replied.

They fell quiet, each content in their own reflections. They didn't need to say any more, as they looked towards the road ahead.

ABOUT THE AUTHOR

Hidden Harm, Ben Byrne's debut novel, has received acclaim as having brought together "specialist insight and a passion for social justice, in a fast-paced crime thriller". Ben's writing is the product of his career as a children's social worker, and draws on his non-fiction publications in the arena of youth justice and safeguarding. In *Hidden Harm* this professional experience is used to develop multiple perspectives, and in doing so, create a unique work of fiction. Having vividly established characters and place, Ben is working on further books in the Gartside series.

Ben lives near London and continues to work in children's services. Any free time is spent trying to keep up with his own children's busy sporting calendars.

Ben's career has seen him champion the cause of justice for those women and children in the most difficult situations. *Hidden Harm* deals with issues of abuse and trauma, which often go unseen, but blight the lives of so many.

A proportion of the royalties from the book will be donated to the charities Safe Lives and White Ribbon. For more information about these organisations go to:

safelives.org.uk

SafeLives, the UK-wide charity dedicated to ending domestic abuse, for everyone and for good.

www.whiteribbon.org.uk

White Ribbon UK is a leading charity engaging with men and boys to end violence against women.

If you would like to contact Ben and sign up to hear about the next Gartside novel, or for information on developments in the real world to end exploitation and abuse, go to:

benbyrne.net

Lightning Source UK Ltd.
Milton Keynes UK
UKHW021249040322
399575UK00010B/974